Hate you too.

Book 1 of The Troubled Series

Torrie Jones

To my Troublemakers.

This ones for you.

AUTHORS NOTE

Please note that this book includes a case that looks at teenagers that commit suicide and mentions of rape. This is all fictional and this is not taken from any event in the present day or any person. This is simply a work of fiction. If in the event this is something that you cannot read, I can completely understand. Please take care of yourself as your mental health and wellbeing is more important.

All characters and companies are a work of fiction. The agency in this book doesn't exist.

TJ x

PLAYLIST
HATE YOU TOO

Made by Rhianna Joel on Spotify:

- ☐ Woman – Harry Styles
- ☐ Unholy – Sam Smith, Kim Petras
- ☐ You Don't Own Me – SAYGRACE, G-Easy
- ☐ Boyfriend – Dove Cameron
- ☐ Under The Influence – Chris Brown
- ☐ Bad Idea – Ariana Grande
- ☐ Let You Down – NF
- ☐ High Enough – K. Flay
- ☐ Circus – Britney Spears
- ☐ Say It Right – Nelly Furtado
- ☐ I Wish I Was There – The Weeknd, Gesaffelstein
- ☐ Chicago – Michael Jackson
- ☐ Sex, Drugs, Ect. – Beach Weather
- ☐ Arcade – Duncan Laurence
- ☐ I Put a Spell on You – Annie Lennox
- ☐ Way Down We Go – Stripped – KALEO
- ☐ Dead To Me – Kali Uchis
- ☐ She – Harry Styles
- ☐ Dangerous Woman – Ariana Grande
- ☐ Friends – Chase Atlantic
- ☐ Do I Wanna Know? – Arctic Monkeys
- ☐ Why'd You Only Call Me When You're High – Arctic Monkeys
- ☐ Love Is a Bitch – Two Feet
- ☐ All The Good Girls Go to Hell – Billie Eilish

CONTENTS

PROLOGUE

Thea

E uphoria.

That is all I feel. Just an intense wave of relief now that I have graduated from the academy. These past three years I have proved to not only myself but also to my family that when I set my heart on something, I do it.

But of course, they aren't here to celebrate with me or support me. That would be a miracle. They weren't supportive of my move to America, or my choice in career, or university. They wanted me to forgive the person who hurt me, move on, get married, have children. I never wanted that.

I had *never* wanted that.

But, although they were never here to support me, I did have my newfound family, Mary, and Frank. My downstairs neighbours, who took me in as one of their own.

Remembering the first day I moved into the building and Mary came prepared twenty minutes later with a cake, saying 'Welcome to the mad house.' and a bottle of wine.

She took one look at me, smiled, and said "Oh, we will get along just fine, dear."

And we have. Just like I get on with Frank.

They have taken me in and although I am not related to them in anyway shape or form, they have acknowledged me as the daughter they never had.

They decided quite early on in their relationship that kids wasn't something they wanted, and instead of wallowing, they did all these amazing things that some people only dream of doing. Although, I know deep down Frank always wanted a son, he knew better than to upset his wife by mentioning it. So instead, treat her to a lifetime of parties, holidays, and gifts. They wouldn't say they're materialistic, and neither would I. They accept who they are and who they are with each other and that is all that matters to them. In Mary's words "Fuck the rest of the world." And that is a motto I live by daily.

With being the only British person in my building, I had been warned prior to my move that the Americans find the British accent fascinating and ask for you to say anything and everything you can just so they can judge you for it or correct you. Something that happens often.

Sawyer Reid being the main person who has tormented me the last three years. The biggest narcissistic womanizer you'll meet. He is good, don't get me wrong, he is a great agent even. But if he could remove his head from the legs of some poor girl who has fallen victim to his charm, he would have got top of the class. Which notably, went to me instead.

"You know James, you should thank your lucky stars that they took pity on you and gave you the top of the class award. I'm not even the slightest bit bitter about it." The baboon whispers over his shoulder in front of me.

"Oh Sawyer, if you're jealous, just say so!" I say sarcastically causing him to grin a sadistic smile at me. "If you cared about your studies rather than getting some, maybe this award would have gone to you." His smile only grows wider, and I feel my stomach turn in disgust.

He leans in close; the stench of his over expensive cologne enters my nostrils, and I am finding it hard not to gag. Why would anyone want to sleep with a man who drowns himself in Dior Sauvage? The scent itself, prior to being stuck with Sawyer Reid five days a week, was one of my favourites. Now? I'm repulsed at the scent even if it is for a moment.

"One day that will be you. And you'll just have to beg me to stop." He grins and I intentionally roll my eyes.

"Sawyer - every time I tell you no, or that's not happening, you seem to find a way to make me more grateful that this is the last day I get to see your face." I smirk. The smile on his face only grows bigger before he turns around.

Thea: 1 – Sawyer: 0. I hope that hurt his ego.

The man has never been told no. He gets what he wants and doesn't ever see the problem with his actions or the way he speaks to people. He has managed to sleep with every girl in our class.

Apart from one: me.

And it makes him itch. Which makes me happy.

Sawyer's name is called up next, and since I'm the last person to be called up as I receive the top of the class award, I can see the corny smile on his face as he receives his certificate and smiles for the cameras.

Oh Reid, always a poser.

I look out onto the crowd and notice a bunch of girls cheering for him. How, and why you would willingly surround yourself with a man like Sawyer Reid, makes me feel sick. I suffered three years, which is enough, and I hope to never see the man again.

"Next to the stage is the Agent who worked hard throughout her time here, who made connections and was never afraid to get stuck in. The top of the class award goes to, Agent Thea St. James."

ONE

Thea

"Venti chai latte for Olive!" I shout.

A bunch of coffee addicted robots stand eagerly waiting for the person to collect their drink.

Instead of waiting for someone to collect it, I decide to continue making the extensive list of drinks. It's only nine o'clock, but I am fully ready for my bed and for my shift here to be over.

Next on my list: a chai latte.

Jesus, I understand it's September, but this must be the worst drink to make – not to mention the smell. I'm sick of it.

After a few minutes I hear someone clear their throat beside me, causing me to leave my long stare of peace. "Is this a chai latte?" A woman stands next to the counter, her chestnut brown hair blow-dried and sunglasses on, my guess is her name is Olive. Her pristine white coat intact, with no wrinkle in sight.

"Yes." I say while a smile, which she doesn't return, not that I would ever expect it. In this city? Saying simple things such as please and thank you? It's unheard of.

"Why didn't you call for me?" She says while removing her sunglasses, to show her model like face.

I smile to her and continue making the next chai latte on my list. "I did." I say while pouring the milk into the cup for the next customer.

I suddenly see fingers click in my face and I look up to see a smug expression. "It's cold. I want a new one made." She orders and I can't help but scoff.

"The one you ordered is right there and has been sat for no more than a minute. But if you were to collect it now, I'm fairly sure it would still be hot enough for you to drink." I say placing the lid on top of the cup and calling out for the next venti chai latte.

"I don't think you understand, so let me explain it because I think there is some broken English." She says getting closer to me, almost knocking the latte off the bar. I narrow my eyes.

"You're going to make me another latte, or I'm going to get you fired." She says as loudly as she can causing people to turn their heads. The atmosphere in the room drops.

I cannot help but laugh and I watch the smug look on her face drop and a wave of anger comes over. "Are you laughing at me?" She questions me, expression laced with disgust.

I nod. "I am, because I would love to hear what you would say to head office about the encounter." I smile at her, and she begins to look around hoping someone will take her side, but no one does – they all look just as annoyed which explains how I'm feeling. I watch as the embarrassment washes over her as she realises that not only is she wrong and out of line, but she doesn't have a leg to stand on.

She sheepishly picks up the chai latte she almost knocked over with her fake tits and walks quickly out of the building. I laugh, some people in this city think they are so entitled. I would have made her a new one if she had asked properly. No harm is treating people with respect.

I put another lid on yet another vile cup of coffee and call out the next chai latte. A lady with the most beautiful red hair, side bangs and perfect facial features approaches the bar. I hand her the coffee with a smile, and she returns it, taking the cup carefully from my hand before peeking through her sunglasses. Giving me a long hard look up and down, she smiles even bigger, nodding as she gracefully places the glasses to sit firmly on her nose.

"You'll do just fine." She says with a nod before walking away elegantly from the coffee bar and everyone, including me, watches her walk away. Mesmerised by her beauty and grace. After a moment of being under her spell, I realise what has just happened. What the hell did she mean by, *"you'll do just fine?"*

I suddenly notice the line of cups forming and decide that I'm going to get through the rest of my painful shift, because there is nothing better than an early finish, going home and falling asleep in the bed you had to leave so early.

Putting the key in the door of my apartment building I feel a sense of relief wash over me. Thank God. I am home.

The door slams behind me and I walk through the entry way, counting my steps till I hear the door unlock and two heads pop out.

My neighbours. Mary and Frank Miller. An unhinged couple that if you met them on the street, you would think they are just a sweet old couple... till they opened their mouths.

Mary, a short woman with white hair and the attitude and vocabulary of a drunk sailor. I love her, and although she is about fifty years older than me, I would consider her my best friend. She always has the best stories not to mention she's stylish for a seventy-five-year-old.

And her husband, Frank. The man who once got arrested for standing up in woman's rights protest because he wore a 'fuck the cops' t-shirt. A taller man, however, not much taller than Mary. His hair being a shade of silver so many people would pay ridiculous amount of money for. He's just as stylish because God forbid, she let him out the house with something she didn't put out for him. He's somewhat quieter than her, however, they are just as odd as each other and it makes me love them even more.

"Any news?" They ask eagerly in sync. Causing me to tilt my head and look up towards my apartment, slowly watching them follow my gaze.

"I've not reached there yet to know." I say tilting my head. Waiting for the penny to drop. Mary looks at Frank, before rolling her eyes.

"Well, run up the stairs!" She shouts causing me to chuckle. Four weeks ago, I applied for my dream job at the I.C.C.O, The International Criminal Communications Organization.

The best job I could go into with a ridiculous

number of benefits, the pay is incredible not to mention it's best criminal justice organization to be in. The job I applied for, something I trained at the academy to do and something I've always dreamed of since moving out to America.

"We know the mail man came. We even offered to take the letters for you. But Ralph laughed and said you mentioned it to him that we weren't allowed to take your mail anymore." Mary pouts causing me to narrow my eyes to her.

"And we both know why." I state before turning on my heels and walking towards the stairs of my apartment. The last time she accepted a parcel or got any of my post, she opened it, and got excited over the parcel.

"I'm just pleased that without a boyfriend you're finding other ways to pleasure yourself, dear." She encourages and a wave of embarrassment come over me while turning to meet their impressed faces. The parcel...was a vibrator. That was an extremely uncomfortable conversation to have. I wanted to die.

"Thanks, Mary." I say quietly walking up the stairs, feeling their stares burn into my soul. I know I'm only going to be met with disappointment. I applied four weeks ago, and I had my exam just after. Now, I understand the process is long but I'm sure that there is a lot of people who would be more suitable for the job, I haven't worked in the field, only studied, because no matter how hard I tried, no one wanted a top of the class graduate from the academy. And I was once told it's because I'm British that I'm not going to get far, and I should give up. So, I put a pause on that part of my life and got a job at Starbucks to pay the bills.

Turning the key in the door and pushing slightly, I watch the pile of letters come in view with my feet and I bend over to pick them up. Placing my bag down next to the entrance table, I flick through them. Bill, bill, bill, bi-

A black envelope. With my government issued name prior to me changing it before I moved here.

Theodora St. James-Monroe

226C Westfield Avenue,

Sin City

SIN245 8D

Well... fuck.

Could this be it? Only a handful of people know my name was Theodora. Changing it was the best thing for me, especially after leaving the United Kingdom. I wanted a fresh start, in a country I barely understood. But this was better than the hell I called home.

"Anything?!" Mary screams up, but I ignore

her, because in all truth, I'm not sure one bit.

I open the letter carefully and remove the documents from inside, turning it to face me I read it like a mad woman.

Dear Miss St. James,

Over the past few weeks, we have interviewed hundreds of applicants who we thought could be right for the job. The Communications Liaison role is something that is so challenging, so rewarding but also, incredibly heart breaking. The role includes being the first point of call for families, law enforcement and other agents and agencies when dealing with tasks such as undercover operations.

The International Criminal Communications Organization is proud of the thousands of cases it has managed to solve, track down and are currently investigating. And we want an employee, who will be the welcoming face to all that they will meet in the role.

Which is why Miss St. James, we are delighted to offer you the role of Communications Liaison starting Monday September 12th at 8am. We look forward to meeting you and welcoming you into the team.

I will see you Monday, if you need anything, please do not hesitate to get in contact.

Kindest Regards,

Agent Nancy Robertson

Operations Manager for ICCO.

I scream.

I can't do anything else but scream. And with the level of uncertainty I'm painting in the room, Mary and Frank start screaming with me.

"I got it!"

TWO

Thea

"Fuck, fuck, fuck, fuck." I shout running around my apartment trying to make sure I have everything for my first day. All documents from the United Kingdom and my right to work in the States. My passport that has my new name, Thea St. James rather than the one I left behind.

This is a new fresh start for me, and I feel grateful that finally, my stars are aligning and I'm able to have my dream job.

After checking for the sixth time that I have everything, I glare at myself in the mirror.

On Friday I was Thea the barista, today – I'm Agent Thea St. James, Communications Liaison for I.C.C.O. Now that is a jump in careers if I ever did see it.

Grabbing my coat from the back of the door, I place it on top of my outfit for today. A black business suit, black heels, and a white blouse. Something safe for today as I'm going to assume there's a dress code and I didn't want to stick out like a sore thumb.

As I come out of my apartment door that opens to the entrance area of the building, I'm met with two happy old people who are smiling up at me, like I've walked out in a wedding dress and I'm about to get married.

"You look fabulous, dear." Mary smiles and lightly pats her eye with a tissue. Oh goodness, I have them crying and that is not what I want.

"Don't cry!" I exclaim before pulling them both into a hug. "I'm going to be back later; I'm only leaving for a few hours." I say while releasing them from my grip. Mary at this point is inconsolable and ushers Frank to speak on her behalf.

"I think what Mary wants me to say is that seeing you, go off for a job you've dreamed of doing since coming back from the academy, it's like seeing you come down in a wedding dress, it's a once in a lifetime feeling."

Huh. You don't say.

"Well, I'll be back later, so, can you two assure

me that you'll be on your best behaviour today? No snooping, no arguing, no shouting. Just a lot of love." I say with a grin. They exchange a look as if to question whether I'm alright but decide to shrug their shoulders and nod instead of arguing with me. *Good choice.*

Giving them both a kiss on the cheek, I make my way out to my car, or should I say Mary and Frank's old car. A Tesla, something I would never have afforded on my Starbucks salary, however now with this new job, I might be able to buy one of my own.

The journey to the job is about forty minutes, with it just being on the outskirts of the city. I decide to follow my Sat-Nav, rather than get lost.

It's currently 7:02am, giving me plenty of time to get there and since I'm leaving the city, there shouldn't be much traffic getting out, it might just be worse coming in later.

Putting on the radio, Taylor Swifts: Don't Blame Me blasts through the speakers and it reminds me of who I was after I moved to America. Freshly heartbroken, new to the city, family who hated her and who decided to do something people told her she would never be able to do.

Taylor brings another level of boss and bad bitch out of you, and no one will ever be able to tell me otherwise. Not long after moving here,

I got Mary into Taylor Swift, Frank was already a Swiftie. Mary took some convincing but will happily listen to her now.

Screaming the lyrics to the song, I dread to think what people around are thinking of me. But looking around at my surrounds, I notice that people are probably shouting at the idiot drivers in front of them rather than some girl blasting Taylor Swift on a Monday morning.

After my morning motivational session, the drive seemed to go quite smoothly, I only hit a few sections of traffic and with that I come face to face with the gates of the I.C.C.O. My heart is pounding out of my chest. Probably because this doesn't feel real.

As I come closer to the gate, I put my window down noticing a man in a black suit and tie, approaching me. As he comes into view, I notice his name badge, Agent Kiro Landon.

"Name?" He questions quite abruptly causing me to be a little off guard.

"Thea St. James, I'm here to see Agent Nancy Robertson." I explain to him, giving him a small smile which he ignores. I don't think he's allowed to smile, none of the Agents are. I feel my heart shatter just that little bit while he walks away from the car and into the hut at the side of the gate.

He's only gone for a short while before he

comes back, a black file in hand. "Here you go, Agent St. James. Agent Robertson will meet you at the entrance. Park your car up on the left." He instructs handing me the file and stepping away from the window. I nod slowly while turning to watch the gates open. My heart does a loop. I've waited for over a year for the title of Agent once again.

I thank the Agent, to which is he gives me a nod and heads back to his hut while I drive up through the gates.

This place is gigantic, and much more modern in person. The photos on Google doesn't do it justice in the slightest. The building itself is all black brick, the windows are gold with a slight twinge of silver when the light hits them. It's hard not to stare at it, it's a complete masterpiece.

Parking was no problem and as I begin to get my things out of the car I notice a red headed lady walking towards me, she walks so elegantly, and I can't help but feel mesmerised like I was the other day. Her hair is curled, and the side bangs are out of her face as they frame it so beautifully. Her flared black pants and green shirt compliment her hair and complexion. The definition of beauty walks towards me, and I begin to question my sexuality for a moment.

"Welcome, Agent St. James." She greets me with a smile, and I can't help but laugh.

"You're the lady from the other day. The one who ordered a chai latte and said, 'I'd do just fine.'" I note and she nods while putting her hair behind her ear.

"Guilty. I wanted to see what you were like before we got to work together." She smiles before walking closer to meet me. "I'm Nancy. Some people call me Nan, Robert or mommy. Depends on if they want something from me." She jokes which makes me laugh nervously. I can understand why, I don't bat for my team, however I could see why some woman would say they are gay from the minute they are graced with her presence. She's extremely electric.

I shake the extended hand; I didn't even notice she had held out for me while I've been so mesmerised. "Thea St. James." I smile at her before releasing my hand as I feel myself become nervous around her.

"Well Thea, let me show you round the mad house." She says while walking towards the building, and I follow her, like she has a collar around my neck and pulling me in on a lead.

Walking through the doors, my mouth falls open at the interior. No doubt it's all black and gold, the staple colours of the company. The receptionists smile our way and Nancy smiles back at the Asian receptionist who begins to blush, and it causes me to raise my eyebrow towards her, Nancy continues to give her googley eyes.

She notices me staring and clears her throat, "Ignore that, come on." She instructs and I decide not to question it further.

She walks me round to the lift where we both enter and silence falls between us. Not an uncomfortable silence, but more of one where just neither one of us know what to say, so it's peaceful. I'm listening, I'm learning. Silence is the best tool, and I don't want to interrupt her.

We stop off at floor one first, while she gives a brief description that this is where the new level agents live, and they sort out files. It's an easy job to have, especially if you're out of the academy. Would have been nice to know. However, there wasn't anything available at the time I left the academy.

"Don't get me wrong, sometimes the newbies are great, like Ophelia – you'll meet her soon. She's the Casualty Prevention Officer. She's the best person that you'll meet beside me of course." She praises herself while we go up to another floor. "Ophelia was in that room four months before the promotion. If Scott, her manager wasn't so good at his job, they'd both have the job title, but at this moment it's not needed." She explains while the lift goes off at floor two and I look out to find an empty room, "This will be a new team of people, I'm going to be recruiting in the new year and then Tuck will be training them in Summer." She explains.

I can't stop myself from asking a question. "Tuck?" I ask and she laughs at me.

"Yes, sorry. You'll get used to people and their nicknames around here. Nicknames are kind of a staple, especially between Tuck & Scott. Tuck is the Head of Undercover Operations. He's the man to go to if there is an undercover sting going on, he's normally the man that's planned it out, prepped his team and someone is undercover."

I can't help but feel grateful for her explanation of his job. I don't doubt I'll meet Tuck sometime soon, but it's good that I can ask him some questions, ones he can answer. I doubt he would just outright tell me about the case he's undercover on until I'm the one handing him it.

Going up in the lift the floors three, four, and five, we see the finance department, the operations team, and the undercover team. However, Tuck was in a meeting, so he wasn't going to be getting a hello.

"So, you're from London?" Nancy asks earning a nod. "I've always wanted to go to London. What's it like?" She asks while watching the numbers go up on the lift.

"I mean, this is from my view, as a British person, but I just say it's overrated. However, you must go. If I didn't live there for as long as I did, I would go like once a year. It's good for a long weekend. Any longer and you get sick. That's just the rules." I explain to her.

She smiles. "Your accent isn't as strong as I thought it would have been. I was expecting you to be extremely British, but I guess if you've lived in America for five years. It just means that you lose it a bit." She explains.

I agree with her. I have lost some of my accent, and I'm grateful. I won't ever forget where I was raised, however I would much prefer to not have so much of my old life with me.

We arrive to the tenth floor, and she steps out, this time it's quiet, but much quieter. This is heaven if I was ever allowed into the pearly gates.

"This is your floor. Not the whole thing obviously, some of these rooms are conference rooms, and there is one of the interns down the corridor, but she only works four days. So really, you're kind of on your own." She explains walking towards a door at the end of the corridor. I'm stunned, I get my own office. I'm not sat with the rest of the team.

"It's so quiet." I say as she pulls a key from her pants pocket and turning to look at me.

"I can move your office if it's too quiet for you?" She asks sweetly and I shake my head quickly.

"I can assure you; this isn't a complaint." I insist and she laughs while opening the door and putting on the light. This must be the most colourful room in the entire building. A white desk sits in the middle of the room in front of a gigantic bookshelf, filled with hundreds of books, more than likely criminology and law books, especially American Law.

A grey sofa sits opposite the desk in the corner with rose gold cushions, blankets, and golden tid-bits, such as coasters and a gold vase with a beautiful bunch of flowers in. I am gobsmacked as I turn to her. Apparently, my reaction catches her off guard and a confused look comes over her face. "I found your Pinterest?" She explains and I begin to nod. Of course, she did. "Is it okay?" She asks curiously, unsure on what expression my face is telling her. But I fucking love it.

"I adore it." I say to her earning me a smile.

"Brilliant." She gleams while taking my bag off my shoulder and places it on the sofa beside me.

"Are you meant to decorate all the newbies offices?" I ask politely.

She grins, "Yes. Something that the organization wants is for their employees to feel like they're at home, considering this will be your second home." She continues to smile before walking back towards the door. "Let's go meet the team."

THREE

Sawyer

Sitting round the round table, I pour a glass of whiskey for each of my men, and the two idiots in the room. It's 5 o'clock somewhere. "Okay, bets on how long she'll last." I say placing $50 on the table in front of my team. "I give it a week." A bunch of them shake their heads, either too busy being pussy's or trying to justify that I won't get what I want with this new employee.

Although it's frowned upon within the company, the only person who would love to tell me to fuck off and get a new job is Nancy, and considering I found myself between her thighs when we first started, she can't say shit considering it would cost her, her job too.

"You never know Sawyer, this one might not like men." Smith, one of my staff laughs along with Scott and Tuck.

Punching Tuck in the arm, who doesn't even flitch, I lean closer over the table getting right in Chad's face. "I can change a woman, even if it's just for one night." I smirk and a laugh from Scott erupts in the room.

"Clearly. That one night with Nancy turned her gay. You really know how to make an impression." He expresses with a smile. The room erupts with laughter and the only thing I can do is laugh with them. Nancy's sexuality was a secret, even to herself for a while. But she announced to the team that she was gay two-weeks after I gave her a good night. I'll stand by my statement; I never turned her gay.

"Moving on from that, come on place your bets men! I wanna see what you got." I laugh while rubbing my palms together. I watch as Tuck moves to stand behind me.

"I can't wait for the day you get a STD Sawyer, and your balls are itching." He laughs and I turn my chair to meet him.

"You think I'm stupid enough to go in raw with any girl I meet?" I query. "I'm saving that for someone special. The day you get all of me is the day you marry me." I wink and Scott pulls a face.

"Oh yeah, the whole half of an inch on your

one-inch cock Sawyer is gonna make all the difference. Atta' boy." He mocks. I decide to turn around and see where my team are placing me.

"You know fine well he's gonna get laid this time next week, the mans a manipulator, not to mention a damn right psychopath." Smith explains earning nods from around the room.

"True." Grayson speaks up from next to me, and I smack the back of his head.

"Have some respect for your superior." I say sitting while pouring a glass of whisky in our glasses.

"I take the bet, 1 week to get the girl in bed." I explain while clinking glasses with them all. Easy bet.

I neck the drink and look up through the conference room to notice that familiar red head walk through with the new prey.

"Here we go boys. She's arrived." I say excitedly while placing all the glasses in the middle of the table and looking back up to see Nancy explain the different teams within the room. And that's when I see it. *Her.*

I don't move for a few moments, stunned at who I see standing in the middle of the pen.

"Sawyer, you look like you've seen a ghost." Scott mocks earning laughs around the room.

There is no way.

I move quickly from my seat and go to stand over the railing looking down on them both. *Why is she here?*

She looks up at me, her eyes go from that soft shade of blue to a dark shade within a flash and I feel my cock throb. *Fuck.*

"No!" We both shout in unison causing the whole room to go silent. Thea St. James, my biggest competitor and not to mention my biggest downfall.

The one woman I couldn't get into my bed stands in front of me, next to the woman who claims I turned her gay. (Not true.)

"I'm going to assume you two know each other?" Nancy smiles while looking at both of our faces. We're both annoyed to say the least.

"What is she doing here?" I question Nancy, completely ignoring Thea, as I should. That woman made me so mad all day, every day at the academy. But I would pay all the money in the world just to hear her moan my name.

"I'm standing right here." She states and I scoff back at her.

"Not for long if I have anything to do with it." I say bluntly, causing her to raise her eyebrow. Fucking hell, why is she the biggest turn on even when I'm angry?

"You don't, Sawyer. But thank you for your

input." Nancy says sarcastically before turning to Thea, her eyes full of curiosity as Thea breaks our stare, for a moment and I feel like I can breathe.

"We went to the academy together." She explains in her sweet British accent. Although it's starting to fade just that little bit, it's still one of the sweetest sounds to come from a human. And if she ever heard me say that she would probably have me done for harassment.

"You didn't answer me Nancy, what is she doing here?" I question once more, this time deciding to ignore Thea's glare.

"Oh Sawyer, she's your new Communications Liaison." Nancy grins wide and I feel my heart stop.

Well, fuck.

FOUR

Thea

I watch the colour drain from Sawyer's face and deep down, nothing has given me more satisfaction than this moment. She's rendered him speechless, finally! Someone who was able to shut the man up for more than ten seconds.

"She's fucking not Nancy, that's an order." He barks at her, and my eyebrows raise. The silence didn't seem to last long, and I turn my head to notice Nancy raise her finger at him, I don't think she liked his tone.

"Strike one pretty boy. Once I'm at three, you're done in this job and your tantrums are someone else's problem. Let me just remind you, I have all staffing responsibilities, not you. Act your salary or walk the plank." She explains rendering the whole room silent, even Sawyer. I get the sense that she doesn't stand for nothing, especially when it comes to Sawyer Reid.

"Thea, Sawyer will be your boss. You'll report directly to him and the Assistant Director, Tilda Shields." Nancy explains and I shake my head.

"I'm sorry, but I cannot work under Sawyer, please accept this as my formal resignation. But I refuse to work with a man as repulsive as him." I say walking away from Nancy and I can hear her stutter behind me.

Gasps begin to fill the room, and I'm quick to hear heels as Nancy chases after me.

"Thea, I understand you don't like Sawyer, but I can put something in place to get you both onto a better page." She pleads while taking my arm in her hand.

"Well, if this isn't the easiest pay outgoing." Someone behind me speaks and it suddenly dawns on me. Of course.

"You're still placing bets on the newbies?" I turn to him, and I watch as the whole row of men fall silent. "Really mature."

He doesn't say anything, and the two men behind him stand there, their mouths wide open, stunned that I'd even know that. "He used to do it all the time at the academy. Yet, no matter how hard he tried. There was one girl who wouldn't let him near her." I smugly say and I watch as a mountain of confused faces fill the room, even Nancy's beside me falls confused.

"That doesn't matter-"

"Well, by the looks on your colleagues faces it does. Because my guess is I've just walked in here and stirred up this little fantasy you've been playing out for the last year." I explain and the colour once again begins to drain from his face. This man cares so much about his reputation and appearance to others that when it comes to anything revolving you, he would tear you down just to make him feel and look better to anyone who was around him. But I don't care. And the thought of bursting his lie in the first hour of being here, really does make me feel good about myself. "Because Sawyer has decided to go silent, I was the one girl Sawyer couldn't tick off his list." I state and the gasps that come from the room, are shocking. This man had the whole office fooled that he's some heartbreaker, he's successful every time, he's never been told no.

And here I stand, all 5ft 4 of me. I stand here ruining his little lie.

"There's no way." A man with long hair speaks from behind Sawyer. "Sawyer?"

Words fail Sawyer and his head falls low while leaning over the railing. "She's right." He admits, and to my surprise that really does shock me. He would never admit anything to anyone. "This is Thea St. James. The one girl I couldn't tick off my list in three years."

"I wasn't one of the girls who fell victim to his charm." I state and I receive a slight nudge from Nancy who looks away. The look itself giving me the answer I need. "No way!" I exclaim and she moves her hand to her neck, indicating for me to shut up.

"He turned me gay." She explains with a slight smile, and I ignore the groan come from the other side of the room.

"Seriously?"

"No!" He shouts making the whole room look at him. He begins to take a deep breath, wanting to compose himself. "I didn't turn her gay." He defends but that only makes me laugh. "But this," He says pointing between us both, "is not going to work, you can't continue working here St. James, I won't allow it."

The silence in the room is deafening as the agents around the room look at us, the stares beginning to make me feel uncomfortable. But I've always been the person to tell Sawyer no, or not to give him what he wants.

"You don't get to make that decision." The stare he gives me almost shakes me to my core. He's furious with me, and I've ruined his perfect plan. "You clearly made a bet prior to me coming in here. And I would like to watch as your colleagues rinse you for every penny you have." I smugly say while turning towards the rest of his team. "Do your worst boys. It's the least he deserves."

Nancy nudges me and gives me a smile. That makes me feel good about standing up to him. The look on Sawyer's face is a picture, and one I will remember till the day I die. I have every intention on ruining this man's life. Just the way he attempted to ruin mine for so many years at the academy. The man will get a taste of his own medicine, and when he does, it will taste so sweet.

"Agent St. James, Agent Reid." A voice from behind us breaks the silence. Turning around I see a tall woman, in what I would call a power suit, her ebony skin glows in the light and the red lipstick she is wearing compliments her skin tone so beautifully. "My office please." She orders and I feel my heart sink. *Well, shit.*

"Is that..."

"Yep." Nancy ushers me, indicating I should follow the woman. That must be Assistant Director Tilda Shields. She has one of the best reputations within the organization. She has cracked down on some of the biggest cases the I.C.C.O has solved, not to mention is an animal rights activist, feminist and someone who has been classed as a 'hard ass' in the American term but also someone who will take you under her wing if you do right by her.

Following her and walking side by side with Sawyer, I feel like we're both in trouble. Surely Shields is one of those women who would not take lightly to her Agent's arguing in the middle of an office setting. Even if it's with Sawyer, who, from what I've gathered in the hour I've been here, is still as insufferable as he was back at the academy.

"Take a seat, please." She orders while holding the office door for us both. We each sit opposite from each other, and the table is that large, I can almost stop smelling Dior for a few moments and I feel like I can breathe.

"You know, in my time here – I've never seen so much hatred towards two of my Agents like I have just witnessed with you both." She begins and I feel my heart sink. She's heard the whole thing. "Agent Reid, would you like to explain to me why Agent St. James can't be the new Communications Liaison? Because what I read from her file, she beat you for the top of the class award, not to mention she did so much better than you in exams, she got stuck in when it came to missions and lastly, she earned the respect from the Director of the academy when she left that year. But all I've just heard in the pen is that you managed to sleep with about 90% of your classmates, you made a list and Agent St. James was the only person who gave you a reality check." She comes down hard on him.

He's sweating, not physically – but if you know Sawyer Reid, you'd know that if he's ever called out for anything, he won't deny it, he will openly admit it, however gaslight you into thinking the reason he is the way he is, because of your actions and the way you were with him. Something I witnessed so many times when it came to his short-term hook-ups with people from the academy.

"In my defence, Assistant Director Shields, Miss St. James made my time at the academy insufferable by bullying, she made me feel inferior about my capability of being an Agent, not to mention she would repeatedly bully me for hook-ups, not to mention false rumours."

I sit there, stunned. I knew the man was insufferable, but he has just bare faced lied to the Assistant Director. The man is sat here playing the victim and I am being portrayed as the villain. You sneaky fucker.

"I would like to come to my own defence here Assistant Director-" I begin, and she puts her hand up stopping me from continuing.

"There is no need, Agent. I know what he is like." She admits while rolling her eyes. "Agent

Sawyer Reid, the biggest pathological liar this company has ever seen. Now if it were up to me, I would fire you right here as you know fine well that initiating sexual encounters or relationships with other Agents, some of them being on your team, is against our policy." She says while pulling out two files. "But now that you know that I am aware of your extracurricular activities outside of office hours, I would like to make one thing clear," She speaks openly while sitting up straight. "*Agent* Thea St. James isn't going anywhere. I won't let you try and decide her future. She has earned her place here at the table, and as much I would like to say you haven't, you have. You are a capable Agent who if given the opportunity, could do important things within the agency. But I will be damned if you are going to bully one of the team because she has more sense than get dirty between the sheets with you."

I feel a wave of embarrassment rush through me, and I close my eyes, praying that this will be over soon. I'm extremely grateful for her to come to my defence, but this is embarrassing.

"Understood, Ma'am." Sawyer sheepishly says and my heart does a loop. It makes me feel so good knowing that he is getting told off for something. Not so much as being shamed for it, but no matter how many times he was told at the academy that he can't, he continued. Like the narcissist he is. Because deep down, he knew they wouldn't kick him out. No matter how many times I prayed to God.

Shields looks somewhat satisfied that Sawyer has agreed, and she points at the files. "In here is your next case, Agent Reid. You and your team are needing to track down an online operation called the K1LLERS." She begins while pulling something up on a screen behind her. "Now this isn't something we would normally take, but because the FBI team that were originally investigating have had to take a case that has taken president, we've been given this one." Shields explains while pulling up yet another slide on the screen.

"Kids?" Sawyer questions and I open the file to find the name and ages of the victims, not to mention crime scene reports. "Since when did my team investigate kids?"

She glares at him. The stare so cold it could cut through him. "Since those kids all took part in a suicide pact that has so far killed six, this is now our problem and because you have a tech wizard on your team that means your team gets the case, Agent Reid." She cuts him off and you can suddenly feel the tension in the room. I remain quiet while they have a stare off and of course, Sawyer is the first to look away, clearly intimidated by Shields.

"Suicide pact?" He questions trying to remain on topic. "How is this a I.C.C.O case?"

"The children involved all belong to a mixture of families from different households and who come from diverse backgrounds. Now, how this case came into the hands of the FBI is because one of the children that died is the Mayor's daughter." She says while putting up a photo of a girl with the most beautiful green eyes and brown hair. She's a child, someone's baby.

"Was there any history of depression or depressive thoughts or contemplations?" I ask and she shakes her head.

"If there was, this case would have been open and shut, however because the Mayor is adamant she wasn't suffering with depression, we've been asked to look at the other five." She says pulling up photos of all their yearbook. Abbie Holland, Jolene George, Sam Blackett, Oscar Todd, Sarah Osman and lastly, Piper Meyers, the Mayors daughter.

"They all died on the same day, and the coroner has determined that they died all at the same time. They were all good kids who had no history of depression or mental health problems that were known, and none were in therapy." She continues and I feel sick, these are babies. Fourteen and fifteen-year-olds who decided to make a pact, but why?

"So, they had made a suicide pact? Where's the evidence or is that just speculation?" Sawyer questions, causing Shields to change the slide to screenshots from the teenager's computers. It looks to be suicide letters.

"This was found on their computers and if you read it carefully-"

"They're all the same. No changes, it's like they've copied each other's." I say reading over the letter and looking up at Sawyer who I think has noticed the same thing as me but decides to look away as quickly as he can.

"Exactly Agent, although the deaths have been proven as suicides, the actually matter in why they died is still being determined." She says turning off the screen and turning back towards us. "Agent Reid, you, and your team are going to be looking into the deaths of the teenagers, use the tech kid too. We need to solve this, and fast." She instructs while Sawyer closes his file. "Agent St. James, you'll be working alongside Agent Reid's team and conducting interviews with the families to establish what kind of kids they were. The parents were only interviewed and a lot of the kids that died have a few siblings. My guess is maybe speak with them, see if they know anything the parents won't know." I nod at her.

My first case, and it's working underneath Sawyer fucking Reid. This is going to be as painful as solving this case. "One more thing before you both leave and get to work." She instructs while standing up in her chair. "Agent Reid, after this case, Agent St. James will be deciding which cases you go on and whether you have to collaborate with other teams, such as Agent Barlow's Undercover team or Agent Wilkinson's Casualty Prevention team. She has my blessing to whip you into shape and I'm certain she will choose ones that will decide whether or not you will continue to be an Agent here. Because, Agent Reid, you are on report, and I want updates from you, Agent St. James. Because if you don't pass your report at the end of the year, you can kiss being an Agent for this organization or any, goodbye." She warns and the temperature in the room goes cold.

She's put me in charge of deciding whether Sawyer keeps his job in three months. Although deep down the thought of this makes me sick, I can also feel the excitement rush through my body.

Welcome to hell Sawyer. This is going to be fun.

FIVE

Thea

As both Sawyer and I exit the room, I suddenly feel the rush of anger walk past me as he begins to storm off. He is not happy about his career being left in my hands, in fact you can see it; because he turns back and stands tall in front of me trying to intimidate me.

"One day I'm going to get you fired, St. James." He warns me and I can't help but smile. "You shouldn't be working here, or with my team. Go back to Starbucks serving chai latte's or whatever you did." He begins before storming off yet again. *Wait, huh?*

Rushing after him, I catch up after a few seconds and stand in front of him, stopping him from walking. "How did you know I worked at Starbucks?" I question and he takes a long deep exhale before looking down on me, his eyes dark and filled with fury.

"I pass it every single day on my way here. Six days a week. And nothing brought me more joy knowing you became another nobody just like some of our other classmates. I did well, I got in here and you got in *nowhere*. Do you not understand how good that made me feel for a year?" He snaps at me wanting to cause a fight. I don't bite because this is Sawyer showing his true colours. Who he really is inside. "I'll be a great employee towards you Thea just so I can pass this fucking report and then the second I do; I'm getting your ass fired. Because I deserve to be here. You don't." He snaps once more before shoving past me and down towards the pen where I'm going to assume he will be giving a briefing soon, once he's calmed down.

His intention is to scare me, he wants me to report him, he wants me to fold and cave. But surely, he should know I'm as stubborn as a mule and I won't budge, and I won't budge for someone like him. The man and his tiny dick can do one. Because that was strike one, Reid. Three strikes in my book and you're out.

"I see that went well." A familiar voice speaks from behind me, and I turn to find Nancy walking towards me. "I've never in the year I've known him seen him so uptight. He's freaked that you're here. You've caused quite a stir." She teases which makes me smile although my heart is still pounding.

"The words I want to use to describe him would probably get me fired." I grit though my teeth and she chuckles slightly.

"Well of course." She laughs. "But Thea, Sawyer is the most insufferable womanizer that exists in this building. What you say about him, 90% of us have already said it, either to each other or to his face. It's the least he deserves. He's horrific." She says while moving down the corridor, the same way Sawyer went moments ago.

"I hate him, Nancy. He just makes me so angry. If I were allowed a gun, I'd happily shoot him just because he's breathing." I begin to admit, and she chuckles lightly before pulling her gun out from behind her.

"Here, take mine. But hold off doing it just yet." She says pulling out her phone. "Let me text the group chat, they will want front row seats." She says placing the gun in my hand.

Her bluntness about the situation makes me laugh, hard before shaking my head and handing her the gun back. "Sacked on the first day for murdering a co-worker? Doesn't sound like me." I say while she straps the gun back to her leg.

"You were about to make my Monday." She laughs a little while beginning to walk back towards the pen. "But I think out of all of us, you deserve to do it. You're the one who's suffered the most." She explains to me quietly and it makes me only appreciate her more. "Besides, I'd happily help you say it was self-defence when it comes to him, he's little bitch really." She says honestly and that causes me to laugh while we enter the pen.

It's a little bit busier than before and I notice there are quite a few people with computers and keyboards who are now working away in the corner.

"Thea!" A voice shouts from in front and I look to see the prick himself signalling me into the conference room where the other Agents are sat.

"Good luck. But remember, my gun is always loaded if you need it." She winks before strutting back out of the pen and taking a right down the corridor.

SIX

Thea

S hutting the door of the apartment block, I can't help but lean my back against it.

It's ten o'clock, and because Sawyer demanded we read up on the cases and listen to some of the FBI's findings, today was just a training day so I can understand what we are looking at in terms of a case.

Now, because there is so much uncertainty on whether this is a suicide or whether they planned it together, the Assistant Director has been on Sawyer's case all day, hounding him for answers that admittedly, he doesn't have yet. No one knows what they are looking for.

There was a handful of Sawyer's team sent to

the houses of the kids to understand if it was something they had been planning on doing for a while, or it was meant to be a little fun to them but ended up with them down in the morgue.

After a few moments of silence, a door swings open, and I hear the footsteps of a small woman in heels and the heavy breathing of a man.

Opening my eyes, I find them hanging out of their door, staring at me. Mary stands holding a bottle of wine with a straw and Frank stands with a plate of food.

"How was it?" Mary asks while pulling a face. "You look like you've had… fun?"

I narrow my eyes at her playfully causing a smile to creep onto her lips. Her wrinkles in full effect while the lasting reminiscence of red lipstick stains her lips. "Guess who is my boss." I say while taking off my heels, still leaning against the door.

"George Clooney!" Frank jokes earning him a slap from Mary. "Okay, I'm out of ideas, who's your new boss?"

"The one man who tortured me throughout my entire time at the academy." I say gratefully taking the bottle of wine and the straw and kissing Mary on the cheek. It takes them a second to work out who I'm referring to, and suddenly, dramatic gasps are heard throughout the entire apartment block as they remember.

"Sawyer!" Mary exclaims earning a nod from myself while I drink the wine quickly. Today has been painful, especially working around Sawyer. "Didn't you know?" She asks curiously.

Still gulping the wine, I shake my head before taking yet another gulp of the fruitiness. "Mary, I wouldn't have taken the job if I knew." I say while kissing Frank of the cheek and taking the plate while my bag is digging into my arm.

"Dear, you can quit. We know how much that boy bullied you throughout your time at the academy. I know you haven't seen him for a year, but has he changed?" She asks as I begin to walk up to the stairs leading up to my apartment. Without even looking at her while I reach my door, I take a deep breath.

"He's still taking bets to see how long it takes girls to fall for him and sleep with him." I say loudly so they can hear me. A sound of disgust comes from both and as I open my door, I turn around to give them a smile.

"Don't worry, I can manage Sawyer, because I'm not going to let him ruin something I've worked hard for. He can ruin his own reputation, but he won't be ruining mine." I say confidently.

Earning smiles from each of them and some goodnights, I enter my apartment and shut the door, grateful that I can drink this bottle of wine, or at least some of it. And have some food. I'm starving.

Leaving my shoes at the door, I walk round to the kitchen and take the covering off the plate. She made pie, and it is the best pie I think I've ever tasted.

I begin to get into something comfortable and set out my clothes for tomorrow, because the last thing I want to do is wonder what the hell I'm going to wear.

From what I gathered and seen on my first day, the attire for I.C.C.O is very much business smart, yet colour wise? It can be as wonderful and wacky as you like. Some agents were in suits, yet ties weren't needed, but as long as you look professional, they don't seem to care.

Going through some of my wardrobe and shoes, I set my eyes on a tartan suit with black heels. The suit itself has a cropped blazer and goes super well with a T-shirt.

Debating on the kinds of shoes, I set for my very trusty and comfortable heels I got from Kurt Geiger. These shoes are about seven years old, yet they are the most comfortable heel I own, and I got them for a great price when I lived back in London.

Although I got rid of so many things that linked me to my past back home, these heels I couldn't seem to separate with. They were my first ever designer purchase and not to mention,

I had saved up two months of wages to pay for them. They were a splurge to say the least, but they have done me good.

They have a history, because for so long when I wore them, I was stuck in a cycle of unhappiness, and I was waiting for the right time to say stop. And it came four months later at a breaking point.

I place the shoes down underneath my suit that's hanging up and I walk through to collect my dinner eagerly. My stomach grumbles at the sight of the pie and an eagerly dig in while scooping up my bottle of wine and heading to my sofa.

This is, in my opinion anyway, one of the best ways to spend a Monday night.

I place my plate on the coffee table and take out the remote to put something on while I eat. Ideally something short and quick like an episode of The Big Bang Theory or Friends. That would do me fine. I've seen them a hundred times, yet they never get old.

Skipping through the channels, I continue to sip my wine in the hopes that it will make me forget about Sawyer and his smug looking face. It makes me angry, just the thought of him breathing, makes me want to put a bullet between his eyes. He deserves it. Although that seems slightly dramatic.

Just when all is well, yet, I've not found an episode of Friends yet, I almost skip past it. But there it is. The smug baboons face glaring back at me while issuing a press conference outside of the I.C.C.O.

You have to be fucking kidding me.

"We are joined now with Supervisory Special Agent Sawyer Reid, Head of Criminal Prevention. Agent Reid, can you tell us why you think looking into this case is a waste of time?"

Open your mouth Sawyer and you're done.

"Of course, Jack, the families in my eyes were incredibly neglectful of their children. All of them had some sort of underlining mental health problems, some of which the families are denying."

Oh, for the love of God, he did not.

"So, in your eyes, you think that the parents are responsible for the death of their children, you don't think any other factor comes into play?" The presenter asks and Sawyer shakes his head.

"No sir, I think that this case is wasting precious time of the I.C.C.O. And there are more pressing cases which need to be dealt with urgently."

I am going to murder him.

After the camera pans away from Sawyer I

turn off the TV. I'm absolutely gobsmacked that the man went on live television and accused the parents of neglect. I place my head in my hands and breathe slowly.

He did that on purpose. He knew that I wasn't there now and going against what I would have advised is a bad idea. He's now not only put me in jeopardy, but now himself. But I care less about his job and more about mine.

Thea: 1 – Sawyer: 1.

SEVEN

Sawyer

I crack open another beer and take a swig, I know deep down I shouldn't have done that press conference. But I wanted to do something that would get a rise out of her, not to mention potentially get her fired.

Taking over another two beers, I place them in front of Tuck and Scott. We decided that pizza and beers was a clever idea since we all had an exhausting day, and my apartment is the closest and in the city.

"I can't believe there was one girl at the academy that had standards and told you where to go." Scott laughs, kicking his feet like a girl as he gets excited mocking me. "It is hilarious because the second you seen her; you knew you were in trouble man."

"He saw his life flash before his eyes. The one woman who said no. I never thought I'd see the day." Tuck mocks with him, taking a gigantic swig of his drink.

"You two done?" I ask taking a bite of my pizza. "So, I failed for three years, I'll eventually get her in my bed. You'll see." I say smugly earning another laugh from them both.

"I mean, you cannot deny there is some severe sexual tension, but Sawyer, that's coming from you. The look in her eyes is pure hatred. Do you want her in your bed? You need to stop doing stupid shit like going on press conferences and labelling the parents as neglectful. Because the second she sees that, you're going to wish you weren't born." Scott explains while picking up another slice of pizza.

"I like annoying her." I say bluntly and Tuck practically growls next to me, earning us both to stare at him.

"You know man, we get it. But there is a fine line between annoying her for fun and just making her life miserable. Because that woman, when she found out you would be her boss, tried to hand in her resignation. So, whatever the fuck you did or plan on doing to her, it needs to stop. I get you want to annoy her man, but all you're doing is making her hate you more and this could either end badly for you, or her. And I would hate to see her career go to waste because of your need to get one minute of fun." He says bluntly. I blink, unsure on how to answer that. I know he is right, and deep down I need to stop testing Thea's patience. But, when she makes my cock so hard it hurts and I can't think straight, all I want to do is take it out on her. But not in the way I want to, so I find other methods.

"I can't believe you're taking her side." I say while I fake being wounded,and yet deep down my ego is battered and bruised from the harsh truth I've just received.

"Dude, that woman has worked hard to get into I.C.C.O. She worked hard at the academy; she's never not worked a day in her life." He admits. I exchange a look with Scott as we both turn back to Tuck.

"How did you find that out?"

He takes a drink of his beer and crushes the can. "Because the I.C.C.O have a full file on her." My eyebrows raise and I begin to feel the curiosity seep through my veins. "I don't know the contents, but what I do know is she changed her name before moving to America."

I look at him, completely in awe as to how I never knew this. "So, her name isn't Thea?" I ask curiously and he shakes his head.

"No, her birthname is Theadora. But she

changed it and got rid of a hyphened last name too. So, she goes by Thea St. James legally."

I look over at Scott who is just as surprised as me at the news. I had never heard of an Agent being hired who changed their name, granted she hasn't changed it completely, but it seems strange to me that she would change it just before her move to the states.

"I wouldn't think too much into it, her name is the same. But they got old police reports and medical records as they do with any Agent who is a potential. All Nancy said was this girl has put up with a lot, and not to take her at face value. She wouldn't tell me anything else." Tuck admits. "And granted, I wouldn't have expected her to tell me anyway."

"It's amazing what you can get Nancy to tell you, considering your friends with me and she knows that you'll tell me." I smugly say, earning myself an eye roll.

"Exactly, that was me telling you that no matter how hard you try, that girl isn't going anywhere." He warns me.

I don't understand why he's protecting her; my guess is Nancy told him more than he's letting on. But will I be able to get it out of him? Hell no. He's as stubborn as a mule, not to mention he's incredibly loyal and a man of his word. You can trust Tuck with some of the biggest secrets that you wouldn't even want to burden yourself to, yet he only offers some judgement but a hell of a lot of support. Which is why people go to him for advice, he's wise, yet he isn't that much older than me.

To a lot of people, he's incredibly intimidating, a hard ass even. But he is loyal, that is something I admire about him. You could screw the man over, and he would give you every way you hurt him and would make you feel so bad about it that you lose sleep. He's also built like a house and completely tatted.

When being the head of Undercover Operations, rule number one is don't have anything that would be able to linked to you, not to mention something they'll be able to remember you by. He's tatted, but in all the ways you can't see, not to mention he's tatted with the most generic things that possibly a third of the population has.

"I think we are just looking out for you man. We get it, you want to win a bet. But that girl isn't gonna sleep with you, I think she's the first one with a brain cell." Scott speaks after a while, earning the attention of both of us. Tuck laughs under his breath, and I look away. "Don't throw your job away because of her. This is all in your head. You have to work with her, get used to it." He bluntly says and deep down I agree with him. I know when I walk in tomorrow, she's going to go mad if she's seen the press conference. That's her job, not to mention I've made a fool out of myself.

I don't believe the families had anything to do with it. I think while looking over the small amount of evidence, I think that something darker is at play. But because I wanted a win, I went above her head.

I close my eyes before rubbing my face and getting up to get another beer, ignoring the stares from my friends. "She makes me so angry, all the time." I admit before slamming the fridge door. "I don't understand. I've never had a woman make me feel the way Thea St. James makes me feel. She infuriates me and even when I don't think about her." I say leaning against the fridge.

"I think someone might have a crush." Scott jokes and I lean over and throw his shoe at him.

"Don't be ridiculous."

"He's right, whether you admit it or not, Thea St. James has a hold over you the way no other woman ever has." Tuck pipes up.

I know deep down Tuck is right, because every single time I look at her, I don't only think about doing unspeakable things that would make any other woman cry, but I would want to cherish her because, she is the purest thing to come into this world, although she is incredibly annoying and obnoxious.

EIGHT

Thea

I'm quick into the office today, I have murder on my mind. Sawyer is playing with fire today and I'm about to make sure he knows it.

I wait in the lift for the floor I need to be on and tap my foot, wishing it would go quicker. Why would he do what he did last night? It was just unnecessary not to mention, harsh on the families. He did it to get a rise, and although I'm about to give it to him, he isn't only a problem for me, but for the Mayor. It was already on the news this morning; the man was having to defend himself.

The lift comes to a stop, and I am met with a group of people standing outside of it.

Oh Jesus, it's the families of the teenagers.

The lift doors open and they turn to me, waiting for me to say something.

My heart is pounding out of my chest as I give them a reassuring smile. "Are you Agent St. James?" A man asks coldly.

"I am. You must be the families of the teenagers." I say softly and they all look around in disgust.

"How could you let him say something like that, I thought you were the person who dealt with anything that goes to the press?"

"I can assure you; I wasn't aware it was being made. I am about to go and deal with that matter and I can only apologise for my colleague's accusation on the national news, it should never have happened." I admit and they look around at each other, the women practically clutching onto their husbands while they let them deal with the anger of the situation.

"He should lose his job! We loved our kids very much; we never neglected them. We loved them." A woman cries, clutching at a teddy bear that no doubt belonged to her child.

"I don't don't think for one second that you didn't love your child. I can see that every single one of you did. I will not stand for the accusations that were made and neither will the organization." I say placing my hand gently on her shoulder. "Can I get you all a cup of coffee?" I ask sweetly while looking around at the other parents.

Their anger seems to have calmed down somewhat with my admission and they nod in agreement. Coffee, the way to most people's hearts.

"Agent St. James, I'll take the families to the meeting room and get them coffees." A woman speaks behind me. She's small, but incredibly beautiful. I give her a smile and thank her before reassuring I will be back momentarily while I go and deal with the situation.

The small woman takes the family down the corridor, and I storm through the door of the Criminal Prevention. "Agent St. James?" Some calls after me and I find the same woman running after me. "The Assistant Director told me to tell you she needs to see you in her office."

"Thank you, Agent…"

"McNeil. Ophelia McNeil." She says while extending her hand and I shake it eagerly. "I work with Agent Wilkinson in Casualty Prevention."

"Oh! Yes of course." I say with a smile, and I quickly admire her outfit. She's so stylish, wearing a black and tan striped suit and white blouse. I am going to need to know where she got it from because I need it.

"I think you should hand him his ass if I'm honest, Thea." She admits after a moment. "Everyone is talking about how much he fucked up, but not only that, everyone has been sat in here waiting eagerly for you to give him a piece of your mind." She says with a grin like an excited teenager.

"Well Ophelia, let me just be honest in saying no matter how you approach Sawyer Reid, he will never admit that what he did was wrong, but will try and point the blame on you." I say softly and she begins to laugh.

"I think you might be the woman who puts him in his place, and I want a front row seat because he needs to be served." She chuckles and I can't help but join in.

"Well, let's hope I don't disappoint." I say leaning over and placing my hand on her arm. "Thank you for taking the families and getting them coffee, I really appreciate it."

She gives me a warm smile, the dimples in her cheeks showing. "It's no problem, I wanted to meet you anyway. You've been quite the talk of the office since we found out about Sawyer's little lie." She laughs again this time it's a hearty one.

"I don't like being talked about, however on this occasion, because it is linked to Sawyer's downfall, I'll happily accept."

Leaving me with a smile she heads over to the

kitchen area and begins to make the coffee's I'm assuming.

I turn on my heels and begin to make my way up to his office. The silence when I walk through is deafening. Everyone knows that I'm mad and with the pace I'm walking and the look on my face, it will show how angry I am.

I push open the door with force and he looks up at me, slightly started. "You know what? You have some nerve Sawyer. That was very courageous of you." I say sarcastically while placing my bag on the seat.

"Please Thea, come in. I'm not busy." He sarcastically says which only makes my blood boil more.

"Sawyer, do you understand what you did last night? You went on TV, and accused the families of neglect."

"Yes, I know. I was there."

I take a deep breath. This is useless. Arguing with someone who doesn't see a problem with their actions, is like arguing with a brick wall. "You need to apologise to the families." I say coldly while taking a seat.

He looks at me as his eyes widen, like I had just asked for him to cut off his own arm. "You want me to what?"

"Apologise."

"No."

My eyes widen for a second. "And why is that?"

"I've got nothing to be sorry for, that was my opinion, why would I apologise for it?" He says bluntly.

I take another long deep breath. I am never going to get through to him. "Fine, Sawyer. Don't apologise. But I've just been told I have a meeting with the Assistant Director, probably about you and your actions last night." I say getting up from the chair and I feel his eyes follow me.

"Good for you. Have fun." He says coldly before looking down at his paperwork and ignoring me once again.

I get frustrated and place both hands on his desk causing him to look at me, this time he greets my eyes with a look of frustration. "Sawyer, I'm going to give you two options here." I explain getting closer. That god awful smell of Dior Savage fills my nostrils and I'm struggling not to sneeze. "Either I walk into that meeting with Assistant Director Shields and hand her your badge since you decided to go against the organizations policies and above my head. Or, you go and apologise to the families, and I'll go into that meeting and tell her that you made a mistake and defend you. Now don't think I'm doing this to save your arse, oh no. I'm doing it to save mine, because no matter how many tantrums you have like a toddler, you still need to be told at the age of twenty-six that your actions have consequences. So, what's it going to be?"

He sits, breathing heavy as he slowly rises from his seat, never breaking eye contact. I've never been scared of Sawyer Reid, but with the way he is looking at me right now, I'd say that he will put me in an early grave. I forget he is my boss and by the looks of it if I continue, that might not last for long.

He stands up straight, fixes his suit and walks away from his desk, slightly taking me by surprise. He opens the door, walking down the ramp as he heads in the direction of the meeting room where Ophelia took the families. Everyone in the room is watching carefully as he stops at the door and looks back at me.

Like something in slow motion, I can see from the corner of my eye everyone looking over at me, waiting to see what I'll do next. I hint at him to keep going and from here even I can see the man rolls his eyes before opening the door and shutting it behind him.

The room is eerily silent as everyone watches to see how the families will respond. I watch as he conjures up some shit probably saying how he's sorry, but doesn't really mean it. But also how it's my fault. Everyone is watching, waiting for something to happen through the window of the room.

The suspense is killing me and as much as I would like to go in there and see what he is saying, the whole room gasps as one of the parents slaps Sawyer across the face.

The nervous laughter and audible gasps that form around the room are hilarious and as much as I want to laugh with them, because he did deserve it, I know I have to put on my stern face.

I only raise my eyebrows. Did I expect one of the parents to slap him? Yes, actually I did. He's a dick.

He leaves the room a few moments later, the right side of his face red and with a handprint. My guess is this isn't the first time he's been slapped, and it probably won't be the last. He looks up at me, waiting for my response to his sudden action.

I decide to not give him the satisfaction of knowing he did good, because that is what he wants – praise. I pick up my bag that I left on the seat in his office and make my way down the ramp, the opposite way and towards the Assistant Director's office.

NINE

Thea

“Come in!” Shields shouts after I knock. I take a deep breath, entering her office and greet her with a warm smile. “Agent St. James, thank you for meeting me this morning.” She takes her glasses off and places them on the table before clicking the remote and playing Sawyer's speech on TV last night.

I place my bag on the floor and stand tall watching the tantrum play on the screen.

“As you can see Agent St. James, Agent Reid's actions could go down as a sackable offence. He has not only accused the I.C.C.O of trying to hide child neglect but also, he has upset the Mayor, and from what I've heard, this isn't the first time he's done it while being the Head of Criminal Prevention.” She speaks clearly, the red lipstick that she wears still complimenting her complexion. "I am currently in talks with the Director as what to do with Sawyer Reid, I would just like to get your opinion on it, Agent."

I stand looking down on her, she wants my opinion on what to do with Sawyer. I think my honest answer should be lock him in jail and throw away the key. However, I am a woman of my word and from what I can see he apologized to the families for his accusations. So, I will keep my end of the bargain.

"Ma'am, after arriving this morning to find a lot of upset and angry parents, I went to Agent Reid's office and demanded that he apologise for the accusations he made. He has done that, and from what I have gathered they seemed to have forgiven him. Agent Reid knew what he did was wrong, not only to the agency but also to the families and I have made sure that he has apologised for it." I say calmly and I watch her eyes widen as signals me to sit in front of her.

"You got Sawyer Reid to apologise?" She asks curiously before pouring me a glass of water and placing it in front of me. "I'll say Agent, if you got that man to apologise, hell must be freezing over. Because no matter what Sawyer Reid does, apologising is not one of his strong points." She admits while taking a sip of water.

"As someone who has known the man for

years, I can agree with you on that. But I'd like to think that with him being on report that he will learn that his actions have consequences. Especially when his job is on the line." I smugly say. She greets my smile as she takes another sip of water, the red lipstick staining the glass perfectly.

"You know Thea, when Nancy came to me with your application, I originally turned you down. I admittedly thought that because you never went into a job in law enforcement right after the academy, that you weren't serious about it." She explains. Her tone is slightly harsh; however, I can't fight with her on it. Jobs in law enforcement, especially in Sin City are like gold dust, and come around once in a blue moon. "But; with that being said, I never realized until she showed me the graduation photos that you were in the same class as Sawyer Reid. So, I called my friend at the academy who told me how you and Sawyer despised each other, he would constantly torment you and, the obvious of course, try and get you to sleep with him. But she said that you fought him, you put him in his place and in some cases, you were the only person he'd listen to." She admits which has taken me by surprise. I feel like my expression is a deer in headlights and I'm unsure on how to respond. Sawyer Reid listening to me is something that doesn't happen often. He doesn't listen to anyone, and if he does, it's so he can get something from it in the end. "I needed someone to come in here and give that man a reality check and a run for his money. And after speaking with my friend, you were the only person I had seen as a perfect candidate. As did the Director. However, although you are still new, you are already our biggest asset. Agents that have met you have said you're well spoken, you're kind and not to mention you're compassionate which makes you, the perfect Communications Liaison."

I sit there stunned almost at her kind words about me, but deep down I can feel anger slightly brewing as to why I was hired. I was hired to keep Sawyer Reid in check, and I can't help but feel slightly bitter about that.

"Thank you, Ma'am, I intend on holding a press conference to diminish any rumours that are circling and defend the organisations reputation. I will have it scheduled for this afternoon." I say while beginning to get up trying to change the subject and she greets me.

"Thea, I understand this might be upsetting as to why I hired you. I would feel the same, especially when you've done nothing but had to work hard, harder in some cases than Sawyer Reid. But I wanted to give you the reality first, I don't want there to be secrets between my staff, and I am an honest woman which is why I'm telling you." She admits.

I take a sip of my water before grabbing my bag. "Thank you, Ma'am, for your honesty. If it's alright with you, I'd like to deal with the mess he's made." I say walking towards the door.

"Of course, Agent."

I couldn't get out of that room quick enough, I practically run and head towards the lift. I can't hide my face; it's filled with fury and a slight bit of heartbreak. I wasn't going to be good enough, if it weren't for my past with Sawyer, I wouldn't have got this job.

The lift closes and goes down to the floor where my office is. I have too much to do, however I need get my emotions intact before I go into a room with heartbroken parents. The lift opens and I head towards my office and to my surprise, it's already open.

I thought I shut the door last night.

I approach it with slight caution and walk in to find a tall, viking like man standing looking over the books on my bookshelf.

"Hello." I say breaking the silence and he turns quickly to meet me.

"Hi, I'm Justin Tucker-Barlow, I'm the Head of Undercover Operations. I don't think I've met you yet." He greets me while extending his hand.

"Thea St. James." I say shaking it eagerly. "I've seen you about." I say with a smile.

"So, how are you finding the job so far?" He asks as he takes a seat over on the sofa in my office. "I saw the press conference; we all told him not to do it. But the man doesn't listen." He jokes slightly.

The thought of Sawyer Reid and his actions makes me blood boil, just the thought of the man in general at the moment. I stand there, not laughing with him and he notices as he stands up.

"Thea, he will never make your life easy, especially if you're working under him. But what I will tell you is if he is out of line and he does something that even you can't control, Scott and I will be the first to tell him or beat him up, depending on what he's done." He admits honestly.

His look is genuine, sincere and for the first time today, I think I smile. A genuine smile. His friends calling out his bullshit is going to help me greatly while I build my case against him on the down low.

"I appreciate that." I say, while I pick up my laptop out of my bag. "I'm sorry, I've got a handful of things to fix. It's been really nice meeting you Justin." I say to him.

"Tuck. Call me Tuck." He repeats, "Everyone else does." He says with a smile. A silence falls on us for a few moments, but it's not uncomfortable.

"I better go. But if you need anything Thea, just let me know." He says sweetly before exiting my office and walking down the corridor.

I walk back over to my bag and grab my notebook and pen and turn to find a redhead standing at my door. "You good?" She asks, eyebrows raised and once again her style is knocked out of the park.

"Were you going to tell me that she only hired me to keep Sawyer in check?" I say walking past her and standing at the door. She's quick to follow me out.

"I mean if I knew, maybe. But I only found out five minutes ago." I shut the door behind her and begin walking down towards the pen.

"Of course." I mock slightly and she grabs my arm, stopping me.

"That is the truth. Sawyer is a dick. Never did I think she was hiring you because of your history with him. She told me that she was impressed with your exam results and your interview. I didn't have any reason to question it, until a few minutes ago. But I still sent that letter, and you are still here, Thea." She says harshly. She's right, I am still here. And I'm off to go and interview some heartbroken families.

"I'm sorry." I apologise quickly, the genuine reaction on her face is enough to make me feel guilty.

"Don't apologise, just make Shields realize she made the right decision to hire you as Communication's Liaison, rather than Sawyer's babysitter."

She winks at me before walking in the same way we just came. The way she walks always leaves me captivated by her gracefulness.

I decide that I've left those families waiting long enough, and it's time to get an understanding of those kids.

TEN

Thea

Placing the glass of water in her hands, I take a seat on the table opposite. "Mr and Mrs Holland, can you tell me about your daughter?"

They cry and so they should. My heart sits here, a twenty-six-year-old Agent, breaking for a family who lost their daughter in one of the worst ways possible. Something I can't even imagine going through.

"She was wonderful." Mrs Holland speaks so quietly. I can't help but smile as they hand me some photos of her from when she was younger. Photos from Halloween, Christmas, what I can only assume is Thanksgiving and her fifteenth birthday. "She was so selfless, and really enjoyed helping other people. She was good in school; she was going to do well." Mr Holland cries placing his head in his hands, he continues to bawl hard. I can't even imagine this, all of these parents, all going through the same heartbreak.

"I want to ask you all a question if it is alright?" I question getting everyone's attention. Mr Holland begins to compose himself slightly listening into my question. "Now, I'm not saying this is a possibility, but do you know anyone that would want to hurt your children?" I ask them.

A bunch of confused faces, begin to circle the room as I look around. "What do you mean?" Mr Osman, Sarah's dad asks. "Do you think that this was targeted?"

I shake my head wanting to defer the questions and theories circulating their brains. "Mr Osman, I am just asking as we need to get a better understanding on why your children died. We have to rule out every possibility." I say to him calmly and he only erupts.

"You sound like a fucking FED. Is that what you are? A FED? Someone who is going to leave us in the dark? To deal with the heartbreak and have to find out the answers on our own?" He shouts and quickly his sister, Marie tries to calm him down, but it isn't doing anything.

"Mr Osman I can assure you; I am going nowhere. No, I am not a FED. I work for I.C.C.O, and I am the person who will make sure you, the families, have voices when law enforcement shuts you out. I am here to find out what happened. I understand you're upset, and I cannot imagine what every single one of you is feeling right now, this is such an uncertain situation. But like I said, I will not leave until we have an answer as to what happened." I reassure him.

It takes him sometime to calm down from his outburst, even with a few of the other parents, taking him to one corner. I meant what I said, I don't understand what they are going through. But I do understand that the FBI left them when they really needed someone.

After a few moments of silence, the door opens and I find Sawyer standing there, his eyes wide as he scans the room. He locks eyes with me, and I feel his annoyance radiate through the room and I watch him struggle to make eye contact with any family member in this room. There is still some tension in the room as to Sawyer's little accusation. "Agent St. James, do you have a minute?" He asks quietly and I get up, giving reassuring smiles to the families before exiting the room and closing the door. I have to practically run to catch up with him as he moves away from the room with all of the family members. "I need you to talk to the siblings. The FBI have already questioned the parents, they didn't know anything. You need to talk to the siblings. Go." He snaps at me before turning on his heels but I'm quick to stop him.

"You're right, the FBI did talk to them. But then they left, and they are unsure on if they can trust us. So, I should help the parents of the kids that died and then I'll have conversations with the siblings." I say turning around only to hear him grunt and I stop in my tracks.

"Agent St. James." He warns, grabbing my arm firmly. "Do as you're told for once. For Christ's sake, if it wasn't the parents putting so much pressure on them, the kids might still be here." He snaps and I am quick to break the space between us. He's furious with me, just because I won't listen to him. But why should I?

"Sawyer, I will not question how you do your job when you actually do it, but I also would appreciate it if you didn't tell me how to do mine. Just because you're as dry as the Sahara Desert over there with leads in that room doesn't mean I am. So, shut your mouth and do something useful, like find the empathy you left alongside your audacity on the floor over there."

The man's face is a picture, he honestly doesn't know how to react before I pull myself away from him, something woman never do. Except me.

As if I would ever let him tell me how to do my job, not to mention try and say it's the family's fault. He knows it isn't, but because he didn't get to choose this case himself.

I think he's frustrated, yet that isn't an excuse no matter how you're feeling.

I walk into the room, and I'm greeted with twelve surprised faces who look at me like they've seen a ghost. "It was nothing to worry about, however I was wondering if I could talk to the children's siblings?" I ask while shutting the door.

Mr Osman is the first person to object. "Absolutely not, Timmy has been through enough I don't need you making up stories to get things out of him. I don't allow you to talk to him." He objects and I give a slight nod while his sister tries to reason with him.

"Mick, maybe she might have told him something-"

"Why would she? She wasn't speaking to any of us for weeks!" He cries and I instantly feel the room go cold. Mr Osman sits down on the chair bawling his eyes out while some of the other parents console him. "We got into an argument, I found out she was dating an older man and I was furious." He says almost as a whisper, and I get down onto my knees to meet him with sympathy. "I told her he was no good and we got into an argument about it, and I grounded her and banned her from seeing him. That was three weeks ago."

He lifts his flannel and begins to wipe his eyes. I look around the room at the other parents who stand, uncertain of what to say. "Mr Osman, can you tell me what the boy was called?"

"Jackson Settler. He's part of the biker club round town."

"Jolene was dating someone too. It was very new though." Mrs George speaks from beside me and looks down at Mick. "I understand your concern, he was older except he wasn't a biker, he was an outcast someone from school. He was a few years older, seventeen."

"Could this be targeted?" One of the other parents speak up and I quickly shake my head.

"Let's not jump to conclusions just yet. But I'm going to need the name of the boy Jolene was dating." I say looking towards Mrs George.

"Isaac Fields. He was extremely weird." She says and shivering as if someone walked over her grave. "He gave us a bad vibe. All of us."

With my current information, I set out to walk towards the room with Sawyer and the rest of his team. The parents would have told the FBI if they had stuck around. But from what I could see, Mr Osman felt so guilty that it was breaking him in half. He wasn't on speaking terms with his daughter, and that is devastating for anyone to hear.

"You got something for us St. James? Or you here to give us some bad news?" Sawyer speaks just as I walk through the door.

"You wish. Actually, I have two names that I need you to look up." I say to him, and his eyes widen while looking me up and down. Why is he surprised?

I ignore his stares and go over to the laptop of the tech guy, who I haven't learned the name of yet. Leaning over next to the quiet guy I can feel him tense up underneath me as I get close to him and look towards him over my shoulder.

"How can I help y-you ma-am?" He stutters and I give him a small smile.

"Could you look up Isaac Fields and Jackson Settler for me please?" I ask nicely batting my eyelashes and he nods very quickly before typing on the computer. I catch Sawyer's expression and he doesn't look the least bit impressed. *Ha.*

"Why those people?" He questions while crossing his arms trying to submit some authority.

Placing my hand on the tech guy's chair, I look directly at Sawyer. "Isaac Fields was dating Jolene George. He was older, seventeen or so. But fifteen-year-old Sarah Osman was dating a biker called Jackson Settler." I explain, causing him to roll his eyes in front of me.

"So, she had an older boyfriend, so what?" He says now standing next to me, that authority still all over his face and no matter how hard he tries to deny it, he's jealous that he's spent three hours trying to understand something or find something out about the kids that I found out in fifteen minutes.

"So, it's wrong. She was fifteen years old; God knows what went on in their relationship. He's a grown man, he should know better." I explain, disgusted with his statement.

He once again rolls his eyes clearly annoyed by me even opening my mouth. "Thea, you can't accuse the guy of being older, we know nothing yet." He says, a smug look coming over his face.

"Actually, Agent St. James is right, Jackson Settler is thirty-four years old." The techy guy admits in front of us, and like we are in unison, Sawyer, and I both lean on either side of the poor guy to see if it's actually true.

"Good god, he's almost twenty years older." I almost cry. How could a man be interested in a child?

"Dirty fucker." Sawyer says clearly and I can't help but pull a face of disbelief to one of his team who begins to chuckle underneath his breath. "Anything on the Isaac kid?" He asks still leaning over the poor tech guy.

"Yeah, he has been in trouble with the law a lot this year." He explains and I once again lean forward and look through Isaacs records.

"That's a pretty rap sheet." Sawyer jokes. "He's had an eventful year. Arson, narcotics possession, theft. Kids just doing it for fun at the moment."

I look at the first date on the rap sheet. What happened prior to this for him to go off the rails and get in trouble with the law?

"I'm going to speak to the school, see if they can give me a reason as to why Isaac has been in and out of jail this year." I say before going to walk off and Sawyer is very quick to stop me.

"Why are you doing that? It's not going to help. And last time I checked, Liaisons don't go into the field to interrogate. You stay here." He instructs harshly, his hand gripping my arm so tight I know he is going to leave a bruise.

"I don't do your job; you don't do mine. I have a hunch." I say, now getting so close to him that he steps back slightly. He hates it, he values his personal space, but he can't respect mine. "Now get off me before I class this as strike two."

He doesn't move for second and all I can taste is his cologne. It's like he's trying to get me drunk with it.

After a moment, he lets go and while giving

him a glare. I walk away towards the family waiting room. *Prick.*

Trying to compose myself, I take a deep breath as I enter the room, all eyes now on me. Hoping I have an answer to the endless number of questions that are running around in their brains.

"I've got a few of the team looking into both of them. So, we appreciate the help with those leads. They are going to help us get a better understanding hopefully of what's happened. But that is all I have for today in regard to questions, but if any of your other kids want to come in and talk about what happened my door is always open and I'm always available for a chat." I say with a smile.

One by one the families head out, clutching one another as they walk towards the lift. Just as Mr Osman is about to leave, I stop him.

"I know this isn't my place sir, but I wanted to say that no matter how much guilt you're feeling right now about Sarah, I can assure you that no matter what she loved you. Please remember that." I say holding onto his arm lightly. After a few fallen tears, he grips my hand and holds it tightly.

"Thank you."

He begins to walk towards the lift, and I run after him and his sister, Marie. "I have a favour to ask." I say to him, causing him to look up, "Whatever you do, do not approach Jackson Settler, and if you are to see him, call us. You have the number for the team. Please don't do anything you might regret." I plead. He is quick to shake his head.

"Agent, I can't agree to that." He says quietly, not wanting to speak to loudly as the other parents hold the lift for them.

"Think of Timmy." I plead. His eyes grow sad once more and he closes them. "Please, Mr Osman. Make me this promise that you'll let us deal with Jackson Settler."

He hesitates for a few moments. Looking up at the rest of the distraught parents that stand in the lift, waiting to go home. "I promise."

ELEVEN

Thea

"Take a seat, Agent St. James." The principal signals me. I smile as I take a seat gratefully, taking in her impressive certificates that line the walls of the office. "I was wondering when someone from law enforcement was going to speak to me."

"I'm surprised they haven't if I'm honest. However the I.C.C.O have just been given the case and I wanted to come and speak to you about a student that's recently been mentioned in the investigation." I begin to explain, and she moves her eyes to the pile of files on the side of her desk and I eye them up with her.

"Pick one." She encourages with a hint of humour in her voice. "I went through the ones who are the most troubling, as I had assumed you would want to speak to them first." Well, this woman is thorough.

"Do you speak to the police a lot, Mrs White?" I ask her sweetly. She shakes her head at me.

"No, however I've seen enough crime shows to know that the weird kids, or outcasts as I'm meant to put them." She says sarcastically, giving me in the indication she honestly doesn't know how to deal with them. "They are always the first ones to be looked at."

I give her a sarcastic grin before getting a bit comfortable in the chair. "Mrs White, I'm just wanting some information on a student, Isaac Fields?"

Her face drops for a second when I mention his name. "Why do you need to talk to Isaac? What has he done?" She quicky defends him and I become confused.

"Mrs White, do you have a connection to Isaac?" I ask bluntly and her face turns sour and cross. I've hit a nerve.

"He's my son."

I feel like my face is a very telling story as to my reaction to the news. "He's your son?" I repeat.

"Yes, now why do you want to speak to him?" She asks harshly, sitting back in her chair giving me the indication she's waiting for me to mention his rap sheet.

"It was to our understanding that Isaac was dating Jolene-"

"False." She quickly shuts me up.

"I'm sorry?"

"I said it's false. He wouldn't date someone like Jolene, she was too high maintenance, not to mention she bullied him as did the rest of that little group." She speaks harshly, her tone flat but a hint of annoyance is in her throat. "That group bullied him for months and no matter how many times I tried to stop it, they continued, but it got worse every time."

She's disgusted with my accusation that Isaac and Jolene were dating, but also that I didn't know they were bullies.

"I am very surprised that none of the other parents mentioned that they knew of my son and the torture that he endured while being here in the presence of the sinister six." She says coldly and I realise what sits in front of me is a protective mother bear that will do anything to protect her son.

"Mrs White, I have to ask this. Where was your son the night the other teenagers died?"

Her demeanour changes and she leans in with the intention of intimidating me. Her musk and lavender scent filling my nose and taking in every bit of oxygen I have in my bubble. "With me, all night." She says, bone chillingly cold.

I give her a nod, noting that I'll not be asking anymore questions about her son and his whereabouts on the night the other kids died.

"Mrs White, do you have documents about the bullying that your son endured? It will help with our case of understanding the other teenagers, but also if you have any other people who have been victim to them, I'd like to take those reports too." I say with a reassuring smile, and she gets out of her chair eagerly.

"I understand you can't prosecute the dead Agent St. James, but I would like these back as I will be making a case against the parents because they allowed it to go on for so long." She says pulling out a box of files from her cupboard. "I think that it has to be one of the weird kids, so you can take their records too." She instructs, placing all of the files in a box and holding it, hinting she would like for me to leave.

"Of course. But I do just have one question Mrs White if you don't mind." I asks sweetly and her cold demeanour changes to a softer one, but I know that the question I'm about to ask, she might end up kicking me out of her office. "Why has Isaac been arrested so many times this year?"

Her face drops and she immediately turns pale in her face. "How did you know about that?

His records are meant to be expunged." She says almost as a whisper.

"Who said that?"

"Mayor Meyers. He said in order for me to not press charges against his daughter, he would make Isaacs criminal record go away. Isaac had a bad few months, the bullying got worse, and he started acting out." She practically whispers, the expression on her face turning to pure anger. "Are you telling me he lied?"

I turn and open the door slowly with the box under my arm. "I'm telling you what I know." I say before exiting the office and making my way down the corridor and out of the school. Although Isaac is looking like a highly likely suspect in this case, I cannot help but deep down think his mother had something to do with it.

She's incredibly protective of her son, but also her job. Why didn't she take Isaac out of that school or have the board deal with the bullying? I want to say that because Piper Meyers and her friends had parents in high places, that the bullying was just seen as a minor issue and because Mrs White had a duty of care, that maybe a donation towards the school was mentioned and it all of a sudden was swept underneath the carpet.

Placing the box in my car; I turn back and look up at the school noticing, clear as day, Mrs White watching and waiting for me to leave. Something isn't sitting right with me on this entire case, and the more I look at this and whatever we can call facts, I believe that something a lot darker is at play. But what that is just yet, I can't be sure.

TWELVE

Sawyer

I stand behind Johnson, the tech guy, while I watch his every move. He can't seem to find anything on any of the teenagers' laptops, which in my opinion, is not a good thing.

I'm struggling to find a motive and any sort of reason as to why this is anything other than suicide. Yes, it is strange for them to suddenly all want to hang themselves, but there is no reason to believe anything otherwise. My opinion is that they put too much pressure on their kids. The older boyfriend theories are just a bit too farfetched for me.

I've ruled out sacrifice and cult relations, and none of the teenagers were sexually active apart from Sarah Osman. That was found in the medical examiner's report. She had sex, more than likely with her older boyfriend, between three and six hours before her death. That makes my skin crawl, she was fifteen, and a thirty-four-year-old man, took advantage of her. That is the only correct way of looking at it.

"Come on Johnson, find me something." I say smacking the back of his head. "I can't still be stood here empty handed when trouble walks through the door." I exclaim taking a long exhale.

"Who sir?" He asks quickly and I can't help but grunt.

"Thea, Miss St. James, the posh brit who doesn't listen to a word I say." I say leaning over his shoulder again, he tenses under me, and I can feel it.

I'm not intimidating in the slightest, but Johnson has always been nervous of my presence. I like having him on my team because he can find things out about people that even they didn't want people to know about.

"I can hear you bitching from across the room Sawyer." The irritating voice speaks behind me, and I turn to give her a fake grin.

"Missed you, darling. We've been so busy here, haven't we Johnson?" I exclaim placing my hand firmly on his shoulders and he tenses. You would think with how he is acting I had a gun to the back on his head.

"Is that so?" She mocks as she places the box down on the desk. "Johnson, has he done anything while I've been out?" She quizzes him, giving him a look. I feel like we're parents, arguing in front of our kid.

I can feel the man start to sweat underneath me, and I know fine well with the way she's looking at him, he's going to crumble. I want her to look at me like that, I'd even let her dominate me if she asked.

"No Ma'am, he hasn't done a thing." Johnson admits and I slap him on the back of the head.

The horror that appears on her face is something like off a picture. "That's assault!" She exclaims and I begin to walk away from her. "Are you alright Johnson?"

I can't help but roll my eyes, shoving past the other agents while walking back to my office. "I'm bored, and I don't care what's in the files. It's just more work for you to do." I shout behind me.

I hear someone clear their voice and I turn on my heels and see trouble standing there with an unamused look on her face. "Do you not want to know what I found out?"

"Not really, cause it's probably nothing." I mock slightly, a smile growing on my face which she ignores and walks towards the board filled with photos of evidence, victims, and possible motives.

"Isaac Fields was dating Jolene George. That we already knew. But not one of us knew that this entire friendship group bullied Isaac Fields and have done for the past few months."

I can't stop my facial expression. *Well shit, that's a turn.*

"So why was Jolene dating him? And why would Isaac date her if she were part of the group that bullied him?" Grayson, one of the other Agents on the team asks.

"All good questions, I'm not sure on yet. But there are a few twists and turns in this case already." She admits, before moving Isaacs photo so it has its own space on the board. "He's the son of the headteacher."

The entire teams face drops, and we begin to try and peace together how that is something we missed when looking into Isaac Fields.

"He can't be. Isaac Fields's mother died when he was three." Reynolds pipes up.

"Ah! It's his stepmother. She's been in his life since he was at least four." Johnson speaks placing his hand in the air. I shoot him a look with a warning, there is no point in getting in my good books now.

"She was incredibly protective over him."

"Doesn't say why six kids died from a suicide." I say harshly and I watch as Thea pulls a face.

"No, you're right it doesn't, but in here is all of the files that she had on every incident with either Isaac or any other child and files on people she labelled as weird." She says, emphasising the weird. She opens the box and begins placing the files on the desk. "She had them all prepared for my arrival, but when I asked, gladly gave me the box with all of the notes on the incidents that happened at the school."

Each Agent takes a file and begins to go through them without any instruction while Johnson begins moving onto the next computer trying to find anything that can help us understand why these kids decided to kill themselves.

"Anything else, Agent Trouble?" I ask, standing in front of her. The sweet smells of jasmine and amber fill my nose and I begin to get excited. The look on her face tells me she's the least bit amused with the nickname, but I gave her the nickname years ago, so it stays.

"That nickname is disgusting." She says, turning her face up causing me to laugh.

"It's the only pleasant one I'm allowed to say in this setting, so it stays." I chuckle and the disgust only grows on her face.

"I don't want to know what goes on in your brain." She says, placing the lid back on the box and pushing it under the table. "I'd probably have nightmares."

"Or the night of your life, sweetheart." I give her a wink and she groans in disgust before turning away from me quickly.

"Just another thing, before I go." She says to the team, meaning fine well she's now going to avoid me. "Mayor Meyers said he would expunge Isaac Fields record if Mrs White didn't press charges against his daughter, Piper."

I scowl behind her; she really is proving to be the smartest woman in the room right now and she's making me look like a fool.

"I found that out in an hour..." She says looking over her shoulder at me. "What have you been doing, Agent Reid?"

I watch as she walks away and towards the door and I groan in annoyance having to ask a painful question. "Where are you going?" I shout after her.

"I am now off to do my job, which entails fixing your mess from yesterday, and asking the family members why they lied to my face this morning."

Watching her walk away from me must be one of the best things in this world. She has me in a trance the way her hair is curled today, and the cropped suit does wonders for her ass. Not to mention with the T-shirt she's wearing, you can see her nipples if you stare hard enough. I close my eyes, not wanting to picture the unholy things that my mind thinks about when she's around me.

I look down at the team who are watching me, smiles on their faces instead of their heads in the cases. "Find something." I instruct before picking up a mountain of cases and carrying them to my desk.

My sex fantasies about Thea St. James have started again, I woke up four times last night thinking about fucking her so hard till she cried, or how I'd use my box of toys on her. Something I've not used for an exceptionally long time. But for her? I'd do anything to hear her beg or scream my name.

Deep down I think she's either a virgin or she's as vanilla as Ben and Jerry's ice cream. Plain. But that doesn't stop the ungodly thoughts I have about her, and that hair of hers. She drives me crazy, and I need her off this case before I either kill her and her sass or I kill myself because I can't control myself around her.

THIRTEEN

Thea

I enter the conference room and am greeted with a bunch of cameras and journalists who begin eagerly getting from their seats and flash their cameras. My first press conference, something that I never thought I would end up doing for a job.

"Good afternoon, thank you for joining me. My name is Special Agent Thea St. James, I'm the Communications Liaison for I.C.C.O." I begin. "Yesterday, a press conference went ahead without my knowledge about the current case the Criminal Prevention team are looking into. Last week, six teenagers' bodies were found and have been ruled a suicide. There is no current evidence to state there was any foul play but since these deaths all happened on the same night, we are currently calling this case suspicious. As of right now, we are looking into every lead we have, however if you have something that would be able to help in the investigation, I urge you to come forward and call our tipline."

Journalists begin to swarm and ask questions even before I've finished, and in my annoyance, I place my hand up. "In regard to the press conference that was held yesterday," I practically shout hinting for them to shut up and let me speak. "The Agent in question has since apologised to the families and will not be making any other statements regarding the case or any future case within the organization. I will now take some questions."

They are like a pack of hungry wolves, screaming at me to answer their questions. I look over and point to a smaller man in glasses and cheap suit. He stands nervously while flipping over his notepad. "John Thompson, Agent St. James, for the Island Magazines, can you tell us why the I.C.C.O is suddenly interested in the case? The FBI didn't seem to want it, so why would the I.C.C.O take their sloppy seconds?"

Ballsy.

"The I.C.C.O took over the original investigation that was led by the FBI as they had another pressing case to attend to, and as per agreement between both enforcements agencies, the I.C.C.O will be taking the lead on the investigation from now on and the FBI has no involvement." I explain and he begins to chuckle.

"So, what you're saying Agent St. James, is the FBI couldn't be bothered to look into the suspicious suicides to six teenagers, so they sent the next best thing who end up accusing the families of child neglect and sending some British bimbo to come to his defence." He mocks me and a bunch of the journalists gasp in horror at his accusations.

"Mr Thompson, I am not a spokesperson for the FBI, but I am for I.C.C.O, and as someone who is actively looking into the case and working with the Criminal Prevention team, we are looking at every possibility."

"I just think it is interesting…"

"Oh! You're done speaking? Excellent! Next question." I say cutting him off. His face goes red with embarrassment before I turn to the next journalist, a redheaded woman who stands just as nervously.

"Shannon McAdams for Files Investigations, Agent St. James." She says with a smile while looking down at her notepad. "There are some rumours that there are a few people of interest in this case, is it a possibility that this is being treat as more than a suicide?"

"Ms McAdams, currently the deaths are being treat as suspicious but the cause of death for all six teenagers is suicide. As this is an active investigation, I cannot answer any more questions on the matter, however we are looking at any other possibility, just to rule it out." I say with a smile. She is pleasant and thanks me before sitting down.

"Ronald Richardson for the Sin City News. Can I ask why they have a Brit currently investigating on an American case and how you work closely with the I.C.C.O with them having a policy of no one other than Americans in their organization." He questions and I deep down want to laugh.

"Mr Richardson, I am both a British and American citizen. Meaning I have the same rights as you, but with this being a press conference about the current case, I see this question as irrelevant and I'm ending the press conference here. Thank you for coming, if you have anything that might be able to help with the investigation, please contact the number on the screen." I say abruptly before leaving the press conference room with a pile of papers in my hand.

My hands are sweaty, and the only person who seemed to ask a genuine question was Mrs McAdams. The rest of them wanted to know why a British woman was working for an American organization. I mean it's not hard.

"Agent St. James!" Someone calls from behind me, and I find Mr Richardson, the last reporter running towards me. "I wanted to apologise if I was out of line in there." He admits and I can't help but chuckle.

"You were, but thank you for your apology. Have a good day." I say turning on my heels. Suddenly he's in front of me stopping me from walking away.

"I was wondering if you were free tonight for dinner?" He asks with a grin, a cheesy one. My insides turn inside out, and I am struggling to keep a straight face.

"No, thank you. Maybe you should make dinner for your partner." I say looking down at his wedding ring, and back up. I watch as he closes his eyes, exhales and chuckles.

"It's not what you think." He says in his defence.

"Have a good day, Mr Richardson." I say walking past him and towards the lift to my office. Some men have some nerve. Nothing worse than a married man or any man for that matter, offending you, apologising and then asking for a date. It is the classic way of trying to get laid. Something I've avoided for so many years, especially with being around Sawyer, he really made me hate men. I was in the stage where I hated men already when I got to the academy, except it just continued throughout my years there and even after I left. I don't want anyone, I don't want to date. I want to be alone, that's the best thing.

I walk quickly to my desk, realising that I now have to call round six set of parents to ask them to come in for a conversation. I don't understand why they lied to me, or why they just failed to mention that their children were bulling the headteachers son.

I open the door, almost jumping out of my skin when I notice someone in my seat.

"Sawyer! What are you doing?" I exclaim as he turns round in the seat and stares at me, shocked.

"How did you know it was me?"

"The mirror, you idiot." I say trying to calm my beating heart. "Jesus, what do you want?"

"I was very impressed today on how you handled those reporters, it was hot." He says getting up and sitting on the end on my desk and looking up at me, a smirk on his face that gives me the ick.

I turn my face at him. "Thanks, I guess." I say placing the piles of paper on the table and opening my laptop to gather the numbers of the parents.

"You know, I appreciate you coming to my

defence in there." He says softly and I look up, confused by his assumption.

"I didn't defend you Sawyer. That is something I'd never do." I practically laugh at him.

I watch as his eyes turn dark for a moment, like the predator inside of him is woken from a deep slumber and he's hungry and wanting to eat. "Trouble, don't laugh at me." He warns but it only makes me laugh that little bit harder.

"Sawyer, just so I make myself clear. We are not going to sleep together, ever. I would rather die than spend two seconds in your presence like that. So whatever fantasies go on in your head twenty-four seven. Block. Them. Out. Because it will never happen." I warn him with a sarcastic grin and look down at my laptop trying to ignore him.

"Thea, have you ever thought that one day you're probably going to cave in and want me just as bad as I want you?" He admits causing me to look back up. This man is completely delusional.

"Like I said, I would rather die. I'm already stuck with you as my boss, I don't need you to give me anymore of a headache by making me fake an orgasm. Now get out, I need to call some parents." I usher him and a grin grows on his lips.

"Darling, if you're wanting to fake an orgasm with Mr Richardson, the reporter, then that's fine, you do that. But you'll never fake an orgasm with me, that I can promise you." He says confidently and I feel my stomachs churn.

"Okay big guy, keep walking." I say shooing him out of my office and he leaves in a chuckle. I have no idea what the hell has just happened, nor do I want to understand it.

Sawyer Reid will be the last man I ever sleep with, even if hell froze over. Because the second I'm to entertain him or let that happen, is the day I lose the bet, and so far, … I'm winning.

FOURTEEN

Thea

I open the door and I'm met with eleven confused faces. I look around and I'm overly concerned as to why Mr Osman isn't here.

"Where's Mick?" I ask Marie, his sister curiously and she shakes her head.

"I don't know, he dropped me off at home and no one has seen him since, I was hoping you could help me look for him." She pleads, tears streaming down her face. "Timmy is asking for him, and I can't tell him anything because I don't know."

I place my hand firmly on hers, giving her a reassuring look. "We'll find him, give me one second." I say clearly before walking back out of

107

the meeting room and into the pen.

"Well, that was quick." Smith jokes as I approach him.

"Mr Osman's missing. His sister is here, yet no one has seen Mick since he left this morning." I admit to them.

"He's probably just blowing off a little steam." Sawyer speaks from the railing in front of his office. "I'm sure it's nothing to worry about." He reassures me. But suddenly I'm puzzled by his reaction as I see him bolt down the ramp and run towards the door of the pen.

In front of my eyes, I notice Mr Osman punching the living daylights out of a man who I can only assume is Jackson Settler, not only that, but he is doing it in a government issued building, and he made a promise.

"You son of a bitch! You raped my daughter!" He screams at the top of his lungs. I watch as the rest of the family members come out of the meeting room in horror as they watch him smack Jackson around.

"Can I ask you to wait in the meeting room please?" I ask them, practically pushing them to go back in. I ask an Agent sitting on the desk opposite to stand in front of the door as I go and deal with the situation.

"Your daughter asked for it, she was a filthy

slut." Jackson speaks up, practically choking on his own blood.

Mr Osman continues punching him until Sawyer comes in and breaks them up, dragging Mr Osman with all of his weight, pushing him down the corridor.

"That's enough!" Sawyer screams in Mr Osman's face. The man looks so broken as we all turn and watch Jackson Settler, slowly but surely get to his feet, clutching his ribs, which are more than likely broken.

"He raped my little girl." Mr Osman cries on Sawyer's shoulder. The man who is incapable of showing human emotion or empathy, is now having to deal with a heartbroken father.

"Like I said, she was a filthy slut. She deserved everything I gave her." Jackson says the cockiness in his voice irritating more than anything and my skin begins to crawl.

"Admission is a powerful thing, Mr Settler." I say as he turns back around. Blood pouring from his mouth and his nose. He needs serious medical attention; however, I won't be getting it that quickly.

"Oh yeah, sweetheart? Is me admitting having sex with my girlfriend a crime, huh?" He practically mocks.

"Well, *sweetheart* when your girl is fifteen, it's

classed as rape." I say smugly while an Agent stands behind him and arrests him. Jackson is so shocked and begins trying to fight with the officers.

"She was seventeen! She said she was seventeen!" He screams in his defence before being dragged away from two agents and away from Mr Osman.

"Mr Osman, you're under arrest-"

"Agent Reid, wait," I say in Mr Osman's defence. "I need to speak to him first before you arrest him."

Mr Osman looks terrified as I lead him away and into the room with the other parents. They all run to him, some calling him an idiot, some of them applauding his actions, mainly the men.

As I turn around, I notice Sawyer standing behind me, watching Mr Osman like a hawk. "Sawyer can you get me the first aid kit." I ask nicely, but he doesn't budge.

He's not took his eyes of Mr Osman.

"Sawyer?" I say quietly, causing him to look at me. "Please?"

He hesitates, before walking away from the door and up to the kitchen bringing back the first aid kit so I can tend to Mr Osman, who right now has a broken hand clearly from punching Jackson's face so many times. "I'm in on this interview." He orders, stepping past me and taking a seat in the corner, not saying another word.

I shut the door behind him, ignoring his presence I kneel before Mr Osman who holds his head in his hands, sobbing uncontrollably.

"Mick?" I ask sweetly. After a moment, he looks up at me, his eyes sad and face puffy. "Can I clean you up?"

He hesitates for a moment when he notices Sawyer in the room, he looks over at me. "You got your bodyguard in here?"

"I don't need a man to protect me, I'm capable of doing that myself. Not going to ask again, last offer. Do you want me to clean you up?" I ask him again, my tone slightly harsh this time.

He is quick to nod, and I put gloves on while pulling out an antibacterial wipe. "You going to tell us why we're here?" Mr Holland speaks, annoyed by the silence.

"Because you all lied to me earlier, and I wanted to give you the chance to explain yourselves." I say, not taking my eyes off cleaning the blood from Mr Osman's hands.

"What are you talking about?" I hear him mumble above me which catches my attention.

"Why did none of you admit that your children bullied Isaac Fields for the last few months? Did you think we wouldn't find that out?" I ask them, annoyance in my voice and they can sense it.

They stay silent. They either thought we wouldn't find out, or that we wouldn't have worked it out.

"Miss St. James, I don't know what you're accusing us-"

"It's Agent, and you're damn right if you think I'm sitting here and accusing you of a cover up." I say through my teeth, glaring at Mayor Meyers. "You of all people especially, who said to Mrs White, the headteacher, that you would expunge Isaacs record if she didn't press charges."

He bites the inside of his lip and decides to keep silent, that's until the other parents notice. "You told her you would do that? For that freak?" Mr Todd, Oscar's dad speaks.

"Of course, I wasn't going to do it. But Isaac and his parents were going to make a case against Piper, I had to protect her. And if you think about it, I was going to be protecting your kids too! Last thing we needed was our kids in jail!"

"The kid was weird, he was odd. Everything they did is normal high school bullying. He was odd towards Oscar."

"He was odd in general!"

"That doesn't matter, your children bullied

a boy!" I shout, frustrated by their lack of compassion for a sixteen-year-old. "No wonder your children were the way they were, you were practically encouraging the behaviour even more so by being generous donors." The silence in the room is eery as the parents hug each other, each of them quietly sobbing. "Your children beat that boy, locked him in the school freezer for hours, took his clothes from the gym, publicly humiliated him on numerous occasions. Do you see a pattern? Your children were bullies and that headteacher couldn't do anything because you paid money to keep her there." Sawyer pipes up from the corner, getting awfully close to the Mayor. "You made sure that she wasn't going nowhere, and neither was her son."

"Mrs George, why was Jolene dating Isaac?" I ask her. She's been awfully quiet in the corner with her husband John.

"Don't know." She says quickly looking away.

"You're lying."

"I don't know!" She screams from across the room at me.

I begin bandaging up Mr Osman's hand best I can, ignoring Mrs George.

"Amanda, you, and Jolene were so close. Closer than a normal mother and daughter." Sawyer accuses while standing next to me, like he's trying to protect me. "You know damn well why she was dating him." He says to her harshly.

He face goes bright red while she looks over at her husband for help. He gives her nothing, just staring blankly at her. He knows that she knows.

"Mrs George, we will arrest you with failing to provide information to a government official if you don't tell us why." Sawyer warns her. I stand up from cleaning up Mr Osman, who sits so quiet, probably not even processing what's going on with all he has just had to endure.

"She was dating him to take his virginity. The kids were going to film it, and publicly shame him." She says before crying.

Disgusted sounds fill the room as some of the parents sit on the floor before some cry.

"Did she film it?" I ask her and she can only nod her head. "Where is it?" I ask her and she rolls her eyes.

"On her computer apparently." She says with an attitude. This woman is making me angry, even Sawyer can see it. This woman has no compassion for anything, especially knowing about what all of the kids were doing and did nothing about it. She's technically an accessory.

"Since I'm probably already going to jail, I might as well help my case." She says while pulling out a green folder bit of paper. She hands me it, and I take it, confused as to how this is going to help her case.

Sawyer and I exchange a look before I open it. My heart drops.

WELCOME TO THE SUICIDE SQUAD

You've been hand selected to join the cult of the undead. Complete the task and you will be welcomed into the afterlife.

Don't, and suffer the consequences.

It's fun.

Just make sure you are out for 10 seconds.

Curious?

Join us Friday!

www.welcometotheundeadk1llers.com

I look up at Sawyer who seems just as confused as me. "There was a rumour going round school for weeks about a fun new game that people are being hand selected throughout the school to play. You play the game; you get welcomed into the party at the end of the school year. But you had to do the task. But you couldn't tell anyone what the task was or that you had been chosen for the next game. It was an exciting secret."

"Did the rest of the kids have one?" Sawyer asks looking around all of the parents. One by one they pull a green piece of paper from their bags. I feel shocked. They all knew that it was a game. All of them knew.

"You wouldn't have investigated their deaths. They would have been forgotten about. But now you know. There was someone else involved."

Sawyer storms out of the room and the door slams behind him. I turn back to the families, and they stare back at me waiting for me to say something, but words fail me. I can't even begin to understand why they would do what they did. Encourage the bullying of another pupil and they hid evidence because they didn't want their kids to look stupid.

I'm not a parent, nor do I want to be. But surely this isn't 5-star parenting?

After a few moments I decide to follow Sawyer out, finding an Agent to watch the door of the meeting room while I head over to where Sawyer stands over poor Johnson who is typing at lightning speed to try and meet his demands.

"I'm telling you the site isn't live anymore. That is why we're getting an error message." Johnson says in his defence which only angers Sawyer more. "Look, I've been on every single one of these kids' laptop there is no link to that website found, they never visited it the day they died or any day before."

Suddenly a box comes up after a few moments, demanding a password.

"So, whoever made the website is either incredibly good with computers or those parents are lying to us again." Sawyer says through his teeth. "We need a password. What could it be?"

"Try Sinister six. All one word." I say to Johnson, leaning over him as he types it in.

Nothing.

"What about with a y? S y? or a 1 instead of the I on the six."

He tries again, this time the screen glitches and six videos come up on the screen.

The videos of the kids and their suicides. I walk away as the screen cuts to them hanging themselves. Agents from all over the task force come over and look at what is on the screen all as horrified as the next, muttering between themselves.

"How did you know?" Sawyer questions me causing me to turn back around. I feel physically sick.

"Mrs White called the teenagers the sinister six. That's how I knew."

"I meant about the y. How did you know to spell it that way?" He asks.

"I don't know."

Placing my head in my hands, I begin to pace. I'm never going to get that video out of my head. Ever.

"Hey," I voice sweetly while placing his hand on my shoulder firmly. "You alright?"

"No." I state clearly. "I never want to see something like that again." I say to him quietly. He nods and me and I feel the weight of his hand on my shoulder somewhat comforting. "Johnson, please delete the website." I ask him, not even looking over at him.

I'm still standing here, looking into the eyes of Sawyer Reid, a man who a loathe more than life itself. He stands here comforting me, something I never thought would happen.

When I don't hear Johnsons fingers moving on the keyboard, I look over. He's waiting for a signal from Sawyer, yet he hasn't stopped looking at me.

"Do it." He instructs Johnson, yet Sawyer doesn't take his eyes off me. And the longer he stares, the more unsettled I begin to become.

I'm the first one to walk away and I head over to Reynolds desk. "Johnson, before you do that, what did Mrs White study at university?" I ask and they begin going over some documents in search of the case on her.

"Biochemical engineering and then a business management degree."

"What about Mr Fields? Her husband?" I ask. They quickly pull out the next piece of paper and I watch as their face drops.

"Computer Technology."

We both look up at Sawyer, waiting to see what he is going to do next. He stands there his hands on his hips, his hair in his face ever so slightly as he thinking on what his next steps will be.

"Johnson…"

"Track the IP of the website? Already doing it, boss." Johnson says with confidence earning a smile from Smith.

"We both know you can't arrest them not until we have evidence."

"Then we wait till we have evidence." Sawyer states clearly. We both know unless we have evidence that can't convict and at this moment this is just speculation.

But then Mr Fields and Mrs White had motive.

"I've been stonewalled." Johnson says furiously before typing quickly on his computer again. "He's good." He says quietly as a bunch of different screens pop up. "But I'm better."

In a split second we watch the IP address be

tracked and bring up a location and the driver's licence of no other than Mr Fields.

My mouth falls open. "Look at you, Mr Smarty-Pants." I say patting Johnson on his back.

He greets me with a smile before turning the shade of a tomato. Sawyer seems to notice this and slaps Johnson on the back of the head, again.

Just as I'm about to protest about the abuse and he notices he places his hand up to stop me from speaking. "Good work, Johnson." He praises, grinning at me like the joker.

I'm surprised by it, as is the rest of the team. But we all know better than to ask Sawyer anything, especially his sudden change of heart to Johnson. So, we all sit in silence, working out our next moves.

"So, Mr Fields created the website, why?" Sawyer asks making everyone pay attention.

"Revenge." I speak up and he turns around.

"Yes, Agent Trouble. But why, and why now?"

Everyone seems to pause after he says that. I don't think it's because they are thinking, it's because of the nickname. Now I haven't heard that nickname since the academy. Something he used to torture me with.

"Agent Trouble?" I question and I watch his face drop. He didn't realise he had called me it.

He turns away from me. "Well, what can I say? It's a great nickname and suits you perfectly." He mocks.

I decide it's probably best to ignore him. "So, why now? Any idea's Sawyer?" I question him, putting him on the spot.

His eyes flash with fear, like he's just been picked on for the answer in a classroom. He stutters and giggles begin to escape from the table. "I know the answer, how about you think for once St. James." He says sheepishly.

I decide to ignore him. "What if he found out about the video?"

"I mean, the only right thing to do is to ask him?" Johnson says, diverting his eyes from Sawyer to me.

"For once, I'm going to agree with Johnson. Let's go and speak to Mr Fields."

FIFTEEN

Sawyer

We exit the car and look towards the house. Nothing special. The Fields family live just outside the city, not far from I.C.C.O. I look over and notice her taking in her surroundings. Thea's fresh meat, meaning she is going to have to listen to me.

I should have brought Smith with me, rather than Thea. She hasn't got a clue in how to interrogate, but since Smith is on another assignment, I'm going to have to deal with little miss posh.

"You going to behave?" I ask her, pulling my jacket out of the car and giving her a glare.

She looks right through me, a cold hard stare while watching her eyes frown slightly. "Who do you think you're talking to?" She questions me.

Trying hard to ignore her attitude, I slam the car door, walking round to her side. "You, clearly. Now are you going to answer me, or are you going to give me a headache?" I ask crossing my arms, showing dominance.

She matches my stance. "You know what, giving you a headache sounds really good, Sawyer." She teases, a small grin begins to grow on her face. "Why did you bring me if you think I'm going to cause trouble?"

I snort. "Because that's all you do. You cause trouble, Agent Trouble."

She pulls a face. "I hate that nickname." She gags, turning away from me and looking up at the house.

"Good, it means I can use it more."

"Why do you hate me so much?" She turns, her voice filled with annoyance. "Is this because I won't open my legs and obey you Sawyer? Is that it?"

"That is exactly right. Why do you have to be different?" I snarl at her almost. She's taken back by my admission, and deep down so am I. My stomach dropped. I didn't even think before I said it.

"Wow," She says slowly and quietly, still stunned by my choice of words. "Why do *I* have to be different?" She questions. The tone in her voice for a second was filled with sadness. "Probably because you are notorious for shagging anything with a pulse."

I raise my eyebrows. She has never sounded more British than she did just then. A small smile creeps on my lips. "Shag?" I question.

She begins to get flustered, "You know what I mean, you sleep with anything that moves. And I refuse to get a disease from you Sawyer, I respect myself too much." She snaps turning round to look back at the house.

As I'm about to object, I watch her face drop and I turn my attention to the front door. There stands Mr Fields. Clearly flustered as he sees us standing here and runs back into the house, slamming the door.

"Good job, trouble." I torment running up the stairs and she's quick to follow me. For once, she doesn't start an argument, because one of them just got us in the mess we are currently in. Chasing down a suspect.

"Sawyer, you can't enter the house!" She shouts as I try to open the door. It's locked.

"Fuck!" I scream, while running round to the side gate. I lift myself up and notice Mr Fields loading a shotgun. *Shit.* "Thea, get back to the car. He has a gun." I say pulling mine from my holster. She's unarmed, and I should have thought better than bringing her with me.

I don't hear her follow me as I kick the gate down, my weapon raised as I lock eye contact with the suspect. "Mr Fields, drop your weapon." I instruct.

He doesn't listen to me, only raises that shot gun to aim right at my head. "Get away from me!" He screams, his arms shaking. Jesus the man is pathetic, he'll hit the tree rather than me at this rate.

"Mr Fields, my name is SSA Sawyer Reid from I.C.C.O. I need you to put your weapon down, I don't want to hurt you." I state to him, and I see fear flash in his eyes.

"They deserved it." He cries, blabbering like a baby almost. "They hurt my boy."

I raise my gun in good faith, raising my hands, hoping he will just surrender. I mean I'm being pretty stupid; my vest is in the car.

"Mr Fields, I need you to listen to me. Because the only thing that will happen if you decide to shoot me is you'll head straight for death row. So, let's work something out together." I plead with him. I hate having to talk to criminals, it's one of the worst parts of my job.

His hands are still shaking as he stares at me, his eyes teary as he works out what to do. I slowly make my way towards him, hoping he won't pull that trigger. "The government lies. The Mayor lied!" He shouts, tightening his grip around the gun causing me to stop in my tracks.

This man is feeling a wave of emotions. Anger, sadness, disbelief, yet with the way he is acting, it's making me question whether he was the mastermind behind this whole thing, or we are being played.

"Mr Fields, we can talk to the Mayor—"

"No! I don't want to talk to the Mayor. He lies, just like you will. I don't believe you're from I.C.C.O. All the government does is lie." He rambles on.

This man has more mood swings than Thea, and I've seen her on her time of the month. You could always tell, because she binge ate chocolate and sweet stuff for a few days and if she were in one of the classes, she would have a hot water bottle pressed to her stomach. She was angrier than usual to me, and that is how I knew it was her time of the month.

"What do you want to do here, Mr Fields? Because you have two options." I state to him. "Either you come with me willingly and we discuss what happened. Or I send you to the hospital and then a jail cell because I can assure you, if it ends badly right now, it won't be me ending up in a body bag."

His eyes flash with fear, probably realizing I have more training than he does.

Slowly, he begins to lower his gun, placing his other hand in the air, surrendering. He's so unpredictable that I place my gun in front of me once more, just in case this man decides to do a full 360 degree turn and shoot me.

The shotgun is placed on the ground and as I approach, I kick it away, go round to behind Mr Fields and lift him up gently. I place my gun back in my holster. The man is sobbing, harder than a man should sob. "I just wanted them to stop." He says through his tears.

I don't have kids, and I don't want them. But I draw the line at taking the law into your own hands, especially when it comes to kids.

Deciding not to console the man, I only place his hands in handcuffs and reach down to collect his shotgun. "Mr Fields, you're under arrest."

As we exit the back garden and make our way back to the front of the house, I continue to read him his rights. He continues to cry but says yes when I ask if he understands the rights as I've read them to him.

We make our way down the stairs, and Thea gets out looking towards me. "You alright?" She asks, her voice calmer and less annoyed than before.

"Of course, trouble." I say placing Mr Fields into the car. "Nothing I couldn't handle. You just sat there and looked pretty." I wink while walking round to the trunk of my car and place the shotgun in an evidence bag.

"Sawyer, you know I haven't got a firearm." She explains, crossing her arms but also standing in front of the car door just in case our suspect tries to flee. *Good girl.*

"I know, darling." I say shutting the trunk. "Cause your job is behind a desk, with the rest of the newbie's." I tease, shuffling her hair before getting into the car. I hear her groan behind me while I shut the door, trying not to smile even harder.

"Strike two, Agent Reid." She says getting into the car and shutting the door. "Once I get to three, you can say goodbye to your job."

I ignore her threat and start the car, making sure to lock the doors, just in case Mr Fields decides to go for a run. Or Thea, not that she would opt for that option. She hates running.

For the next twenty minutes, the only thing that can be heard is Mr Fields' light sobbing. Thea never turns around, and I can't tell if it's fear that's stopping her. She's never been in the same room, or car in this instance as a killer, let alone a serial killer. Of course, innocent until proven guilty and all that crap.

But deep down, something is telling me this guy played a part, I'm just not sure if he was the one who did everything.

Making the website, yes. But actually, instructing the kids to play? I think that could have been someone else. Or, it could have been his wife.

She had motive, opportunity, and with her husband setting up the website, he could have easily helped her navigate it so she can talk to those kids and instruct them on what to do.

We make our way to the gate of the building, and they open straight up for us as we continue down the long stretch to the building. Mr Fields has managed to stop crying for the moment, and as I look at him in the rear-view mirror, he's taking in the beauty and structure that the building has to offer.

For something so modern, it holds an old-fashioned twist. Because that is what the organization does. Looks into more effective, old fashioned and reasonable approaches and strategies to take down criminals and their empires. Something I've very much enjoyed doing since starting here as a newbie.

Both Thea and I exit the car, and I'm grateful for a moment of the gust of wind to pass through so I don't have to smell her sweet smell any longer. She's intoxicating, and I would like to be drowned in the perfume she wears.

It has never changed in the years I've known her. At one point, it was all I needed to smell to get me by and I tried everywhere and at every store to try and get the perfume, but I still don't have a clue who it's by.

Pulling Mr Fields from the car, Thea waits for me to see what our next moves are. Instructing our suspect to stay where he is, I go into the trunk of my car and pull Mr Fields' shotgun.

Leading him into the building, we head for the elevator. First thing I need is a cup of coffee, and I need to write an incident report. I would hand it off to Thea, however because she wasn't next to me when I had to get Mr Fields to surrender, it's my version of events versus his. So, I need this right.

The elevator doors close, and the silence is deafening. However, it's just how I like it, Mr Fields has finally stopped crying and that is peace in itself.

Looking over at Thea, her curled blonde hair placed behind one ear, I never noticed she had her cartilage pierced. It's a tiny gold stud, something that is well in the guidelines of working at the I.C.C.O.

I'm broken from my long stare to my phone ringing. Pulling it out of my pocket, I place the phone to my ear. "Yes, Smith?"

"Sir, did you just come into the building with Mr Fields?" He questions and I groan in annoyance.

"Yes, why?"

"Er—" He stutters until I hear a loud conversation in the background. *"You might want to take him to a different floor. The parents are here, and they want to speak to Agent St. James."*

I look over at Thea who meets me with a puzzled look before I hang up on Smith. "You are going to the pen. I'm taking Mr Fields here to a different interrogation room." I instruct her before clicking the button for floor 10.

As it was the next one to pass, the elevator comes to a halt and I instruct Mr Fields out and begin to walk down the corridor, leaving Thea behind in the elevator.

This floor is a hell of a lot busier than ours. This is Undercover Operations. Something Tuck has perfected in his time here. He has solved and closed down some of the biggest criminal enterprises. Some that started well before any of us were born. He has quite the track record, because not only is he loyal to his staff and the organization, but he's loyal to himself. He has always maintained that if something were going to go wrong, he would protect his family first. As he understands the risks, works them out and if there isn't a safe outcome, will go for the one with the least amount of damage.

I sit Mr Fields down, not saying a word to him as I attach his handcuffs to under the table. He's a mastermind that's for sure, but I just can't place how he is involved in this until I speak to him.

He doesn't say a word, but I feel him watch me leave and the door slams behind me. I don't want to be in the room with him any longer than I need to be.

I leave the interrogation room and head in the direction of Tuck's office. It's right at the bottom of the hall, and I can see Scott is there looking over something on the desk.

"What brings you to this neck of the office, Sawyer?" Tuck teases handing me a bottle of water on arrival and then handing one to Scott. "Has your little crush pissed you off again?"

I laugh at them. "Funny." I say and they exchange a look between them. "You alright if I leave a suspect in your interrogation room?" I ask.

Tuck frowns. "You know you can. Everything alright?"

I move over to sit on the edge of his sofa. "Yeah, Smith said the parents were waiting at the elevator and instead of telling them we have a suspect in custody, and then walking in with him…"

He nods. "Say no more."

"I hear you took Thea out." Scott teases and I watch Tuck's eyes widen.

"Not like that." I issue, giving Scott a look of disgust. "I brought her along to interview someone." I explain and they both begin to grin. "Until we started to bicker, and then he ran into his back garden and pulled out a shotgun."

Their faces drop. "Is she alright?"

My eyes widen at the question. "What do you mean is she alright? I told her to stay back at the car. You should be asking how I am!" I exclaim and Scott places his hand to his chest and laughs, hard.

"Man, we know you can handle yourself. And by the looks of it, your first thought was to protect Thea, which I think is sweet." Tuck teases and I get up from the chair of the sofa.

"Alright, well thanks." I say and they begin to laugh as I exit the room. "I'll be back for my suspect in a few hours."

I begin walking down the hallway. "Reid!" I hear one of them call after me. causing me to turn back on my heels and head to the direction of the door. "If you're here, where's Thea?"

"Oh, I sent Agent Trouble to deal with the parents." I smile sadistically.

They exchange a look. "You sent her into the pack of vultures?"

"I mean, I can't be sweet all the time now, can I?" I wink and begin to make my way towards the pen.

SIXTEEN

Thea

The lift doors open, and I am met with the angry faces of the parents. What could they possibly be angry about now?

"What are you going to do about this?" Abbie Hollands' father says shoving a phone in my face. I take it from him and read the headline:

Suicidal Teenagers Bullied Headteachers Son, Should the I.C.C.O Still Investigate?

Oh, bloody hell.

I begin to scroll down, reading through it quickly. It labels the parents as incompetent, neglectful and they also encouraged the behaviour. I mean, they didn't do much to stop the bullying from going on. At the bottom, I notice the author. Ronald Richardson, the gentleman from Sin City News. Brilliant.

Just up from his page, you can see a lengthy paragraph about me, my work, and some false facts about my history. I hate reporters.

"I'm going to deal with this. Why don't you all go home, get some rest and I will call you with an update." I instruct them. They all begin to look between each other. "Is there something else?"

Mayor Meyers steps forward. "Do you have a suspect?" He asks.

"We have a person of interest. But who that is I cannot tell you at this time. So please, go home. Get some rest." I explain to the parents.

They decide not to argue with me and begin to make their way to the lift as it has now opened for them. They group together and the lift closes and then shoot down towards the bottom floor.

Taking a deep breath as I make my way back into the pen to see if Johnson managed to find the video of Isaac Fields and Jolene George, Sawyer comes out of the woodworks.

"How did it go?"

I scoff. "Well, let's just say I'm going to have to have a conversation with that reporter from earlier, you know the one that asked me out?" He nods. "Well, he decided to put out an article about the teenagers and their bullying of Isaac Fields."

"Great."

"Yeah—"

As we approach the table, Johnson grins back at us. The little wizard has something. "What have you got Johnson?" I ask him eagerly as he pulls a laptop towards him.

"So, I had to search high and low for that video, but I found it. It was in a folder, and when I clicked it, it produced a timer. It was going to be released on Friday after school finished." He says with a smile.

Sawyer groans beside me. "Get on with it, Johnson."

His smile is quick to fade as he turns back to his computer and begins typing. "Jolene had someone add a passcode onto the file. It was her birthday, so not very secure. However, the video isn't of her sleeping with Isaac Fields." He says looking back over at Sawyer. "The video is of Isaac admitting that he liked or loved Jolene. Only for her to diminish and embarrass him." He explains pulling the video up.

She tries to seduce him; however, Isaac becomes incredibly uncomfortable and pushes Jolene away slightly. Like Johnson says, Isaac admits that he loves Jolene, and how she is so different to what he thought. In a split second,

Jolene begins to laugh like a maniac, belittling Isaac and making him look silly. Accusing him of being a simp, labelling him as embarrassing, and explains how this was all a lie to get him to admit something.

Isaac becomes distressed and leaves Jolene's room in a hurry. Her still laughing before going over to the camera and turning it off.

"So, there is no sex tape?"

Johnson shakes his head. "Apparently him admitting that he loved her, was better."

"It's emotional. Having that emotional admission was more than she needed. She didn't need to sleep with him, cause that would make it look worse for her too. The emotional turmoil was what she needed, and he gave her that." I explain.

Sawyer gives me a look, which I decide to ignore. "Johnson, did you stop that video going out?"

"Yes, boss. All the kids had the same video on their laptops. They have been noted and there was no timer on them, so it won't be going out on Friday."

"Ok, great."

"Johnson, where was the video going to be distributed to?" I ask leaning over onto the desk.

"Er—" He begins before typing something

onto Jolene's computer. I couldn't even begin to explain what I would be looking at if I knew how to. A bunch of numbers, letters and god knows what begins to fill the screen. "The website for the student newspaper." He says, opening up the website.

Classic student articles, changes to the food, petitions, old articles. "Who is on the student newspaper?" Sawyer asks.

Johnson clicks on the section labelled 'our reporters.' One by one, the headshots of teenagers fill the screen. But two, very quickly catch my eye. "Oscar Todd, and Piper Meyers." I say pointing them out.

Sawyer stands tall and places his hand on his hips. "Smith, Greyson. Talk to the kids on the student newspaper." He instructs and they gather their things. "Johnson, look for anything to say if Mr Fields did this alone, or if his wife is involved. I'm going to interrogate Mr Fields before he starts screaming for a lawyer." He says before leaving me in the pen.

"Well, I better go and speak to that reporter." I tell Johnson, giving him a weak smile. "This is going to be fun."

SEVENTEEN

Sawyer

With a file in my hand, I burst into the interrogation room down in Undercover Ops. "Mr Fields—"

"I want a lawyer." He cries immediately. I decide to ignore him.

"You're Isaac Fields' father, correct?" I say slamming the file on the desk and taking a seat.

"Y-yes." He stutters. "He is my only son."

"Excellent." I say opening the file and pulling out screen shots of the video. "Mr Fields, can you explain to me the extent of Isaac's bullying?"

He takes a long deep breath. "It was awful. They took his clothes, publicly shamed him. They locked him in a freezer. Beat him after school."

He explains while the tears begin to fall down his cheeks. "You know, Agent Reid, those kids deserved everything they got. They bullied my boy for months, got away with it and were encouraged by their parents. Nothing was going to change!" He screams at me.

"Mr Fields, can you tell me what happened?" I ask him softly.

"No." He objects. "I want my lawyer."

"You'll get them. But I need to know why." I say as nicely as I can. This man is testing my patience. Although, I'm meant to stop questioning him, right now, I couldn't care less. I have to have something when Agent Trouble comes back from her meeting with that nasty reporter.

"Because the same thing happened to me! No one did anything to stop it. They deserved it." He snaps at me.

My blood runs cold. This is darker than we thought.

"Mr Fields, what did you mean by that?" I ask him and he shakes his head, anger fuelling his face.

"Lawyer." He says pulling back and sitting further on the chair. He's done talking, I've got something at least.

I get up pulling the file close to me and exiting

the room. My guess is this is something linked with Mr Fields' past. Clearly by how he worded it, he was bullied too, which is why he's the way he is in protecting his son. I mean, I can't blame him for wanting to protect him, but killing the six kids that bullied him? That is next level extreme.

"Sawyer!" I hear a familiar voice break me from my thoughts of the case. Scott runs towards the elevator as he greets me with a smile. "How did the interrogation go?" He asks, clicking the button and turning to me.

"Well, he gave me something. This is something that could be linked back to his time at high school. He said he was bullied." I say. He nods but for a moment doesn't say anything. "How are things going with you?"

He meets my face surprised. "Yeah! Good, man. I mean Ophelia is great to have on my team." He says looking at the numbers change as we go through the floors.

"Still gonna deny you have a crush?" I say as the elevator comes to a stop and the doors open.

"Yep." He says sheepishly, following me out.

"You know, you should tell Sophie. It isn't fair if your heart is in another place." I explain before coming to a halt outside the doors of the pen.

He meets my face, surprised. "Relationship advice from Sawyer Steven Reid? No thanks."

He says patting me on the back and turning in a different direction down to a different department. Rude, but not wrong. I wouldn't take advice from me either.

Scott and Sophie have been dating the better part of ten years. They met in high school, he realised he wanted her for the long run, and through the academy and her moving away for two years for nursing school, they made it work. He's always been a hopeless romantic, however they couldn't be more different. When they were together, he was a gigantic nerd, now, he spends more time here than he does at home. He won't ever admit it, probably because he will see it as a failure, but his relationship was done with Sophie years ago. He was just holding onto see if something was going to get better.

Entering the pen, Johnson meets me, file in hand as he scrambles to get his words out. "Boss, it's all linked, all of this." He says pulling a board from the corner and my eyes widen with the use of red rope, photos of all of the parents and their kids and the Fields family. "Woah…"

"He's been like this since we got back." Smith says, his eyes wide while he scours over the board.

"I'll get to you two in a minute, Johnson speak before you go into cardiac arrest." I instruct him and he takes a deep breath.

"So, Mr Fields went to Sin City High, so did all of the kids' parents apart from Mayor Meyers, he was older. But his wife was in the same year as the rest of them." He explains showing a photo of them all.

The photo, at the bottom dated 1993, shows all of the parents at some sort of pool party.

"I've spoken to some classmates of theirs, turns out that this group," He says pointing at that same photo. "bullied Mr Fields for years. He was in the hospital more than 10 times. They shoved his head down the toilet, locked him in a freezer—"

"All things there were doing to Isaac Fields." Greyson pipes up. "Do you reckon that the parents were encouraging the behaviour because they knew who Isaac Fields' father was?"

"I think that's exactly what they were doing. Mr Fields almost confirmed it. He said that nothing was done when it was happening to him." I say placing the file down and looking up at Johnson's board.

"So, like Thea said. It is revenge." Smith says.

I take a long deep breath, "For once, I think we're gonna have to admit that Agent Trouble is right."

EIGHTEEN

Thea

As I get closer to this bar, I know deep down this is a set up. Mr Richardson's assistant explained how he had left for the day, but he was expecting my visit, therefore he will be at Frankie's bar downtown. My skin crawls at the thought of this. But he's putting out damaging things into the press, and I have to be here to put a stop to it.

As I pull into the car park, I make sure that I start recording on my phone. Just in case he decides to spin this on its head and claim it's a date, which it isn't, I need my arse covered. Especially when speaking to a reporter.

I should have instructed he come to headquarters. This whole thing is sketchy.

I get out of the car and grab my bag as I make my way to the door of Frankie's. I've never been here; however, I know Frank and Mary have. It was where they used to come when they were younger. It never used to be as fancy as it is, especially for downtown.

"Hi, can I help?" A lady with auburn hair and red lipstick greets me in a waistcoat, shirt, and pants.

"Yes, I'm looking for Ronald Richardson?" I ask and she gives me a smile before turning and pointing to a booth. Great.

"He's right there." She instructs. I make my way over. Grossed out by the atmosphere and the fact he is sat in a booth.

"Agent St. James. I knew I would finally get you for a drink." He says with a grin as I stand in front of him. He begins to signal the waiter before I shake my head.

"I'm not staying long Mr Richardson." I say before his smile fades.

"This can't be a date Miss St. James; you have to have a drink. It's on me." He insists.

"Mr Richardson, I'm not having a drink with you, and if you continue to ignore me, I will be inclined to call your wife." I snap back at him. His small smile fades, and his face begins to fill with fury.

"What do you want Miss St. James?" He snaps at me.

Ignoring his tone, I place my bag on the seat hopefully my phone can pick up the conversation.

"You released a very damaging article today regarding the parents and the teens that died today." I state clearly and he begins to laugh.

"Hardly damaging, Miss St. James. I'm just doing my duty as a reporter to get the word out about the little brats." He laughs.

I don't join in, which he is hoping I do. "I need your source." I snap.

He continues to laugh. "Well, you won't be getting that now, will you?" He queries. "All my sources remain confidential."

"Mr Richardson, I know who your source is, I just need you to confirm it." I snap back at him, and he raises his eyebrows at the tone of my voice.

"Miss St. James," He whispers getting closer to me across the table. "this attitude you have towards me, it's just built-up sexual frustration. I know a clever way to get that out." He teases and I immediately want to throw up.

"Mr Richardson, if you continue, I will have you done for harassment." I warn him and he laughs.

"Oh, Miss St. James, just to clarify. I have more authority in this city than you do. So, it's your word against mine. And I know who the police would believe. A Sin City resident, over a posh, petty British girl." He barks back at me.

I can't help the smile that grows on my face. "It is amazing what comes out of a man's mouth when his ego's bruised. Let's get one thing clear, Mr Richardson. I work for one of the biggest agencies in the world. So, I think I might have a little more authority over you here. Because I knew this whole situation was a set up." I say getting up from the table and turning my head. "Either you call off your photographer, or I will release this audio," I say pulling out my phone showing him I've been recording this entire time. "to your wife and your employer." I say, a smug smile on my face. "Because this whole conversation is going to ruin your career."

"You fucking bitch." He says getting up from his seat.

"Ouch. Well, I've been called a hell of a lot worse from men like you. But the only person in the wrong here is *you*. And you know it. So, unless someone calls you out for your behaviour, you'll continue to do it. Because men like you, don't change." I say putting my phone in my bag.

"You're blackmailing me—"

"You were harassing me." I snap back. "There

is evidence outside of the press conference room, I have a recording right here and I called your assistant and she said that your intention here was to trap me into a date. That poor girl has to put up with so much just to get her pay at the end of the month. Work for one of the worst newspapers in the city, and under the sleaziest boss going. So, what is going to be? Do I get that name now?" I ask him.

He's eyes are panicked because he knows he's been caught for his crimes. He begins debating what to do. The clogs in his brain working overtime.

He closes his eyes and takes a long deep breath. "Rachel White. She's the headteacher of the school where the kids went to."

I give him a smile before walking past him and out of Frankie's bar. There is no way in hell I'm letting this man get away with what he's just said to me. I never made a promise, and he is, in my mind is one of the most dangerous men on this planet because he thinks that what he has just said to a woman is alright.

NINETEEN

Sawyer

Johnson, Smith, Greyson and I have been sat going through old statements from when Mr Fields was at high school. It's clear as day that the parents of the teenagers that died were the culprits in Mr Fields' years of torture.

Isaac and Mr Fields suffered almost identical methods of bullying. It's as if the parents gave them a handbook, or a seminar of how to bully a Fields.

Smith and Johnson had worked out that Oscar Todd was the tech guy in the group and had been able to lock the video on all of the kids' laptops and have it scheduled to go up from Jolene's laptop. He was making sure it was going to be live, and Piper was in the middle of drafting the story on it on her laptop.

These kids had meetings on how to bully this kid, it was in their calendars. Which makes this even more sick.

"What do we think was the breaking point?" I ask them and then begin to exchange looks. "I know it's getting late, but we need to produce something final, even if it's circumstantial for now. We can figure out the facts later."

"The video? What if something like that happened to Mr Fields?"

"But I don't think he knew about it. Or at least he's claiming he didn't." I explain. I tried to speak to Mr Fields earlier, who was in the middle of talking to his lawyer. A pompous, smug dickhead. Paul Foster. He was in our class at the academy, yet he ended up working for his dad's law firm.

"Sorry I'm late." I hear a sweet voice come from behind. "I was threatening a reporter." She says causally and my team and I exchange a look.

"Seriously?" I ask her as she takes a seat at the top of the table.

"Yeah."

"St. James, you're not meant to threaten reporters." I say with a grin. Her face becomes annoyed.

"Well, when this one has the same disgusting thoughts as you Sawyer, I seem to have to show my authority." She snaps at me.

Well, that's me told.

"What have you found out…" She begins before her eyes wander to the bottom of the table. "Who made the board?" She asks alarmed taking in each corner which is now filled with theories, dates, and more photos. We have also added a timeline or .

"That was me." Johnson pipes up giving Thea a smile. She grins back before getting up and walking over to the board.

"That's fabulous!" She says, praising him. He begins to go a bright shade of red and I slap the back of his head when she isn't looking. "Sawyer, apologise." She snaps, not bothering to turn back.

I look over at Johnson and mouth 'I'm not sorry.' He ultimately gets up from his chair and begins to present his findings.

Thea listens carefully watching as each of my team presents what we have learnt so far and instead of watching and listening to them, I find myself entranced by her beauty.

When she's concentrated, she frowns slightly to indicate she's listening and understanding. She likes for people to know she's attentive in what they are saying, that they have her full attention.

"Sawyer, what is your take on this?" She asks turning to me. I'm not used to being called by my first name, especially by my team. But I'll let her call me it, just so I can hear her pronounce it in that angelic accent of hers.

"I think that Mrs White has to be involved somehow. I just can't work out how." I say sitting back in my chair.

"Can I give my theory?" She asks and I can't help but groan and shrink further into my seat.

"Not a Thea theory." I groan. I watch as confused faces begin to form on my teams faces, and as I look over to Thea, her face is disgusted.

"A Thea theory?" She questions.

"When we were at the academy, she always had a theory about a case, or had a theory about the assignment—"

"And all you did was ask some poor helpless soul if she wouldn't mind opening her legs for you." She snaps back and laughter begins to erupt along the table. "He's still bitter he never got the top of the class award." She says winking at Smith before giving me a long hard glare.

I stare back at her, her eyes a shade of playful blue while a smug smile resides on her face. I want to smile at her, I can't help it. She does things to me, only men who actually like their woman could relate to. Except I hate her. I hate her. I hate her.

"Tell us your Thea theory." I say impatiently. She rolls her eyes and pulls out her phone.

"I just got coerced into a date with Mr Richardson, the snobby reporter who asked me out after the press conference yesterday, who is also married." She says sitting down. "I spotted the photographer the second I walked into the bar, yet I still sat down and listened to what that man had to say." She explains.

My blood begins to boil at the thought of some man speaking to her in a way that I would. He clearly upset her, because when she's distressed, she rubs her hands together, like a coping mechanism. Something I caught early on in missions, or undercover operations while at the academy.

"Ronald Richardson wrote an article about the parents and the children that died. The article had pieces of information that only us, and the parents of Isaac Fields would know." She explains, taking off her suit jacket and putting it behind the chair. You can see the bra straps and my mind begins to go to places I know I'm not allowed.

I distract myself my looking at her face, which ultimately makes me angry, and I feel my cock throb with excitement. *Jesus fucking Christ.*

"So, you're saying that the Fields family leaked the information to the press?" I ask trying to take my mind off my thoughts.

She turns to me. "No Sawyer, I'm telling you. Because I got confirmation from Ronald Richardson that Mrs White was the one to leak the information." She says with a small smile on her face. "However," She says before the smile falls. "I had to put up with some vile words from him before I threatened him to give me the name of his source. Which he did." She says and sits back in her chair.

"Let's go through this one more time." I say standing up and heading over to the board. "These six kids all died almost a week ago. They died of suicide. Now the reason this happened was they were each given an invite to join the undead, this invite—" I say picking up he piece of paper. "urged them to do it, but they couldn't tell anyone else." I say to the team who nod in agreement.

"These six teenagers all bullied another boy called Isaac Fields, now his stepmother is the headteacher and was pleading with the board and to the Mayor to get him moved to a different school, but every single time the request was denied." Thea says pointing at the Fields family.

"So, they took the law into their own hands?" I ask Thea who nods her head.

"Mr Fields seen the level of bullying and the similarities of what he went through, and it was happening to his own son. Something must have been the trigger. But I just can't work out what it is."

"Mr Fields has been through years of therapy, I mean the man lost his wife when Isaac was three and they only moved here under a year ago, because that is where his new wife, Rachel White, got a job at the new and improved Sin City High School." Greyson says while looking up from his file.

"But what was the stressor? Why now? What happened or what changed?" I ask my team and silence falls around us.

"Johnson," Thea speaks softly after a moment. "Can you check if there was any events on at the school within the last two months, anything that would put all of the parents together." She asks walking round behind him as he begins to look up the school calendar.

"There was a parent teacher conference six weeks ago." Johnson says looking over at Thea. "Could that be it?"

Thea looks over at me. Johnson is right, I just don't want to admit it. "Give me a minute." I say walking out of the pen and down the corridor to one of our interrogation rooms. I had two of my agents move Mr Fields up here before his lawyer got here.

I hear the sound of heels move quick behind me and I stop, slowly turning around staring down at her. "May I watch your interrogation?" She asks nicely.

I glare down at her before turning on my heels. "No." I say as I begin to walk away.

"Sawyer!" She shouts after me, causing me to come to an immediate stop. I slowly turn back to her; she begins to walk towards me. "I was only asking to be polite," She says breaking the space between us. "I'm watching your interrogation." She says coldly before opening the door and entering.

For Christ's sake Thea.

Taking a long deep breath, I enter the room. The smug bastard I once called a friend at the academy sits greeting me with a sadistic smile. "Sawyer, took you long enough." He says rising from his chair. "We were just leaving, as you have nothing to charge my client with. Let's go Mr Fields." He instructs before I slam the door behind me.

"Sit down." I instruct him and he begins to laugh. "Sit down, or I'll make you." I warn him this time.

The smile drops from his face, and he sits reluctantly. "Sawyer, you don't have any reason to charge my client." He snaps.

"Sure, I do. He confessed in his garden, didn't you, Mr Fields?" I question.

He looks over at his lawyer, "No." He lies. "I didn't do anything to those kids." He lies again.

"Mr Fields are you sure?" I question him, and he nods quickly. "You see Mr Fields, you were aware I was with my colleague at the time of your arrest, correct?" I ask him again. He nods once again. "Well, she made sure that just in case I was to get injured that it was recorded on video. But you also admitted that the kids deserved it did you not? After our conversation earlier?"

"That conversation should never have happened and won't hold up in court, because you went against the law and continued to question him even after he asked for a lawyer!" The pompous dickhead continues.

I'm sure he loves to hear the sound of his own voice. "Whatever, that doesn't matter. Mr Fields there was a witness to your admission, therefore there will be someone to testify when you have your day in court. So why don't you save us all the trouble and start talking." I instruct.

The man is sweating and crying. There isn't a video, but I needed something. So, I might have needed to throw Thea under the bus. He looks over at his lawyer and he's rendered speechless. I want to guess that he has never had to defend his first murderer, just by the look on his face.

He gives him an encouraging nod. "I made the website five weeks ago." He admits and I sit further in my chair.

"Why?" I question.

"There was a parent's night the week before. And because Isaac was still very new to the school as was my wife. We didn't know the extent of the bullying until that night. That seemed to trigger something in the kids and the parents, because that's when the worst of it started." He begins to cry, and his lawyer pulls out a packet of tissues. "Three days after, Isaac was locked in the freezer and then on the Tuesday the following week, they had taken his clothes and got rid of them. I was just setting up a website to scare them, but the more than Isaac got bullied that's when we—"

He stops. "We? Who's we, Mr Fields?"

He takes a long deep breath. "You're going to work it out eventually, but my wife and I were coming up with a plan to make the parents and the kids hurt." He explains while gently wiping his eyes. "I told her I would sort this, but she insisted on joining me in this to get justice for Isaac. We pleaded with the board to let us move him, but every time more donations popped up and more money in our account, extra money from the board to keep our mouths shut, like did they think money was going to fix this?" He begins to get angry. "My son was being bullied! And since that night at the parent teacher conference, it got so much worse so fast. It had to be done." He says, sniffling, and sits back in his chair.

"Mr Fields, what exactly did your wife do?"

He wipes his nose again. "She placed all of the invites she made in the kids' lockers. It happened so quick because we found out what Jolene George had said to Isaac, and it just made us angrier."

"Mayor Meyers. Why did he say he would expunge Isaac's record?"

He shakes his head. "I don't know, but I knew my wife wanted to make him think that she could trust him. She hated Mayor Meyers, because the more he spoke about Piper and said that she was a private school kid, it made my wife angrier that he would lie to his people."

"So, she hates politicians?"

"Oh, like nothing you've ever seen. She was signing petitions to get Mayor Meyers off the board all together, she constantly wanted a city not ran by corruption." He explains.

I sit back in my seat. "Any reason why?"

"Her father was a politician. She has some trauma there."

It's all making sense now. I knew he couldn't have been the mastermind behind the whole thing. Rachel White wanted revenge and because the Mayor's daughter was bullying her stepson, she sees this as a way for him to step down.

"Mr Fields, the night of the suicides. Who was instructing the kids on what to do?" I ask.

He begins to cry, it's more of a sob this time. "I couldn't do it. She said I was pathetic, and I had to leave the house. I regretted everything but I couldn't stop her. And I knew deep down unless this happened, Isaac wouldn't have been able to live. They would have ended up killing him, and I couldn't lose him too." He sobs.

"Mr Fields, I think anyway that you look at this, you were going to lose your child." I explain harshly and he places his head on the desk and begins to bawl.

I raise from my seat, his lawyer quick to follow my movements. "Speak to the DA?" He questions me.

"I will, but I can't promise anything." I say opening the door and shutting it behind.

As I walk down the corridor, I feel someone grab my arm and drag me into the room. *Oh shit, I forgot she was watching.*

"What the hell, Sawyer!" She exclaims, looking directly at me with fury. "You've just lied to a lawyer?"

"Oops?" I say sarcastically and she groans.

"That's all you have to say, really? You have just thrown me under the bus!"

"Good, might get you out of here quicker."

"Wow, Sawyer, and just when I thought we were working as a team." She's quick to respond. I can see the hurt in her eyes, but surely, she expected this of me?

"Silly of you to think so."

She's hurt by that and storms past me, leaving me in this room. Well done, Sawyer.

TWENTY

Thea

I decide that with the way I'm feeling after Sawyer's little outburst, it was probably best to go to my office to calm down. It's almost eleven o'clock, and realistically, I've been assisting in this case as a case Agent, rather than doing my actual job which is dealing with the press.

I place my head on the desk and groan super loudly. He's such a git, why does he have to be like that? He knew what he was doing, yet he still threw me under the bus to save his own arse.

This is strike three, in my option, Sawyer shouldn't work for this agency or any as far as I'm concerned. His lack of empathy is apparent in anything he does whether it be working with people, or being an Agent of the law, he forgets the honour code.

As I raise my head, I'm startled as I notice a man sitting in a chair opposite from me. It takes me a moment to realise who is sat across from me. "Oh, my goodness, Director Sinclair." I say rising from my seat and extending my hand.

He shakes my hand. "Don't worry Agent St. James. Is everything alright?" He asks softly, his broad southern accent is impressive, and I find myself captivated already.

"Yes, I apologise." I say sitting back down, clearly flustered.

"No need to apologise. How is the job going? I see that press conference went well earlier. You handled the questions very well considering they were like vultures." He begins to chuckle.

"Well, Sir, the job clearly does come with challenges, however, I seem to be picking up those challenges and dealing my cards accordingly." I explain.

"You talking about Agent Reid?" He questions me. I'm taken back at how with the sentence I've just said, he concluded that Sawyer Reid is the reason I am feeling the way I am. "Agent St. James, Agent Reid has only ever been able to listen to one woman in his life, it used to be his mother, but from what we gathered through Assistant Director Shields, is that you were the only woman he would listen to in the academy." He explains softly.

"I don't believe he would listen to anyone." I laugh back.

"Well, I watched you put that man in pause, and turn him around to face you. If that were anyone else, he would have kept walking." He explains.

Although I've never believed it, some girls in our classes always said I had Sawyer wrapped around my little finger. I always ignored what they were saying because he only ever had one thought in his mind and that was sex. And I was still recovering from losing everyone I loved.

"As much as I don't get on with Agent Reid, Director, I would like to think that I've helped solve some of this case they are working on. However, I've been distracted, and I will be resuming to my job title duties. Which is why I'm assuming you're here?"

He shakes his head. "I was just here to introduce myself; I know you were all working later, and I watched how angry you left the watch room. So, whatever he said, note it down, Agent." He instructs me before rising and I meet his stance. "You know Thea, Sawyer is a capable Agent when he puts his mind to it. But when he thinks with his dick, he doesn't think straight. So not only are you a distraction to him, but you are also someone who is going to make sure he works harder than he's ever worked before. So please, don't think you're here to be Sawyer's babysitter, because you are much more than that." He reassures me before walking towards the door frame. "But I don't care if he is a capable Agent, Thea. Three strikes and he's out." He says and I feel the temperature in the room drop by ten degrees as he walks away.

I don't doubt Director Thomas H. Sinclair has my best interests at heart with me being a new recruit, but I can be sure of one thing, he is adamant that Sawyer Reid is on his last warning.

I decided to go home after my conversation with the Director. I really didn't feel like having another conversation with Sawyer Reid, or his team tonight. Plus, I'm useless while the start to piece together the bits of the puzzles and make arrests in this case.

Mary and Frank weren't waiting for me, maybe because it was the middle of the night when I got home, and I would feel really guilty if I woke them up. I did write them a note and put it under the door for them, so at least they know I'm home safe.

I made frozen pizza when I got home, I think I might have ate something or someone if I didn't get food in me.

I devour the pizza and take a sip of my wine

with a new straw. I'm so pleased I didn't finish this bottle last night and left some for today, because I needed it.

Today has been tough, it has been mentally draining not to mention I'm struggling with Sawyer. The way he is baffles me because I have never known a man as insufferable.

I'm going to have to explain the exchange between Sawyer and Mr Fields' lawyer to the Assistant Director tomorrow, because if it comes up in the case notes and the trial that there is no video presented, they will question my credibility. And Sawyer's, but that I don't care about.

I look over at my bed in the far room and decide that I've missed it too much and I'm going to need to get a few hours of sleep to be somewhat pleasant tomorrow.

I make sure my alarm is on for the morning as I dive into my bed. It's the hardest goodbye, but the happiest hello.

TWENTY-ONE

Thea

I t's been two days. I've avoided Sawyer Reid with all of my might because he only seems to have a need ot upset me. Since he decided to throw me under the bus, I decided to do the same thing to him. Because karma is a bitch.

Nancy told me they are currently prepping to arrest Rachel White, Isaac's stepmother, for her involvement in the killings.

I wouldn't be much help either, if things did go south, then I would probably end up dead.

I'm not big on carrying a gun, however I do have a gun licence and I do have one in my apartment. It's only a small pistol. But it will do the trick if I ever need to use it.

Currently, I'm writing up a press conference speech for a case Agent Wilkinson and Agent McNeil are currently dealing with.

It's being held later today, and so I will be once again, on the screens of the residents of Sin City, I'm just hopeful that Ronald Richardson from Sin City News isn't there, probably because I went by his house yesterday and explained to his wife what had happened. She was obviously upset however she found credit card transactions to prove he has clearly been having an affair. She also apologised for her husband's behaviour at the press conference on Monday and said she will be kicking him out of the house and asking for a divorce.

I feel bad for ruining a marriage, however with how she worded it, it seemed she needed a push to leave him and me turning up was that push.

Women have to stick together, especially when entitled men such as Ronald Richardson and Sawyer Reid exist on this earth. We are practically fighting for our lives.

I rise from my seat and gather my things, hoping to catch either Scott or Ophelia before this press conference, just to double check the facts.

"Agent St. James?" A gentleman says at my door. I can only see his head, and not his body.

"Yes?" I say curiously, before he comes into view with the biggest bunch of tulip's I've ever seen. "My God."

He places them on my desk and hands me an iPad of some kind to sign my life away. "Thank you." He says with a grin before leaving my office, leaving me with these flowers.

"What the hell?" I say while looking around for a little card. I find it at the other end of the flowers and open the card eagerly.

Welcome to the team!
Johnson

I can't help but smile. The card is unnecessary as are the flowers, and as much as I like Johnson, I'm caught off guard.

"How odd." I say moving the flowers over to the end of my desk and gathering my things to find Scott and Ophelia. "Very odd…"

I begin my journey to the department in the hopes of finding both of them. It isn't a big deal if I don't, yet I would like to just confirm a few details.

Walking down the hallway, I recognise that laugh anywhere coming directly from their office.

Great, Sawyer's here.

As I enter and turn my head, I notice him immediately, somewhat surprised by my appearance and I roll my eyes.

"Hey, Thea. What's up?" Scott asks sitting on the edge of the desk.

"I was just wondering if we could go over a few details before the press conference." I ask him and he nods, giving Sawyer a look.

"I'm going. But, Thea, I'd like to see you in my office after you're done here." He instructs before leaving the room and I can take a breath.

I am not looking forward to that meeting.

Scott watches him leave before instructing Ophelia to shut the door. "I know that look, what did he do?" He asks crossing his arms.

Ophelia comes to sit beside me. "The tension between you two is ridiculous, Thea. What has he done this time?"

"He put my job in jeopardy and proceeded to make me feel like it's my fault." I explain. Scott's face drops and without saying a word clicks a button on his phone and holds it to his ear.

"Yeah, man. We have a code blue. Yep. If you could get here as soon as possible... great." Before he hangs up the phone.

"What was that?" I ask him and he begins to grin sadistically.

"Nothing you need to worry about." He explains giving me a wink and exiting the room, shutting the door behind him.

I look to Ophelia who shrugs her shoulders. "When it comes to those two, I tend to not ask questions. Especially if it involves Sawyer." She says before shoving me slightly. "Come on." She encourages. "Ask me those questions."

TWENTY-TWO

Sawyer

I sit in my office flicking a pencil. She hasn't spoken to me in days, not that I deserve it. And the more she makes me wait in this office, the more nervous I become.

I never meant to upset her... well I did. But not the way it was intended. I know she wants me to apologize, but that is something I don't do. It gives me a rash.

She infuriates me because she is being unreasonable.

Okay, she's not.

No, she is.

I decide to get up and pace because she's ruining my thoughts and my day by being stubborn.

The door slams behind me and as I turn, standing in front of me is Tuck and Scott. "Hello?" I ask as I look between them.

They don't look happy with me and that could be for a number of reasons.

"We made an agreement when that poor girl joined this agency, that if you did anything stupid, which happens a lot may I add, that we will take matters into our own hands for how you treat her." Tuck says as he stands taller, trying to intimidate me.

"Oh, here we go, she's blabbed to the big boys. What did she say?" I ask, my amusement growing.

"How about you tell us your version and we will decide how to go about it." Scott says matching Tuck's stance.

"Alright." I say taking a seat on the sofa. "When speaking to Mr Fields' lawyer, I might have lied and said she videoed the interaction while Mr Fields held a shotgun to my chest, when in fact I told her to stay at the car. I lied and got a confession, but it also puts her job at risk." I explain and I watch their face turn to stone and they both take a long exhale. "But in my defence, she deserved it."

Scott throws his hands in the air and walks

away whereas Tuck just stands there taking a longer breath than usual. "You are completely incapable of empathy, or any sort of care towards that girl. Get a grip of yourself, Sawyer." Tuck practically shouts at me. I've never seen him this frustrated with me, and it's over a girl?

"You're butt hurt because she won't sleep with me. She's the first one with a brain cell and actually the first woman besides Nancy and Ophelia who I would like to class as a friend. So, get your shit together, Sawyer. Because as much as we love you, and we do. We will help her put the final nail in your coffin." Scott threatens and I begin to stand.

"What is this? Some sort of intervention?"

"Yes! Because you don't care about your job, and you don't care about anyone but yourself—"

"That is how it's meant to be!" I shout back. "I'm meant to care about Agent Trouble, that's hilarious. All she's caused me and is going to cause me is trouble because that is all she's good for!" I shout moving past them and I stand next to the door. "She didn't work to get here like the rest of us, she belongs out there making chai latte's and giving the worst customer service known to man. Because after my three-month report is finished, her ass is getting fired." I say swinging the door open and I am met with fury.

The silence in the room is deafening and not

in a good way. The air is freezing cold, and the look of her face is frightening me.

"Strike three, Sawyer." Thea says before turning on her heels and walking down the ramp as Ophelia and Nancy wait for her at the door of the pen.

I turn back to my friends, who look just as shocked as the rest of the Agents in the room. "Fuck."

TWENTY-THREE

Sawyer

I t's been two weeks since what happened in the pen. She won't come near me and when she needs to deal with the team she will only deal with Johnson, Greyson, or Smith and if my name comes up, she avoids the subject all together.

I have only seen her when I have purposefully tried to pass her office. She must have seen me because she's started shutting her door this week.

Somehow, I'm still here, I still have a job and as far as I'm aware she hasn't went to Assistant Director Shields about me just yet.

But that is the main word, *yet*. I know she's gathering more evidence against me, probably trying to add harassment to the endless list of things I've done.

Because she has me so on edge, I'm debating handing myself in. Nancy will not look at me and I don't know Ophelia well enough to ask a favour, all I do know is they've been keeping an eye on her.

Johnson said she was crying yesterday, and as someone who knows Thea St. James the longest in this building, she doesn't cry, not often anyway. It's always been one of her strong points, that she's always so put together and I feel like I've broken that within her.

I don't doubt that I hurt her feelings, because the second it left my mouth, I knew I would regret it and I *did* regret it. Because her face broke me, and it's all I've been able to see when I close my eyes for the past two bloody weeks.

I want to talk to her, but that won't help my case.

It will only make it worse, and I don't want to be doing that.

Tuck has been away undercover for the last ten days, and it's rumoured he's coming back today. Scott has spent time with me, but only when he knows Thea, Nancy and Ophelia aren't watching. I'm the worst person to be around, according to everyone in this agency. And deep down I agree with them.

"Boss, we have an arrest warrant of Rachel White." Greyson says at the door. We didn't have enough evidence a few weeks back to charge her yet, so we had to gather more evidence against her and issue stakeouts. She started driving past Mayor Meyers house almost every night. More than likely trying to intimidate or, she's found her next target.

One of the other team agents, Evans, he was the last person on the stakeout.

"Let's go." I instruct.

As we pull up to the Fields' house, we notice the family car is no longer there, but Evans is, and he looks to be asleep. Fuck's sake.

I launch myself out of the car, "Evans!" He doesn't respond even when I almost rip the door off the car. That's when I notice the blood. He's not breathing. "Smith!" I call for him and immediately he's by my side checking for any sign of life.

"Come on, Evans!" Greyson shouts behind me. The kid isn't older than twenty-three. He's a bright agent, who works well with the team and any other team he works with.

"He has a pulse, but barely. I'll call for an ambulance." He says while pulling out his phone.

"Greyson, Johnson, you're with me." I instruct while we make our way towards the Fields house. I don't take likely to someone abusing my Agents unless it's me.

"Greyson round the back, Johnson you're up front and centre with me." I say pulling my gun close and check the front door. It's unlocked.

I push the door open, and to my surprise there stands seventeen-year-old Isaac Fields, with a shotgun.

And it's pointed right at us.

What is it with this family?

"Isaac…" I begin to plead, and he moves the gun right to my head.

"Everything was going right; everything had a place, and we had a plan. But you fucked it up!" He shouts at me. "Sawyer Reid, is it? Head of Criminal Prevention at the I.C.C.O. That's very impressive." He taunts, a grin begins to form on his face behind the shotgun.

"You've done your research on me, Isaac." I praise and he moves the gun ever so slightly.

"You know, you had my vote when you publicly shamed the parents, I mean you got the facts wrong. They were bullies. As were their sadistic kids. But you had my vote until that stupid British woman decided to make the world feel sorry for them again." He almost shouts. The way he spoke about Thea only showed anger, and not control.

"You're angry with her?" I ask him, never moving my gun from in front of me. He begins to laugh through his anger. I feel like I'm staring at the real-life Joker from Batman. This kid is so damaged that he thinks this is okay, and better yet, he's got a severe hatred towards Thea and that is making me nervous.

"Of course, I am! People like her need to see reality and what those people are like. Mom has gone to talk some sense into her." He praises with a smile and that sends a rush through me so I can't see straight. *If they hurt her...*

"Isaac, where's your mom?" I ask him as calm as I can. "I don't want to shoot you, and neither do my men." I say while Greyson gets behind Isaac pressing his gun to his head.

You can see the fear flash in his eyes. "You brought back up?" He questions with a smile.

"Course he did." Greyson says growing more impatient as the seconds tick by with Isaac's lack of information. "You going to give us the gun? Or you going to be known as the kid who couldn't listen to instructions?" He snaps at him.

Greyson has never been one for small talk, especially in a standoff, and that is why I have him on my team.

Isaac thinks for what feels like forever before he puts the safety back on the gun and surrenders it to Greyson. Johnson is quick to get the man to his knees, placing handcuffs on him while I put my gun back in its holster.

"Boss, see to Thea. We have him." Greyson reassures me.

I can only nod, running out of the house like a mad man, in the direction of our SUV. "Smith, he alright?" I ask before getting in.

"He's gonna be fine, they're almost here. Where you off to?" He asks.

"Thea is who they want, I'm on my way back to headquarters." I say getting into the SUV.

"Keep me updated!" I hear him shout through the glass. Without putting my seat belt on, I put my foot down on the gas in the hopes that the security in that place is worth what they pay for it.

TWENTY-FOUR

Thea

That meeting was uneventful.

The undercover operation Tuck was under managed to get seized by another agency. Which means Tuck got arrested and had to prove who he was and that took hours. It was just a lot of him swearing at the other agents in that agency and calling them all bastards.

His mug shot is hilarious though, and I want to use it for his birthday next year. He's got a black eye from resisting arrest, and it only took me thirty minutes of telling him to shut up, did he actually listen, and they agreed to let him go, as long as we cooperated on the investigation and Tuck was to testify. I couldn't agree to the second part as of Tuck's job, and they seem to want to fight me on it, so let them fight.

I scroll through my phone, case file in hand; as I make my way towards my office. I'm hoping to leave a little bit early today as I promised dinner with Mary and Frank. Since I stopped working directly with Sawyer and only working with his team, I've started to really enjoy this job.

I want him to worry intensely as he thinks I'm going to Assistant Director Shields, but I haven't decided if I want to do that yet. I would feel guilty for ruining someone's career, even if it is Sawyer Reid's.

Opening my door, I place my files on my desk and head round to take a seat. I have so much to do. The Criminal Prevention team are currently going to arrest Mrs White for her involvement in the suicides of the six kids.

I am somewhat grateful this case is ending. I've been struggling to get the images of the six teenagers out of my head since I started. I know with some therapy I'll be able to move on, but they are beginning to haunt my nightmares.

"Agent St. James?" Someone says that causes me to look up. "You have a visitor." He says and I begin to get excited. I don't get visitors, or at least I haven't in the past two weeks or so.

I rise to meet them and to my surprise a lady in a white coat, sunglasses and what looks to be like a wig greets me at the door. Just as I begin to question her, I notice the gun that is pointed right at me through her bag.

She tilts her head down, dazzling me with her eyes and I know immediately who I'm dealing with. "Thank you." I say to the Agent, and they exit the room with a smile.

She fakes one too, and watches carefully as the Agent makes his way down the corridor, and towards the lift.

The minute he is out of sight, she turns to me, takes off her sunglasses and looks me up and down. "Take a seat, Thea." She instructs, pulling out the gun. "We're going to have a chat." She says before kicking the door shut behind her.

TWENTY-FIVE

Sawyer

I'm not going the speed limit. I have to be doing at least eighty. I've tried calling Thea for the last twenty minutes, I've tried calling the reception and I've been calling Nancy, Ophelia, and Scott nonstop.

I try Nancy again, hopefully she won't send this call to voicemail.

My heart dances when I hear her pick up the phone. "Sawyer, I don't have time for you, if it's urgent, call another female Agent that might give a shit—"

I groan in annoyance, "Nancy! Thea's in trouble!" I scream down the phone at her and she only groans back.

"Sawyer, I don't want to be involved in your

foreplay, ok? Just tell Thea how you feel, and she will just deny you. Which will be funny." She begins to giggle.

"Nancy, listen to me. Mrs White is in the building and she's looking for Thea." I say harshly and she goes quiet for a second as I hear her do something on the end of the line.

"What are you talking about? I thought you went to arrest Rachel White?" She questions.

"She wasn't there, but we got a lovely greeting off her son as a held a shotgun aiming it right at my head!" I shout at her hoping now she will see the severity of it. "She has a gun I know that, and because Isaac has convinced his Mom that Thea is the problem, they are going to try and take her out too. Now will you please check on her!" I scream, and suddenly she puts the phone down on me.

"Damn it!" I say clicking on Scott's number again and this time, he answers.

"Dude, I love you and everything, but what the fuck is wrong with you?" He questions, his voice playful.

"Scott, our suspect for this case is going after Thea." I explain and I hear him rise from his seat.

"Where is she?"

"I think in her office, Nancy is on her way, can you go with her?"

"We're on our way. Ophelia, take my phone keep Sawyer on the line." He instructs and I feel completely helpless. I haven't been on my game these past two weeks since I upset her, meaning that the arrest of Mrs White was put off until I got my head sorted out.

I can hear conversations Scott and Ophelia are having with other Agents about Thea. Her office is isolated, and it just so happened to be the day that the intern isn't working, and she wouldn't be in her office.

I'm going almost ninety miles an hour, but if it means I get to Thea quicker in the hopes to save her, then I don't care about the risk.

TWENTY-SIX

Thea

She's pacing around my office looking for something to do. She hasn't said a word other than instructing me to sit and from the way my phone has been blowing up with calls from almost every Agent in the building, my guess is Sawyer managed to work out she's here, cause he's been calling me nonstop.

"How can I help you, Rachel?" I ask becoming impatient. "Whatever you think I can offer you, I can promise you that isn't going to happen."

She turns to me, and I begin to look into the eyes of a maniac. "Thea," she begins, still pointing her gun at me. "what I want, is for you to make a press release, saying you made a mistake by defending those god-awful parents, and you retract your last release." She instructs and I scoff at her.

"That isn't happening. And let me tell you why." I explain leaning forward. "Because I can't do a press release, or conference without contacting the media, meaning I need to use my phone to do so. Which, you won't allow me to do. So, really whatever you came here for, is flawed." I explain and her nostrils begin to flare in anger as her brows frown to me.

"Miss St. James—"

"It's Agent in case you forgot. You've come in here with an empty threat and not a lot of action. You were hoping that at the click of your fingers I would have that press conference ready. In the middle of a government building. I mean it is very ballsy, and stupid—"

She aims the gun behind my head and shoots, missing me by a few inches. My mouth falls open in shock. My god, this woman is crazy.

I stand to meet her, and she angles her gun once again. "This time it will be through your head." She snaps at me.

I decide not to play god. This woman clearly hasn't thought out a plan thorough enough to see it to the next step. She likes the thrill, the excitement and thrives off the chaos. Something I'm clearly not giving her.

She's sadistic in the sense that she will happily see how this plays out in the long run. Will she take me as a hostage? Shoot me? Who knows.

"You're coming with me." She instructs. Opening the door still angling her gun at me. When she opens the door, she fails to look behind her and see the swarm of Agents, including Nancy, Scott and Ophelia all pointing their guns in the direction of Mrs White, and she has still not noticed. "You're going to do what I asked so move it, Missy." She instructs me, moving me away from my desk, still not noticing the swarm of Agents behind her.

"There is only one problem with your plan, Mrs White." I explain trying to control the smile on my face,

"And what is that? Huh?" She taunts which only makes the smile grow on my face.

"Turn around." I instruct her and she begins to laugh, still pointing the gun at me.

She turns around with so much confidence that when she sees the Agents you can see her legs buckle.

She turns back to face me, her gun still in her hand and the only thing I can think of doing...

I punch her in her face.

And she falls, to the floor and the gun flies across the room. Everything begins to go in slow motion, and I look up to watch everyone in sync follow Mrs White fall to the floor.

My hand begins to hurt like a bitch but I'm too shocked that I punched a prime suspect to think about my throbbing hand.

I look up at my friends who show a mixture of excitement, happiness and shock. "I cannot believe I just did that, and this must break some sort of guideline…" I begin before looking down at Mrs White, "But that felt amazing." I begin to laugh, as does everyone else.

Guns are lowered, while a bunch of Agents head into my office to collect her gun, and her from the floor. They do check she's alive and to my surprise she begins to stir only moments later, and I feel myself taking a breath. Thank god, I didn't kill her.

"You alright?" Scott says placing his hand firmly on my shoulder bringing me back to reality.

"I think so." I say softly.

"I mean you didn't have to make her pass out." He jokes with me, and I can't help but laugh with him.

"I imagined it was Sawyer. That's why I hit her so hard." I joke and everyone begins to laugh, Ophelia stands on the other side of me giving me a hug.

"We are just pleased you're alright, Sawyer sounded so panicked when he called." She explains and I turn to her.

"What do you mean?" I ask her softly and she clutches my arm tighter.

"Sawyer called all of us at least a hundred times to get our attention. If it weren't for him, this could have gone a lot worse." She explains, squeezing my arm.

As I look down the corridor, to my surprise. I see him standing there, breathing heavy. His vest still on from the arrest and he looks to me with relief. God knows what is going on in his head, but also, why does he care so much?

TWENTY-SEVEN

Sawyer

This time, I've been avoiding her. I haven't seen her since the incident in the office, and that was two days ago. I did, however, brief Assistant Director Shields on why our case went wrong and how Thea ended up the target.

She blamed me, and I would too. She also asked about why Thea hasn't been more involved in our cases like she was in her initial days.

I decided to be the better man, and explain to her what I said about Thea, how she heard the whole thing and how, if she took this to Nancy properly, I could be written up and out of a job, which even I know I deserve.

I've never been a man to admit to my faults,

I'm very aware I label everyone else the problem, sadistic some would say, but when I heard from one of the Agents that there had been a gun shot on Thea's floor, I did expect the worse.

I did however hear from all the Agent's that witnessed it that when she punched Rachel White that she pictured my face, and I did laugh because I know that I deserved it.

For the past two days, all I've done is fix the messes that were made, fill in our reports for the DA, and every hour, check on Thea as I pass her office. She's started to leave her door open, not sure if it's an invite to actually apologize, or if it's so she can see who is coming down the hall.

Today, she's wearing flared black trousers, a white shirt, and a cropped blazer jacket. All the women here have individual tastes, yet Thea has to be the most out there in terms of style. Every day she surprises you with something exciting, whether it be a new hairstyle, new outfit, or a new pair of shoes.

Yesterday's hair was one that I will remember, it was in a half up and half down bun, with slight bits of her fringe at the front to frame her face.

I have another meeting with Assistant Director Shields in an hour about my behaviour, and because Thea hasn't gone directly to her about the incident; I've been told this is so I can meet the person who will be training me on how to speak and respect woman. So basically, I'm going on a training course in how to be a decent human being.

I would like to think she had something to do with this, or Nancy told her and she's laughing at the thought. I don't need to be told how to speak to woman, I do that on a daily basis, I get any woman I want, when I want them just with a smile.

However, the woman I want, just so happens to not want me in the same way, even if my motives are mainly sexual.

"You know if you stare at the wall any longer, you might start hallucinating." A familiar voice says to me from the door of my office. "I hear you're being a big boy and fessing up to Shields about what you said to Tuck and Scott about Thea." Nancy says, coming into view and taking a seat on the couch.

"Here to mock me because of it?" I say sarcastically.

She grins at me. "No, Sawyer. But I do think it was incredibly good of you to do what you did." She admits, causing me to look at her.

"Why are you here, Nancy?" I question, becoming annoyed with her presence. She smiles lightly, ignoring my tone of voice before rising from the chair.

"She's kept that door open hoping you would speak to her." She says walking round to the side of my desk, trapping me in so I can't leave from this conversation. "She knows better than to expect an apology, however I know she wants to thank you." She says leaning and placing her hand on the desk looking down on me.

I look up to her, a surprised look. "Why would she want to thank me?"

She snorts. "Because without you and your persistence to contact someone from the Agency, Thea is alive. So, I would take it if I were you." She says softly, but ultimately shoves me. She turns on her heels and stands in the doorway, "I'm having a party tonight, Sawyer, and you have to be there. It starts at eight." She instructs before leaving me in the room, rendered speechless.

Nancy throws great parties, but that isn't what is running through my mind right now.

She wants to thank me.

The woman who is as stubborn as a mule, will not let anyone, let alone a man, walk all over her. Wants to thank me, for doing something as simple as making a few calls.

I know that this is what she wants, to show her authority, and that it will show she's not going anywhere.

Which I know has to change.

I can't be this good man people are hoping to change me into, that is something that will never happen.

I can't be the same Sawyer Reid I've been for the last twenty-six years if she's still here.

> I'm losing this bet, and I can't have that. I need to show I'm never going to change, how I only have one thing on my mind, and how she's going to have to leave straight after I get what I want.

I decide to go to Nancy's party, which, might I add wasn't a decision that came easy.

She's gonna be there, Thea is going to stand there is one of her fancy outfits, drinking wine, and mingling with her new co-workers. And I am going to avoid her like the plague.

Nancy knows a lot of people, and by people, I mean men. No doubt to try and set Thea up with one of the other Agents, however if I know Thea, she'll be polite and tell them she's not interested quite early on.

She never had a relationship when she was at the academy, or at least that's what I was told. She moved over here when she was twenty-two. And in the three years we studied together she never went back to London. Spent all of the holiday's here. And I always thought that was strange.

I opt for a white t-shirt, olive green shirt, jeans, and a pair of my fancy shoes. Putting on my regular aftershave, I make my way down to my car so I can stop and get some beers before I head to Nancy's apartment.

This party is for Nancy to show off her new refurbishment. She decided to do her entire apartment out as she said the previous colours and furniture wasn't her anymore. Whatever the hell that means.

It's colder than it has been, and I instantly regret not bringing my jacket. Nancy however lives on the top floor, and it can get unbearably hot, so I try to look on the bright side.

The drive to Nancy's takes longer than normal as a lot of people decide to hit the streets tonight and the city is filled with people having drinks, food and spending time with friends or family.

The only time I ever do anything is when I'm with Tuck, Scott, or it's all of us at a party. And I'm a workaholic. So, I don't have time for my family, and by that, I mean my brother, Andrew.

My Mom died in February; we all expected it. She had cancer for the last year and by the end of January, the doctor said to start planning and prepping for the hardest goodbye. And it was.

She was the only person who has able to keep me in check about my behaviour. To her, I was her sweet Sawyer. Until she left the room.

My brother and I haven't spoken since Mom's funeral. Even then it was a few sentences and one-word answers.

We've always been different in the sense that he looked down on me for not wanting a family or a wife and deciding to sleep around. In a drunken row at Christmas when I was in the academy, he accused me of being a man-whore and a child because I refused to own up and find a woman who would whip me into shape.

And until we found out Mom was dying, that was the last time I saw him. My choice in lifestyle angers him, and his wife. Don't get me wrong, Shelly is lovely, as is my nephew, Dustin. But that life is something I don't want.

I see myself as Sin City's most eligible bachelor. Because what else could I be? Sawyer Reid: the man who decided to let a woman control him and produce more offspring into this world that would cause chaos and destruction? Deep down thinking about it, I would be gracing the world with my presence, just in the form of smaller humans.

But then, I know that would be a disaster, and I wouldn't want a hand in raising the child. My brother decided to be a feminist supporter and become one of those stay-at-home dad's while Shelly went back to school. We've always had to work hard for what we wanted. And my

Mom always had to lend Andrew money as with him not working and taking care of Dustin, the money was tight.

I would offer, but I'm not close enough to my brother and his wife for them to start relying on me financially, however, if he was desperate I'd give him it. I'm not that shallow. Cause more often than not, it goes on food, and clothes for little Dustin. Who I do love dearly although my brother thinks I don't.

I managed to pick up some cans on my way here, and I get out of the car moving quickly to Nancy's apartment block.

After a few moments, she lets me in the apartment building and I'm grateful when I'm hit with heat as I walk through the door. I know later on I'm going to be warm, so I'm pleased I opted for a t-shirt in case I do get hot.

She opens the door, and I'm met with a rather happy version of Nancy, who undoubtedly started drinking from the second she got home. "Sawyer Reid." She greets me, standing away from the doorway allowing me entry.

"Nancy." I say back, looking around at who is already in attendance. Tuck and Scott stand in the corner in their normal party attire. Tuck is in a shirt and jeans whereas Scott is in a thin turtleneck and jeans.

Ophelia stands talking with another female

Agent. I don't remember her name; however, I know she was number 226 in my accomplishments.

A bunch of other Agents stand talking in groups or pairs while Nancy's party playlist blasts through the speakers. She stands in front of me, wearing a green blouse, black jeans, and heels. "You look nice Nancy." I compliment her, to which she pulls a face.

"Don't kiss my ass, Reid. Go mingle." She instructs, taking my beers away from me and handing me a cold one from the fridge.

Thanking her with a grin, I make my way over to Tuck and Scott. "Here he is. Mr nice guy," They tease patting me on the back and I start shushing them.

"Don't say it too loud. Can't have people thinking I'm starting I'm starting to have a heart. Got to keep the reputation up." I tease causing them both to laugh. "How was prison?" I ask Tuck who punches me in the arm slightly.

"You know, I spent forty minutes in that jail cell thanks to Thea." He praises her, a grin growing on his face. "I have never in the years I've worked in law enforcement, seen a man of that agency quiver the way that Agent did when she started speaking to him. It was so impressive."

I scoff. "We would have been able to get you out of prison?" I say between Scott and me.

Scott shakes his head. "Tuck had so many reasons for them to arrest him, that it would have taken us months to convince them. You know how that agency is, they will drag their feet when it comes to undercover Agents." Scott explains and I find myself struggling to argue because I know it's true.

That particular agency has a reputation of putting undercover agents from other agencies such as I.C.C.O in danger by putting them in jail cells with people they've been investigating and then telling them who they are.

It's been to court plenty of times, but the judge always throws it out and says there was no foul play meaning the families of those Agents that have been killed or injured while in their custody, don't get some sort of answers or justice.

"I heard she's not coming." Scott says looking over at Nancy's door. I turn my head to him, and he catches me staring. "Your little troublemaker. Nancy said she wasn't going to come tonight." He explains looking to me.

"Any reason?"

They both shrug their shoulders. "Something about a family emergency. She had to leave the office early too."

I frown. "She has no family here. Her family's in London." I explain and they look to each other. "She moved here on her own, I found that out from the academy, she doesn't talk to her family back home."

Tuck gives me a stare. "Do you know why?"

"Not a clue."

He avoids my look and proceeds to look out the window of Nancy's high-rise apartment that gives relaxing views of the city.

"Wait, she has neighbours. They are older." Scott says, causing me to divert my eyes. "Maybe that was who she was referring to."

This time I shrug my shoulders, but with how Tuck has just acted when I mentioned Thea's family back home, it is giving me the indication he knows more about her than he's letting on. Especially about her family.

He mentioned it her first day here, when we were all having pizza at my place, he said not to take her at face value.

I feel like my friends know more about a woman, who I have known for the better part of five years, than I do. And that isn't sitting right with me.

TWENTY-EIGHT

Thea

Opening the door to Frank and Mary's apartment, I move Frank in with the wheelchair. Nothing to worry about, the man fell off the path and broke his ankle. However, Mary decided to almost give me a heart attack and tell me he was skateboarding. At least they got a good giggle.

"Okay, Frank. Stand up, I'll get you to the bed." I instruct and he begins to argue.

"Thea, I promise I will be fine, please." He begs and I shake my head.

"Get in the bed or I will break your other ankle. Then that will teach you." I warn him. He turns back to look at me, horror on his face that I would even suggest such a thing. "Sorry, get in the bed. Please." I beg this time.

Without any arguments, I manage to get him into the bed, and I rest his ankle. "You know, Mary is quite capable of taking care of me." He praises his wife.

I look behind me, and I'm met with a crazy lady grinning at me. "Clearly, it took her a whole twenty minutes to call an ambulance to get you to the hospital because she couldn't stop laughing." I say narrowing my eyes.

"Oh! Thea, it was the most pathetic fall!" She laughs again, this time causing Frank to join in. "It was hilarious." She laugh's holding her chest.

As much as I try to stop the smile on my face, I can't help it. These two really are trouble. The fact she called me telling me he had been skateboarding and because Frank is that wild, I full believed he would do it.

They are unhinged, and carefree and that is why I love them the way I do. They say I keep them young, however they keep me happy. Because they are my family.

"Are you going to be alright, Frank?" I ask hoping to get their attention. They are laughing that hard at the situation that I might have to have an ambulance on standby. "Mary, stop laughing. He could have been hurt badly!" I plead with her, but it doesn't do me any good.

"Thea, he will be fine. I'm going to make some soup, I'll put the TV on, and we will be fine.

Please, get ready for your party." She pleads with me as I tuck Frank into the bed.

I quickly turn around. "How did you know I was going to a party tonight?" I ask curiously and a look is exchanged both of them. I frown my brows. "Spill it!" I demand.

Mary groans. "Well before Frank took a dive off the pavement, a sweet lady called Nancy called instructing us to do all that we could, to get you to the party." She explains and I raise my eyebrows. "We just didn't predict the old bastard on the bed would fall!" She laughs, and Frank joins in.

They are useless. "I'm going to get sorted. Call me if you need anything." I say, leaving them in their fits of giggles, hoping they don't die of laughter.

I run up the stairs to my apartment and try and think mentally what outfit I could conjure up in twenty minutes. My hair only needs a quick touch up, as does my makeup. I'm just unsure on an outfit. I haven't been to many parties, not because I wasn't invited it was just because I didn't like the atmosphere. However, I'm looking forward to seeing all of my other co-workers, and meeting some I've passed in the corridor.

I take off my heels at the door and head into my bedroom, looking through different combinations of outfits, hopeful to find something that will work.

I decide on a long-sleeved bodysuit, black pants with a white stripe down and the black Kurt Geiger heels. That will be comfy.

After fixing my hair and makeup, I pack a bag and make my way out of the door, not forgetting my leather jacket as it is colder outside.

Making my way down the stairs, bottle of wine for Nancy in hand, I see the other neighbour in our building, Alister I think his name is, locking his door. I know he works nights at a museum, but that's all I really know.

"Hey, Thea." He greets me as I come into view.

"Hi Alister, you alright?" I ask politely and he nods. He's shy sometimes and although in the five years I've lived here, I've only seen him about six times, he's always nervous when I speak to him.

He's not very tall, has blonde hair and blue eyes just like me. He's currently dressed in his work uniform as he puts his backpack on. "Off somewhere nice?" He questions, making his way towards the front door of the apartment building.

"Just a party with some friends, are you off to work?" I ask stepping back and knocking on Mary and Frank's door.

"Yeah. What are you doing?"

"Seeing if these two are behaving before I go." I laugh and Mary swings the door open.

"Oh, dear. You look fabulous." She says quietly and gives me a kiss on the cheek. "Frank!" She screams to get his attention. "Just so you're aware, she's dressed like a hooker!" She says giving me a wink and I can hear Frank protest in the background before she shuts the door.

I look over at Alister, who is just as shocked as me that Mary just called me a hooker. "Do I?"

He shakes his head quickly, before opening the door and waiting for me to go through and I do, as quick as I can. I will be having words with Mary tomorrow about that.

"Nice seeing you, Thea." He says before turning on his heels and walking down the street and away before I can say anything.

Following my Sat-Nav, I park at Nancy's apartment in under ten minutes. That isn't so bad, and I never realised she lived so close.

I pick up my bottle of wine and my bag and exit the car, making sure to lock the door. She lives in an incredibly old building, it used to a watch factory she once told me over lunch. She's had it renovated to Victorian chic, her contemporary style that she's found, and she's obsessed. I don't even know what Victorian chic is, so whatever I'm about to walk into. I know it's going to be a surprise.

She lets me into the building, and I decide to go into the lift to get up as I know it's one of them on the top floor.

Once the lift reaches the top, I watch as the door opens and right in front of me is Nancy's apartment. Number 7460A.

I knock and for what feels like a few moments of forever, she answers the door. And I manage to find myself captivated once again. "Took you long enough." She teases as she stands aside to let me in.

"Sorry, my neighbour was at the hospital."

She meets my eyes. "Mary and Frank? Are they alright?" She asks curiously, but her eyes flash with fear.

"Oh yes. They're fine. Frank fell off the path and Mary's laughing about it." I chuckle as does she.

I hand her the bottle of wine and she gives me a grin. "My kind of woman! What can I get you to drink?" She asks opening the fridge.

"Do you have lemonade?" I ask her, looking in her fridge.

She turns quickly. "With vodka?"

I frown my brows. "Just lemonade, please. I'm driving."

She doesn't like that answer but pulls me

something out of the fridge anyway. "Here go you, Miss boring." She teases before pulling out the bottle of wine and pouring herself another glass. "So," she whispers getting close. "do you see anyone eligible?" She says softly.

I turn to her. "Eligible?" I query and she smiles.

"Yes. As in someone you would sleep with, or even date." She says sadistically and my mouth falls open in horror.

"Is this what this is? You're trying to set me up!" I whisper loudly and move away from the crowd of people.

"No, we are." Ophelia says coming into view. "I don't even want to think about how long it's been since you had sex. So, you need to get some, ASAP." She teases holding onto Nancy's hand.

"I don't like this intervention." I say honestly and they both begin to chuckle.

"We know." Nancy speaks looking over at Ophelia. "But you need to meet someone." She says leaving her grip from Ophelia and turning me around. To all the other Agents in the room. "So, who we starting with first?" She says eagerly.

TWENTY-NINE

Sawyer

T he more I stand here the more I feel sick. Nancy has introduced her to every single Agent in the room, some of which she's had longer conversations with than me in the years I've known her.

I'm not jealous. That is something I won't ever feel. But it's beginning to anger me the more she speaks to the male Agents in the room. You can tell if they like her, it's simple biology, and so far, Edison, Rogers and Kent are on my list to kill. Because they have found more reasons to talk to her during the night and that is just angering me more.

"You know, if the wind changes, your face will stay that way." Tuck teases causing me to break my stare towards Thea.

"Huh?" I ask and they both laugh.

"Will you just stop being a bastard and apologize? You can't be standing here territorial of a girl who you won't speak to because you're afraid of her." Scott teases.

"I'm not afraid of her!" I protest and they exchange a look.

"Yes, you are. Because you know deep down, she's who you want." Scott explains.

I scoff. "Sexually, yeah."

Tuck rolls his eyes. "Sawyer, you wouldn't be this territorial of anyone. Because you know she makes you feel other things, she makes you feel emotion which is something you hate, and you struggle to feel in any other capacity. Go over there and talk to her or I will call her over." He warns me and I roll my eyes.

He always delivers empty threats—

"Thea!" I hear him call behind me and I shoot him a look, of if you continue, I will shoot you myself. She looks over but ignores him as she's in another conversation with a female Agent. She was number 208.

"Stop. I'll talk to her eventually. I just need to find the right time." I instruct and both of them look over at each other and decide it is probably best not to test me.

Ophelia signals Scott and he walks away

quickly, like she has him on a lead. "Has he ended it with Sophie?" I ask Tuck, to which he shakes his head.

"Nope. The idiot was looking up engagement rings the other week." He explains and my eyes widen.

"What? He's thinking of proposing to her?" I ask.

Tuck nods his head.

Scott is just denying is feelings for Ophelia at this point, and he's just causing more problems for himself in the long run. None of us doubt that he doesn't love Sophie, but they are two different people now than when they were before the academy and before she went to school.

Tuck has tried speaking to him about where his heads at, and because it's what he thinks he should do. The man has ran with what he thinks is right, which is in fact wrong, and he has decided to take a leap.

"I can't see Sophie saying yes, can you?" I ask Tuck honestly. He's probably discussed this with Scott, laid out everything that will happen, and Scott still has it in his head that Sophie is who he's meant to be with.

"Honestly, no. But it's none of our business." He snaps a little at me and I turn to see Scott walking in our direction. The tone of his voice was a warning.

"Ophelia had a question." He says straightening himself out.

"Did she get to answer that question or were you too busy eating at her face?" I tease to which he looks at me in horror.

"You're disgusting." He says, fixing his jeans and his turtleneck.

"I know. But I'm also right."

We all clean up Nancy's apartment., so she isn't waking up to a mess in the morning. She got a little white-girl-wasted and ended up passing out about an hour ago. After that, little by little people started to leave. And the only people left were Scott, Tuck, Thea, Ophelia, and me. One of the Agent's I now have on my hit list, Rogers, offered to help and clean up but Thea was sweet and said he should go. Yes, yes you should.

"Thank you for helping." Ophelia says giving us all a smile. "I'll stay with her tonight. Make sure she's okay." She says sweetly and all of us nod.

Nancy hasn't been one to handle her drink well, especially when she's emotional. Turns out the Agent she was dating, was also dating another Agent, so Nancy decided to end that quickly. She's upset she didn't see the signs.

We all know about this as Johnson is a

blabbermouth when he starts speaking and decided to let everyone know on the team what happened. Apparently, the Agent Nancy was going out with didn't like that and starting to publicly shame her. She was very embarrassed.

Tuck and Scott are the first to leave and I hang back for Thea just in case she needs a ride.

She shuts the door and jumps back when she sees me. "Did you forget something?" She asks softly.

"Er—no. I wanted to know if you needed a ride home?" I ask her and she seems taken back by my offer.

"I have my car but thank you." She says with a smile before clicking the button for the elevator to go down. She has that perfume on again. The one that makes me feel drunk when I'm around her and I'm about to be stuck in an elevator. Great.

We both enter awkwardly, and I have never known to be so quiet around her, I feel as though I'm walking on eggshells.

I try to block out the smell of that perfume for as long as I can as we reach the bottom floor.

We exit in silence and leave Nancy's building, awkwardly waiting for one of us to say something.

"See you Monday, Sawyer." She says and

begins to walk away, and I feel my heart hurt.

"Thea," I call after her causing her to stop and turn around. "let me at least walk you to your car." I offer walking towards her.

"That's very nice of you." She says awkwardly, and I chuckle a little.

"It is." I agree. I don't even know where it came from.

"I've been wanting to speak to you for a few days." She says as we walk down towards her car. "I wanted to say thank you." She speaks in the purest voice.

"What for?" I ask curiously. Although I know what it's for, I just want to hear her speak.

"I know you did all you could when you went to deal with Rachel White and Isaac Fields. So, when she turned up at the office. Although it caught me off guard, I knew you would work it out." She praises me.

I can feel my cheeks getting redder and redder then more I stand with her, and I would like to think it's because I'm uncomfortable. "You're welcome." I say eventually and she walks in front, unlocking her car. "A Tesla, on a Starbuck's salary?" I query playfully.

She scoffs. "It's my neighbours. They got a new one and they're letting me use their old one till I can afford to either buy it off them or buy my own. But that is a future project. I have too much going on right now to think about." She blabbers.

"Are you close with your neighbours?" I ask curiously. I realise that I don't know that much about her, probably because I never thought to ask.

"Very. They are my family." She says with a smile. It's genuine. I don't want to press into it too much in case I go over the line. So, I decide to ask those questions eventually or if they come naturally in conversation.

"How did you like Nancy's tactic to get you a suitor?" I tease.

She raises her eyebrows. "Suitor?" She mocks lightly. "Are you alright, Sawyer?"

I become embarrassed. "You know what I mean." I laugh it off looking away from her and that stupid smile on her face. "Did you like any of them, that is what I'm asking."

She seems taken by my choice of words. "Like any of them? Sawyer, are you jealous?" She asks, you can hear the humour in her voice.

"No." I'm quick to respond. "Just seemed to everyone in that room that you were very desperate to find someone." I answer without thinking.

Well done, Sawyer.

The smile drops from her face, and she rolls

her eyes. "Goodnight, Sawyer." She says abruptly almost hitting me with her car door as she steps inside and slams the door.

A few seconds later she speeds off.

Well, I have just royally fucked that up.

THIRTY

Thea

Desperate.

Who the hell is he of all people calling *me* desperate? The man can't go five seconds without having to shag something with a pulse and I'm desperate for getting to know my other co-workers? Please.

Sawyer ruffled my feathers on Friday, and I can't be sure if it was just to make himself look good, which it didn't; it made him look like a twat, or if it was a reaction when I asked if he was jealous.

I know he was, because for the entire night he was staring directly at me whenever Nancy or Ophelia introduced me to any male Agent in the I.C.C.O.

Deciding to ignore Sawyer's outburst, I walk through the entrance way of the building, completely ignoring my surrounding while scrolling on my phone. "Agent St. James!" I hear someone call after me.

As I turn, I see a young male Agent head towards me with a bunch of flowers, all assorted colours, and smiles at me. "How can I help?" I greet.

"These are for you," He says, handing me the large bouquet of flowers.

I look back up at him for confirmation that he's being serious, and he is. "Thank you." I say turning on my heels and walking towards the lift.

Who is sending me flowers first thing on a Monday morning?

Earning looks off my fellow Agents, I make small, uncomfortable smiles while heading towards my office.

By the looks on the other Agent's faces, flowers aren't delivered here often as they gleam at me curious as to the sender, and probably the reciever.

I reach my office and place the flowers on the desk, hoping, actually praying, that there is a card so I can see who has just caused me the embarrassment.

It is a sweet gesture, however, I've been here under a month, and so far, I've been given two bunches of flowers. One by Johnson, and this one by a stranger.

I search eagerly for a card and find it on the side of the bouquet. *Come on James, open your eyes.*

Opening the envelope, I can't stop the look on my face as I read the card.

Great to finally get to know you.

Maybe we can go out sometime.

See you around, Miss St. James

Kent.

Oh, dear god.

I place the card down and rub my temples. Kent was lovely, don't get me wrong. But the man still lives with his mother and made a few derogatory comments about women, and how they are meant to be mothers. The whole situation made me feel slightly uncomfortable.

"Someone has an admirer." I hear someone speak behind me, and there stands Nancy, with yet another bunch of flowers.

"Please tell me they are for you." I say as she walks towards me, laughing lightly.

"I wish." She laughs. "The only time I ever got flowers was when everyone found out I was gay, and the last person I slept with was Sawyer, so Tuck and Scott congratulated me for embarrassing him." She teases placing the flowers next to the ones from Kent. "So, who are these from?" She asks lifting up the card and reading it. "Huh," she says after a moment.

"What?" I ask curiously.

She waves me off. "It's probably nothing, but Kent said that he would never send anyone flowers. He thinks they are a waste of money." She says looking over at me and then back down at the flowers.

"That is weird." I say picking up the card in the other bouquet. "I have an idea who sent these."

"So do I." She says standing next to me while I open the card. I feel a wave of sickness come over me. "Well, that is painful to read." She moves away.

"Is he normally this forward?" I ask her turning around to meet her gaze as she stands at the door. The flowers are from Rogers and although they are beautiful, the card is disgustingly forward.

"The man had four beers and it took all of his might to talk to you. Unless he was drunk out of his mind. He didn't write this." She smiles.

I grab my file and meet her at the door. "So, you think this is a joke?" I ask her as we make our way towards the lift. "Cause I don't want to be a joke."

She shakes her head. "I don't know, Thea. It's weird. We haven't seen him yet. So, let's speak to both and try and mention it, unless they do it first." She explains the plan while the doors open, and we are met with both Kent and Rogers. They stare down at me, both having a letter in their hand.

"Agent St. James." They greet me and exchange a look. "We were wondering if we could have a meeting." They say looking over at each other again. "All of us." They say signalling Nancy.

Her eyes light up and she nods to them both. "Thea?"

"My office?" I say turning on my heels and walking away from the uncomfortable feeling and they all follow us.

It's not even a thirty second walk to my office but with every step I feel like I want to kill myself. I have no idea what this meeting is about, but I get the feeling it has something to do with the pieces of paper in their hands.

"Agent St. James," Kent begins as we approach the office. "we had a great night the other night getting to know you. But this is a bit far don't you think?" He says holding up his piece of paper.

I look over to Nancy, who is just as puzzled as myself. I hold out my hand to look over the bit of paper in his hand, not knowing what to expect.

I go bright red. The shade of a tomato. Oh my god what is this.

The letter goes into detail about sexual fantasies I've had about Kent since Friday. Including kinks, I suddenly now have. How I want his children one day. The list goes on.

I am mortified and my face undoubtedly shows it. "Agent St. James, you didn't write this?" Rogers questions and I shake my head, still in disbelief and hand the letter over to Nancy for her to read.

She turns the same shade as me, however, tries to hold in her giggles to which she fails miserably. Her shoulders begin to rise rapidly, and the tears begin to form in her eyes. I'm trying not to laugh as I am so embarrassed, however, this is ridiculously funny.

"Men, I can vouch for Thea, she didn't write these." She giggles handing Kent his letter. "But I think she might have an idea on who did." She says giving me a look.

I can't understand what she's trying to say, I don't know anyone who would want to—

Sawyer.

That prick.

I feel the anger rush through my body. Why would he do this?

"Agent St. James, Edison got one too. We checked his desk and there was the same letter. He's off to see family for the next week, so we thought we would save him the uncomfortableness of it." Rogers explains and I nod.

"Of course." I say, still trying to understand it all. "I'm so sorry, this must have been traumatising to read." I say and they both nod.

"Yeah, I mean we talked about it, and we're into you know—" He begins, his face blushing slightly.

"I don't, sorry." I say, hoping he'll continue.

"We're into like regular sex. You know, what the weirdo's with kinks would say is vanilla?" He says, emphasising the vanilla.

I exchange a look over at Nancy who is intrigued, but still mouths the word 'boring.'

"Someone's popular with the flowers." Kent says looking behind me.

I turn, completely forgetting about the flowers. Trying not to cause them any more distress, I decide to not mention them. It would only cause more problems and I am about to commit a murder.

"Can I keep your letters? Is that alright?"

They are very quick to hand them over. "Yeah. We don't want to read anything like that again." Kent explains.

"Are you that traumatised?" I ask curiously, but I'm also horrified. "Have you never read a romance book?"

They look at each other. "Why would we? Woman are meant be submissive to a man, and I think that this talk about sex and kinks is not in gods will. Woman are meant to not have control."

I narrow my eyes. "In any situation? Women are meant to be submissive?" I ask. Nancy stands closer to them, crossing her arms. We aren't going to like what we are about to hear.

"Of course. Just how woman are meant to give men children and keep the house clean—" Rogers starts and Nancy points towards the door.

"Enough!" She demands. "Out of Agent St. James' office before I demand you both on a course on how to speak to women." She warns.

They scurry out of my office, like kids who have just been told off by their mother. "Well, that was hell." I say picking up the letter and reading it again. "Why would he do this?"

She gives me a look. "He knows he crossed the line, but he's also still trying to win that bet, Thea. We both know this was to make you look bad and to get you your first warning. All it has done is made him look stupid." She chuckles taking the letters out of my hands and placing them in my desk draw.

"Can I borrow your gun?" I ask her and she chuckles, walking back round the desk. Picking up the file I need and placing it in my hands.

"Later, we have a meeting." She instructs leaving my office. I follow along, like a dog on a leash, because we are extremely late for this meeting with Assistant Director Shields.

THIRTY-ONE

Sawyer

I've not seen her since Friday, but I'm on high alert.

What I did to her, to cause her an insane amount of embarrassment, I deserve to be in the six-foot grave she's digging for me.

I did enjoy the look of disgust on her face when the flowers came into headquarters. Or when they turned up at her office. That I really did enjoy.

She doesn't like them.

Meaning that I might have a chance to win this bet. A new bet was placed between my team a few days after Thea joined, just before she heard my conversation with Tuck and Scott, that as long as I get her into bed and get her fired. I get the full pay out.

It's a sweet deal to me. I need her to hate me to have hate sex with me and that will be one of the best sounds in the world.

Hearing her moan my name.

Fuck. I'm getting drunk imagining it.

"What did you do?" Tuck asks standing in the doorway of my office. "Nancy said you've done something. So, I want to hear it from the horse's mouth. Spill it, Sawyer!" He demands, slamming the door.

He's not in a playful, or in a, understanding mood. He's pissed off. And it's directly aimed at me and knowing how Tuck is with the other females and how protective he is. I need to make sure he is away from me before I admit anything.

"Sit down." I instruct, standing up tall. We are the same stature, I am just a little smaller on the arms wise, and he is two-inches taller. But this is my office I need to show off some sort of dominance.

He does what I ask, but it feels like forever, and I can finally take a breath when he walks away and takes a seat on the couch. "I haven't got all day. The Director wants to see us both. So, I need you to hurry this up." He instructs.

"I might have sent flowers to her from the two of the three men that talked to her at Nancy's party on Friday." I laugh.

He stands up after a moment and rolls his eyes. "I'm hoping to god that this meeting with the Director is to discuss the fact that you're out of a job, Sawyer. Are you joking me? Why would you cause her that much embarrassment?" He asks me, more like shouts.

I notice a few people begin to look in our direction as my door is still open and I tell him to shush. "You're going to attract people!" I inform him.

"It was stupid, and damn right out of order Sawyer!" He shouts again.

I roll my eyes. "She might leave! This will be a win here!" I explain to him.

He groans pushing his hair behind his ear. "You are the most insufferable dick I've ever met in my entire life. You think with your dick, you don't think with your head or your heart because that hurts too much." He shouts and I practically run to close the door.

I'm about to object, but he quickly cuts me off. "Don't bother, Sawyer. You've been insane for as long as I've known you. I dread to think what you put that girl through at the academy. But this behaviour only got worse when your Mom died." He snaps at me. My eyes widen, he and Scott are the only people who know that my Mom died in February, I never thought he would use it against me. "The way you treat women is disgusting, it's harassing and it's unbelievable to witness because we know that your Mother would never have let you do half of the things you've done to Thea. You would have a conscious. You would think of the outcome. But since she died, the only thing you've thought about is winning, all this is about is getting that ten seconds of fun." He snaps again.

I take a seat on the end of my desk, I'm trying not to show it, but I know he's right and I am out of order. "She brings anger out of me, Tuck. I can't explain it." I say hoping he'll hear me out. "She was a barista a month ago. That felt amazing knowing she was no one. But here, she's the Communications Liaison. She can publicly call out on anything I do. She keeps me in check. I for some reason decide to listen to her." I explain.

"Treat her with respect, Sawyer. That's all she's ever tried to do to you. Even though you don't deserve it." He says harshly walking past me to the door. "I hope this meeting we walk in to see Thea; she's sat there with a file. And you lose your job. Cause after this little tactic. You've well and truly fucked it."

He storms out of my office and down the ramp leading to the door out of the pen. I really hope that when I walk into this meeting with Director Sinclair that trouble isn't sat there with her evidence to ruin my life.

But I really do deserve it.

I'm behind Tuck towards the Directors office. It's on a whole different floor and I've been here a handful of times to help out on the Undercover Operation catching the killer and arms dealer known as Tony Delsavo. He's been untouchable for the last two years, and I was brought onto the taskforce to try and have Johnson track and locate Delsavo on numerous occasions. Tuck has three men undercover in Delsavo's world of crime. This meeting is a monthly update to show what Johnson and myself have found out.

Tuck opens the door and sits at the long desk in the middle of the room is the District Attorney, Director Sinclair himself, Yazmin Ferroway with the local police, and Simon Romero from the FBI.

Fresh faces to the taskforce. Unusual.

"Agent Tucker-Barlow, Agent Reid. Take a seat." He instructs.

Without a second thought, we take a seat at the last two remaining seats at the table. "Director." We greet him warmly and he looks around the table.

"Agent Reid, you know Yazmin Ferroway and Simon Romero, right?" He asks, turning over to them. "You worked with them before on a previous case am I correct?"

I nod. "That's right, Sir."

The atmosphere in this room is colder than a freezer and I can sense it. Something isn't adding up and I can't work out what it is.

"Agent Tucker-Barlow. I want to bring you to something we found out earlier today." Director Sinclair explains, slightly eyeing me up. "A security breech was reached this morning at 7:25am, and private and very damaging documents about the Delsavo case has gone public, to the media and has been shared to other people within the office." He explains.

I turn my head and notice Tuck is furious, as he should be. He's risked his life and his men to try and bring down Delsavo. And some idiot as leaked it all? Who the hell would do that? And who would do it with access?

"Who?" Tuck asks as calmly as he can.

All eyes turn to me, and Tuck's are not far to follow. I begin to feel nervous. Something isn't right.

"Agent Reid. Care to explain?" Director Sinclair asks, and I frown my eyes.

"I have no idea what you're talking about." I admit and he rises from his chair, doing the button up on his jacket and collecting a file from his desk.

"There is no doubt in my mind Sawyer that in your year here at I.C.C.O, that you have become a very well known, hardworking and capable Agent. You're close rate is one of the best in the agency, however your mind has since been on something else, which is why I think you didn't realize what has happened." He explains, standing over me and placing the file on the desk.

"I don't know what you mean." I repeat and he shakes his head.

"Sawyer at 7:25am this morning, it was your login and your access that leaked the information to everyone." He explains opening up the file and right in front of my eyes, shows me that my login did in fact send the information to people.

"Sir, I can assure you this wasn't me. I got into the office at 7:40 this morning. I wasn't even here." I explain and he shuts the file.

"Agent Reid, you have ruined an investigation that is two years in the making!" He shouts, accusing me, ignoring my alibi. "Agent Tucker-Barlow's Agents are all dead because of you!" He shouts and me.

"I wasn't here! It wasn't me!" I defend myself.

He laughs. "Oh really?" He says turning on the TV and security video begins playing of me sat in my office at a time of 7:25am, on todays date.

"I wasn't here! Check the log with the hut Agents, that video has been fabricated!" I accuse and he turns to me.

"They all went on record to say they saw you come into view at 7:10 this morning. The three Agent's on duty all vouched for it and have given statements." He explains and I look over at Tuck.

He's stunned, but you can see the anger on his face underneath. "I didn't do this Tuck, I swear." I plead to him.

He looks away from me and around the table. "What happens now?" He asks, ignoring me.

"Sawyer Reid will be arrested for breaking company policy and assisting a criminal in a murder. All three of your men are dead, Agent Tucker-Barlow. I'm sorry." Yazmin says to Tuck who nods as a thank you, but then looks at me.

"Arrest him." He says looking over at me. His eyes are cold, hurt, and afraid.

I raise from my chair, backing away from the other people in the room. "I didn't do this." I plead with them as they rise, reaching for their guns. "I wouldn't put my job at risk!" I explain and Director Sinclair scoffs.

"You should have thought about your job before you started harassing another co-worker." He explains and I look over at him.

Thea.

She did this.

I decide not to plead my case anymore and I take off running, pulling both doors open as I make a run for the elevator and out of this building before security is called.

THIRTY-TWO

Thea

I approach the lift patiently, going through my notes with my meeting with Assistant Director Shields. I decided that this is the last time I was going to let Sawyer Reid get away with anything and informed her about everything that has happened.

She was surprised, but she did say she expected it. Sawyer Reid was one more problem away from being sacked. I was just the Agent that lit that fire to get it going.

She assured me that this wasn't my fault and asked that I make copies of those letters to send to Director Sinclair and she was going to schedule a meeting with him sometime this week.

The lift doors open, and I step in, hoping for a relaxing and quiet day ahead.

This morning has me feeling a handful of emotions, angry, sad, and embarrassed for the most part. Why Sawyer would write that I'm into BDSM, or that have an oil fetish is beyond me. BDSM, yes. Oil, absolutely not.

There are a lot of things Sawyer Reid doesn't know and will never know about me and what I like in the bedroom. The man is clearly a sadist, and why I would subject myself to someone like him when there are dominants out in the world that actually know how to give me a fun time.

The lift stops at floor seven. Director Sinclair's floor. I know in Tuck's diary he had a meeting with Sinclair this morning about an undercover operation that has been going ahead for years.

I'm on the need to know for that.

I'm startled when the doors open and there stands a frantic Sawyer, who looks as if he's just had the worst sex in his entire life. "Sawyer?" I say and he stares at me, struggling to form a sentence.

A bullet flies past my head and lands in the metal boards of the lift. He turns around to see a woman with her gun raised, giving him a warning look. He moves me out of the way and pushes the emergency button on the lift and it shuts them immediately. Bullet's start flying towards us and as he go up to the top floor of the agency.

"Sawyer, what the hell is going on?" I shout at him.

He places his hands around my neck, making me drop my notes from my meeting with Shields. "Why did you do it, huh? Wanted to see what I looked like in orange?" He snaps as I struggle to breathe.

"Sawyer- I. didn't." I plead and it only makes him squeeze harder. "Sawyer, I can't breathe!" I plead again and this time, he sees the fear in my eyes and decides to let go.

I gasp for my breath holding onto my neck coughing, hoping, and praying for air to reach my lungs. "Why did you do it?" He shouts at me, punching the side of the lift, as me fly through the floors.

"What are you even talking about, Sawyer? Do what?" I cough and he groans.

"You released the documents on Tuck's undercover operation that killed three of his men." He accuses and I stand tall.

"I most certainly did not! How dare you accuse me of that!" I shout.

He begins to laugh. "Thea St. James, always the victim."

"Me, the victim? How about you explain

how I supposedly leaked documents, Sawyer?" I demand and he places his hands on his hips. The lift suddenly stops, and he draws his gun without a second thought. "Sawyer, what the hell is going on?" I ask and he places his hand up, telling me to be quiet.

We aren't on a floor, and if we are the emergency button isn't opening the doors. He puts his gun away for a minute and pulls the doors open ever so slightly which reveals a group of masked men, armed Agents, pointing guns directly at the lift doors. "Oh shit." He says shutting them and glass begins to fly everywhere.

I can't stop screaming. I'm frightened, I'm being shot at, and I'm being accused of something I didn't do. I watch Sawyer as he pulls put the electric wiring of the lift and tries to look at each individual cable.

"Fuck it." He says and cuts all of the cables with some sort of pocketknife.

Oh, dear god.

The lift begins to creak, and I look over at him in horror. "Hold on." He instructs. Suddenly the lift begins to drop, and I hold on, screaming Sawyer's name as we fly from the top floor of the building to the bottom.

I'm going to die. This is how I die.

No more than twenty seconds later, the lift hits the bottom floor, and my ears begin to ring.

I can't move, but I can hear gun shots and some sort of alarm.

"Thea?" I can hear someone shout as they stand over me. "Thea, get up." Sawyer instructs and that is when I feel it, the pain.

He tilts my head, and I watch his eyes widen when he sees something. Without saying another word, he lifts me up bridal style and takes me through what I seems like an underground car park. He reaches one side of the car park, and opens the door, putting me in the passenger seat.

He straps me in carefully, shutting the door and heading round to the other side.

I'm in and out of consciousness, but he starts the car no problem and reverses out of the space like a maniac. Everything begins to go fuzzy, before everything goes black.

THIRTY-THREE

Thea

I feel a wet compress on my head, and I stir at the uncomfortable feeling. Jolting myself awake, I'm surprised to see Mary and Frank in front of me. Frank is sat in his chair, while Mary sits in front of me on a dining room table, pressing the cold material to my head. "Thank god you're alright, dear."

Taking in my surroundings as I sit up, that's when I feel it.

The pain.

"Dear, you're going to have to lie down." She instructs me, forcing me back down to the sofa. "You have a concussion."

"You're not a Doctor, Mary." Frank explains and she shoos him away.

"Don't need to be to know this girl needs serious medical attention." She says placing the compress back on my head.

Suddenly Sawyer appears from the kitchen, and I sit up slowly. His body is closed off as he looks frightened over at Mary. "I didn't know where else to go." He explains sheepishly.

"Did you tell them that this is your fault?" I snap at him. He raises his face to look at me, a lack of emotion is on his face.

"They gathered. That's why Mary punched me." He explains.

I look over at Mary who smiles back at me. "I've waited years to do it." She admits, causing me to press my lips together. "You should be proud of me."

"I am, Mary. Slightly jealous you got to do it before me." I tease looking back over at Sawyer.

His expression is still emotionless, still quiet. Yet, that doesn't surprise me. "We can't be here long. The first place they are going to go is our apartments." He explains casually, and I look over at Mary and Frank.

"You're joking? I'm not harbouring a fugitive, Sawyer!" I shout at him, and he avoids my stare.

"Love, you don't have much choice." Frank

says pointing at the TV.

I get up slowly and make my way towards the TV as he turns it up so I can hear.

"Breaking News!

I.C.C.O have released a statement that they are currently looking for the following Agents in relation with an incident that occurred earlier today. Agents Sawyer Reid and Thea St. James of Sin City are currently wanted by all organizations regarding information. If you see the pair, please do not engage as they are severely dangerous."

I fall back onto the chair, stunned as my face is being plastered all over the news. I.C.C.O know I wouldn't assist Sawyer in anything. How I've clearly been taken hostage by the insane man who stands there, smiling. "Is this a joke to you, Sawyer?" I ask coldly. "What the hell is wrong with you? Are you trying to get me fired?" I shout.

"Yes!" He screams back and I sit back stunned. "I planned this whole thing, Thea. I leaked the intelligence documents on Tuck's biggest case to date. I made sure to almost kill you as I thought it would be fun." He jokes. "Do you not see that this is so much bigger than we thought? In the space of an hour, they've released our photos and names to the press. This is bigger than us, Thea." He shouts.

"Stop using the word us! I'm going to the building, demand that they look at the cameras in the lift and I'll assist in any way I can to have you arrested." I warn.

He rolls his eyes. "Thea, for once listen, will you?"

"I suggest you word that better, son. Otherwise, I will be inclined to commit a murder." Frank warns him.

Sawyer takes another step back. "Fine. But let me be realistic here, Thea. We are now fugitives. Meaning we are going to have to work together to stay out of a jail cell. You aren't going back to the I.C.C.O because they would have already edited the video of the elevator to show that you helped me escape. And I will throw your ass under the bus. Because I don't doubt for one second you didn't have something to do with this." He snaps at me.

I look at Mary and Frank. "So, let me get this straight, Sawyer. You jumped to the conclusion that I'm the one framing you for the leaked documents? That I hate you that much that I would risk my job by leaking documents, to have you fired?" I explain. He nods confidently. "Well, you're the dumbest person in the room then, aren't you?" I snap back.

He doesn't like my tone and charges towards me. "Back up." Mary warns him. Her fist is raised, and, in this lighting, I can see that she isn't joking. She's warning him.

It takes him a moment, and he does back up a few seconds. "Thea, we're gonna have to work together." He explains.

I scoff. "I would rather end up in that jail cell. Because that is probably better than the hell, I would subject myself to being on the run with you." I admit.

He's slightly taken back by response but composes himself. "Will you stop being a troublemaker and do as you're told?" He demands again.

"No, why should I? You got me into this mess, as you always do. You get me into the worst possible situations that I have to get myself out." I explain.

He doesn't fight me this time, only takes a long deep breath in the hopes to keep his composure.

Just as he is about to explain something, he turns to the window, and his eyes widen. "Last chance, Thea. You can die here or end up in jail. Or live and get your reputation back?" He explains backing away from the window.

"Go, we can hold them off." Mary explains. My eyes go as wide as saucers.

"Absolutely not, what if they hurt you?"

She scoffs. "They won't hurt a harmless old lady!" She teases, rising from her chair and heading over to the cupboard behind Frank.

"Thea, we have to go now." Sawyer reminds me, and I stand to my feet. This is the stupidest idea I've ever had. Agreeing to become a fugitive with Sawyer fucking Reid.

"Here." Mary says handing me a small envelope. I quickly open it while following Sawyer towards a window leading to the alley way. It's money, and a lot of it. "You'll need it. We'll tell everyone you're innocent, now go!" She demands and I run to meet Sawyer at the window. He helps me out and that's when he hear the bang. There goes the front door to the apartment building. "Sawyer, get her killed and I will kill you. That is my promise." She warns him. He doesn't do much other than nod. I think he's frightened of her.

"Thea!" I hear someone whisper to me. Turning around, I notice Alister, our neighbour, standing next to a car. "Here, take this." He demands placing the keys in my hand. I'm startled, and he can sense that. "We know you're innocent. Go, before they get you." He instructs looking up at Sawyer.

"Thea, come on." Sawyer says heading towards the car.

"Thank you." I say placing a kiss on Alister's cheek and running towards the driver's side of the car. That was nice of him, considering I barely know him.

I put my seat belt on and hit the gas and drive out of the alleyway, away from the building. "What is the plan, Sawyer?" I ask him. He looks around nervously, noting anything that may or may not be a police car or government car. "Head out of the city. I know a place we can lay low."

THIRTY-FOUR

Sawyer

S he drives as calmly as she can towards the outskirts of Sin City. The place I'm taking her to is so off the map that they shouldn't find us.

The cabin we are heading to I bought as a retirement plan. I wanted to live in the middle of nowhere, where I could enjoy the peace and quiet of what the outskirts of the city had to offer.

"Sawyer, where are you taking me?" She asks again.

"Trust me—"

"I don't." She quickly responds. "Why should

I?" She snaps, turning back to look at the road. "You've not only manage to ruin my life in the worst way possible, but you might also have just got my neighbours, killed or arrested."

I scoff. "Mary and Frank will be fine. I'm not worried about them." I explain.

"Well, I am." She snaps again, this time I see the tears in her eyes. "They are my only family out here. I don't know why I've been so stupid to join you in this. I haven't thought any of this through." She cries softly.

"Thea, you're safe with me." I say softly. "I know this has nothing to do with you. But I have full faith that when we get back to normal. They will be fine." I explain softly, placing my hand on her leg, in a sign of comfort.

"Sawyer, remove your hand from my leg before I turn this car around and hand you over to them." She warns and I'm quick to remove it before she bites it off. "You said in the lift you thought it was me, and you said at Mary and Frank's that I was in on this. Why?"

"Because I knew eventually, I was going to get fired cause of what I did to you." I explain and she looks over slightly. "I deserved it though. What you decided to do. Just didn't think you would try and get me arrested and thrown in jail." I tease.

"This isn't me, Sawyer." She admits. "I have no idea why you would think I'm that advanced, or that I know anything about the case Tuck was working on."

I take a long deep breath. "I'm sorry for accusing you."

She turns her head quickly to me. "Don't do that. I'm not forgiving you, because I know it is all shit, Sawyer. Get your act together." She says, shifting uncomfortably in the driver's seat.

I begin to laugh. "I applaud your honesty. Love you, trouble."

She groans. "Hate you too."

As we approach the cabin, I watch her eyes look over it, concerned. Granted I haven't had a lot of time to fix up the outside, the inside is pretty nice. "Home sweet home." I joke, getting out he car as it comes to a stop.

"Home? Sawyer, are you planning on murdering me? This is the cabin out of horror movies." She says getting out and looking around. "Oh my god, you're a serial killer. You kill people on the weekends." She says dramatically.

"I do, it's an extracurricular activity for me. A bit like sex." I tease.

Her face turns horrified. "You are disgusting."

"I know."

I get the key from my pocket and open the door. Outside may not look nice, but inside is one of the proudest things I've done to date. It's back to its original beauty. There was an old original fireplace I was determined to save; I put in new flooring and turned this place into a comfortable retirement cabin. I was incredibly happy with my project.

"Wow, who does this belong to?" She asks looking around. It's freezing in here, and I head over to start the fire so we can get warm.

"Me. I bought it back in February." I explain, attempting to set the fire alight.

"Any reason?"

I stop what I'm doing and look back at her. "My Mom died. So, I needed something to do to deal with the grief." I admit honestly, which catches her off guard.

"Sawyer, I'm sorry. I didn't realise she passed." She says sympathetically.

I wave her off. "It's fine, I don't go announcing it. I try not to think about it too much." I admit. The fire roars to life and I feel myself become calmer.

"Why this colour scheme and vibe of the cabin? I wouldn't say this is your style?" She says, changing the subject.

"Really?" I say raising from my position. "You should see my apartment in the city, it's a bachelor pad." I tease, to which she rolls her eyes.

"It's probably got more STD's than most people in Sin City." She says playfully, and I pretend that hurts my feelings by clutching at my heart.

"Funny, trouble." I say taking a seat on the couch. "But I'm clear of everything. In case you were curious." I wink.

She groans in disgust. "I wasn't, but thanks."

She takes a seat on the chair opposite from me. "So, what is the plan?" She asks as I lie down and begin to get comfortable. "Surely you've thought of something."

I pull a blanket over me, hoping she will stop talking. "We wait it out, things will come together. That's the plan." I admit.

I hear movement in front of me and pull the blanket away to see she's standing. "I'm sorry, you're telling me to sit here and wait for a miracle?"

"No." I snap back at her. "Wait for them to come to their senses. All we can do." I say getting comfortable and close my eyes again.

"Oh, I understand..." She says, which causes me to open one eye. "You don't have a plan." She says smugly, crossing her arms.

"I do indeed! It was exactly what I just said." I snap at her, and she laughs slightly.

"The great Sawyer Reid doesn't have plan.

That is one for the books." She says walking away from my view and heading in the way of the kitchen. "Pleased that I'll be getting the one bed in this place, Sawyer. Thank you for being such a gentleman." She teases and I rise from the couch.

"You will not, you can sleep on the couch!" I demand and she turns very slowly, the look on her face unimpressed.

"Wow, you're going to ruin my life and then tell me I can't have a comfortable place to sleep? That's nice of you." She snaps.

"You'll be perfectly fine on the couch. I mean I haven't changed the sheets since I last stayed, and I had a lady friend with me." I say.

She groans in disgust. "You are absolutely disgusting, Sawyer!" She screams at me.

"What?" I object. "I didn't realize I'd end up having someone over, who isn't welcome, FYI." I explain, to which she only roles her eyes.

"Well, like it or not, Sawyer, you're stuck with me. You dragged me into this mess. You're going to get me out!" She shouts back at me.

"Why would I help a Starbucks barista who can barely make a chai latte!" I shout at her.

She lets out a squeal. "I make brilliant chai latte's not that I would ever make you one, I would have to spit in it!" She shouts at me.

"You wouldn't dare." I test her.

She narrows her eyes, "Wanna bet, Sawyer?"

I growl, out loud. "You have to be the most insufferable woman I have ever met! No wonder no man would go near you!" I shout at her.

She gasps in horror. "I'm insufferable?" She questions, her eyebrow raised while her face is filled with disbelief. "Let me just remind you that you were the one who's currently under investigation for leaking documents, which happens to be a very Sawyer Reid like thing to do, just to get back at me! Also, you have to be the most dangerous man on the planet, because that dick of yours has been in more woman than I've had hot dinners!"

I blink at her, my face clearly filled with disbelief. "Are you calling me a whore?"

"Absolutely."

My eyes widen at her admission. "At least I could get some unlike you. There's probably cobwebs down between your legs with how long you've gone with no one touching you! Yet I wouldn't blame them!" I snap at her. This time her eyes widen, and she begins to head towards the bathroom, not saying one word to me.

"Where are you going?" I ask.

"Away from you. I'll sleep in the bath." She says. It's not even five o'clock, but she does need to rest, especially with the head injury she has. I can't have her dying on me while we are on the run.

"Thea!" I shout at her, stopping her in her tracks. "Lie down, please." I plead.

She stands there with her face unimpressed as I hold the blanket for her to take.

After a few moments of silence, she walks towards me, glaring me down. "You better have washed this." She says pointing at the couch, taking the blanket out of my hand.

"Of course." I admit to her, and she takes a seat slowly, kicking off her heels. "You need to rest." I admit, and she nods. She gets comfortable and closes her eyes not saying another word to me. I'm not saying sorry. She will need to apologize first.

I decide to head into the kitchen and think of a plan. She can't be walking around in what she wore earlier. Her t-shirt is covered in blood and her black and white plaid pants are ruined in dirt, blood and sweat. So, they need to be taken to the trash.

I can't seem to work out why someone would accuse me of doing this to Tuck or to the agency. Director Sinclair was determined not to hear my side of the story, how he had concluded and how the video he showed the rest of law enforcement showed that I was the one who sent the documents, although it was clearly a fake video.

To be fair, it could have been taken at any point, and the date and time altered. When I came back to work after my Mom died, I was doing eighteen-to-nineteen-hour shifts to try and keep myself focused. Once I got back into my normal schedule I was here at decent times and leaving normally. So, where this video has come from, really does confuse me.

I've been undercover a few times before. But I've never had to hide as a fugitive. This is new to me, but in case it ever happened I did want to become prepared. I look under the sink to find the bag I packed in case of emergencies. A few extra guns and rounds of ammunition, a burner phone, and a laptop. I managed to somehow get Wi-Fi out here.

I turn on the burner phone, thankfully that can't be traced, and I open the laptop. I don't know what I'm searching for, but I need something in order to prove I'm innocent, as is Thea.

It's peaceful when she isn't speaking, and I can focus on what I'm doing. But I know I don't have long, and I'm going to have to keep checking on her and the blood coming from the back of her head.

Mary is right, she needs medical attention, and I'm hoping that soon, I can get her to a hospital without a target on our back.

I take the phone out, it's an old phone, so old it still has snake on it. But it will do the job.

The logo of the phone flashes on the screen and I try and wait patiently for the thing to start up. I miss my old phone, as in my iPhone. I feel like I'm back in middle school with this old thing.

I begin to pull out the other guns I have and place them on the counter, double checking they are all here. I'm going to have to teach sleeping beauty over there how to shoot a gun. I doubt she's had any experience since we left the academy.

A text pops up on the screen of the phone and I immediately become alarmed. No one has this number, it's not registered with anything, so how can someone have it?

I open it and my brows raise.

Boss, it's Johnson. Call me back.

I really do underestimate this kids' talents. However, I'm sceptical that this could be a set up. So, if I do call, it will be on my terms in case he decides to hand it over to the big boss.

As I'm about to hit call, the number flashes on the screen.

I decide to step outside, not wanting to wake up her royal highness.

I answer, reluctant to speak first.

"Boss?" I hear Johnsons whiny little voice speak on the end.

"Johnson, you alright?" I ask him.

"We're fine here. Are you? Is Thea? We heard she's injured." He asks. I can hear the panic in his voice. He likes Thea, not in the way that I thought. But he cares about her because she showed him kindness and compassion.

"Johnson, I can't talk to you—" I begin.

"I'm calling from a burner phone at Nancy's. The whole team is here, Nancy, Greyson, Smith, Scott, Ophelia, and Tuck." He says and I feel my blood rush in anger.

"Tuck is there?" I ask. Not bothering to mask my tone of voice of pure disapproval.

"Sawyer, I know you didn't do this. I'm here to help, we all are." He explains calmly. "We saw the elevator footage, man."

"Is she alright?" I hear Nancy speak up. "Sawyer, is she alive?"

"She's alright, for now. I need to get her some sort of medical attention. She has a concussion, and she's bleeding on the back of her head." I explain.

"Oh, god." Nancy cries. "Sawyer, Tuck explained what happened in that meeting. Sinclair went after you, and we think we know why."

"I'm listening." I say sitting on the porch of the cabin.

"So, in Tony Delsavo's diary, there's been secret meetings for the last year with someone called TS. We couldn't work out or place who that is. At first, we thought it was Shields, but we had her followed on the night one of the meetings were being set up. She didn't leave her house; she spent the night with her husband and her dog and watched a movie. It isn't her." He explains.

"So, you think it's Sinclair?" I ask. I mean, the way he accused me so easily made me question whether he was involved, but that seemed like such a jump.

"We know it is." Johnson speaks up. "I hacked into his financial records using one of my online aliases that says I'm in India if they were to track it. He's been getting paid every month, $2 million and it's coming from an offshore account that has been linked to none other than Tony Delsavo himself." He speaks.

"Tuck…"

"I didn't know." He comes to his own defence. "The money wasn't being monitored because it was a separate business, we only found when Johnson here did some serious digging."

I take a long deep breath and take off my suit jacket which is ruined. "So, what do I do?" I ask and the other side of the phone goes silent. "First thing I need to do is get Thea to a Doctor. But we are currently being hunted, so any idea's you have will be greatly appreciated." I say sarcastically.

"My brother is a Doctor." I hear Greyson pipe up.

"No way is your brother a Doctor, Greyson." I say in disbelief. This man should be a model, not a Doctor. However, a man with a soft side would get more ladies, so you have to hand it to him.

"Yeah! He's a trauma surgeon at Sin City General Hospital. I can explain the situation?" He explains.

"I'll come with you. This has to be dealt with correctly." Tuck offers.

"I need a plan guys; Thea is sleeping inside." I explain looking through the window to watch Sleeping Beauty rest peacefully.

"Where are you? Maybe we can work together?" Ophelia asks and I shake my head although they can't see it.

"They could follow you. As long as you don't know our position, we will live." I explain putting my hand though my hair. Mary was nice enough to pick all of the glass out when we reached the apartment. Suddenly something dawns on me. "Why now?" I ask and I hear some people mumble in the background of the phone. "Why now? Why did it have to be today?" I question again. "Johnson, did Sinclair get a pay out in the last forty-eight hours?"

"Nothing." He says quickly. "It seems sudden, why would he pick you to be the person to take the fall?"

That's when I hear a gasp. "Because Thea and I had a meeting about you today, Sawyer, just a few hours before Sinclair cornered you."

"Meeting about me?"

"Thea didn't appreciate the letters that you sent to Kent, Rogers, or Edison." Nancy explains.

"What letters?" I ask, my voice filled with curiosity.

"Sawyer don't play dumb. The inappropriate letters you sent to them labelling Thea as some sort of sex pest?" Nancy explains, and my eyes widen.

"I sent the flowers, Nancy, not the letters. That wasn't me." I explain and suddenly this starts to make more sense. "They needed her to come forward about me, didn't they? They needed the final nail in the coffin."

"It's looking like that, yes." She admits. "Johnson, there should be cameras in their office. Can you see who placed them there?" She asks, and the tech wizard works his magic.

"The camera's cut out at 7:00am. They didn't come back on till 7:50am." He explains and suddenly this is starting to all make sense. "The hallway cameras are cut too." He says with a long exhale.

"Who's tech savvy enough, other that Harry Potter there, who could hack into my login and leak the documents, take out the I.C.C.O's million-dollar security system and hack the information to release it to other agencies who have been wanting him. This makes no sense, guys." I state, placing my head in my hands.

"Sinclair is in deep, and it seems it might have gone on longer than a year. Only thing I can think of is Delsavo told Sinclair he had to cause a distraction, or he was going to release that he's been in on it the entire time." Scott says.

"Not a bad theory, but we need proof." I say harshly. "What are they saying about Thea?"

"Just that she's in on it. Why did you strangle her in the elevator, Sawyer? You tried to kill her twice in two minutes."

I had forgotten about my anger outburst. "I thought she had done it." I admit, and I hear Nancy and Ophelia laugh.

"You've lost your mind if you think Thea St. James had something to do with it." Nancy laughs. And I begin to chuckle. She's right, Thea knows the basics of technology, and she's a theorist and likes the evidence and statements in front of her. She wouldn't know how to hack into a system as equipped as I.C.C. O's.

The silence that falls on the other end of the call gets me unsettled. "The letters are making me feel nervous. Someone who was at the party had to be the one who wrote them Nancy." I explain.

"I know, we are looking into it." She says softly. I have full faith in my friends, that they will help prove our innocence.

"Greyson, call your brother. I'll see to Thea first, then we can work out a plan of action to prove our innocence." I explain and say my goodbyes and hang up the phone. I hope that when I walk in there, she's not dead. Cause I would be going down for murder if that's the case.

I walk in and close the door gently, if she isn't dead, I don't want to wake her up. I walk round to the couch and look at her peacefully sleeping. Her shoulders rising as she dreams about probably placing her hands around my neck and killing me. That I deserve.

I gently place the back of my hand to her cheek. She's sweating, too hot for what she's normally meant to be. "Shit, Thea!" I say trying to shake her awake.

She groans but doesn't come back to the land of the living. I move her forward to check the back of her head. There is so much blood. Oh, shit I should have checked on her earlier. "Thea if you die on me, I'm going to pull you back from hell myself!" I shout trying to get her to wake up. She's dripping in sweat.

I pull the phone out of my pocket and begin to dial the number Johnson gave me in a panic. Out of nowhere, she rises, panicked, and punches me in the balls.

I hit the floor, groaning, almost screaming in pain. "Thea! What the hell?" I say clutching to my crown jewels.

"Sawyer! I'm so sorry!" She says kneeling next to me. "Are you alright?" She asks holding my face.

"Are you? I tried waking you, but you wouldn't budge! I thought you were dead!" I shout, still clutching my prized possessions. "Thea, I think you've made sure I can't have children." I whine, almost on the verge of tears.

"I sleep like I'm dead!" She shouts, a smile starting to grow on her face. "I think it's a good thing if I make sure there are no spawns of you. Saved the world the trouble of your offspring." She teases, letting go of my face.

"You're a bitch." I say sitting up, still in a serious amount of pain.

"I know." She smiles, rising slowly from the ground. She reaches over next to me and picks up the phone. "Who were you calling?" She asks. The smile slowly dropping from her face.

"I was about to call Johnson back, so he could tell Greyson that his brother needs to be brought up to speed a little quicker. His brothers a Doctor, and your head needs to be seen to." He explains.

"I see." She says quietly. "Anything else I should know?"

I take a seat on the couch, indicating for her to sit with me. "That Thomas H. Sinclair is the reason we're in this mess."

THIRTY-FIVE

Thea

After Sawyer's extended explanation as to why he and the rest of the group think Thomas Sinclair is linked with the notorious murder and crime boss, Tony Delsavo, I sit trying to process all of the information given.

"Do you think Shields knows?" I ask.

Sawyer shrugs his shoulders. "I don't know. I really don't."

"All this is speculation." I say rising from the sofa as I begin pacing. "I don't even have a theory." I say feeling deflated. My head is pounding, and I can feel my eyesight starting to dwindle the more I stand up. I sit back down on the chair opposite him.

"You don't have a Thea theory? That's heart breaking." He jokes with me. My face must tell a different picture as he kneels to the ground, holding my head in his hands. "Hey, focus." He whispers calmly to me. "I'm gonna call Greyson, see where they are and tell them where to meet us." He explains, trying to keep me awake, although my vision is blurry. "Thea!" He says, causing me to jump. "Stay awake." He responds, letting go of me and turning around and reaching the phone.

"My head, Sawyer…"

"I know, trouble. I know. I'm sorry." He repeats over and over, waiting for the phone to answer.

"Greyson?" He asks and I feel the relief rush over his face. "I need you and your brother to meet us somewhere, she's not good, man." He says keeping my head up, rubbing my cheek lightly.

This isn't the Sawyer Reid I know. This man couldn't care less if he injured you, or that you could be dying. He's the type of man to put you out your misery by shooting you between your eyes.

"Yeah, meet us at Rosewell Bank." He says before putting the phone in his pocket and reaching for his keys. He runs over to the kitchen, and I watch as best as I can as he puts things into a black duffel bag. "Come on trouble. Let's get you some help." He says lifting me lightly and leading me out of the cabin and towards Alister's car.

He places me in gently, putting my seat belt on and heading round to the driver's side of the car. "I need you to stay with me." He says while putting his seatbelt on.

"I'm trying." I say softly, my eyes becoming heavy and all I want to do is sleep.

"Look at me." He demands. "Trouble." He says reaching over and turning towards him. "Eyes on me. No where else, and not closed. Understood?" He says. I manage to agree, and he drives out of the entrance to the cabin, and to Rosewell Bank.

It feels like forever and a day until we get there. Rosewell Bank isn't anywhere near where we were, but I know Sawyer chose it because there are multiple exit routes if we were to be cornered and when we turn up it isn't Greyson, Tuck and Greyson's brother standing there to meet us.

He pulls into the car park of Rosewell Bank and watches until Greyson, Tuck, and who I'm assuming is Greyson's brother, exit the car in a rush.

"She has an open wound on the back of her head." I hear Sawyer say as he makes his way round to my side of the car. "She's got slurred speech and she can't keep her eyes open for long." He says opening the door for Dr Greyson.

Someone tilts my head. "Thea? Can I take a look at you is that alright?" He asks and I manage to agree. "Where does it hurt?" He asks sweetly.

"My head." I say reaching for the back and he pulls my arm down to stop me from touching it. He tilts my head forward to get a better look.

"She needs stitches, and it looks to be getting infected." I hear him explain. "Thea, I need to give you some pain meds, is that alright?" He asks softly.

"Yes, anything." I manage to say.

"She has a concussion, but I can do what I can for now. The second you can, you need to get her to a hospital, Sawyer." He explains to him. Dr Greyson places my head back on the headrest and begins looking for things in his medical bag.

"Greyson, do you know anything else?" Sawyer asks.

"We think it was Edison that framed you, we've managed to clear all of the other people at the party." Tuck explains.

"How did you manage to work that out?" I manage to ask.

271

"Edison went to a prestige college for technology and computing, also, Johnson managed to find him, and his alias and he is apparently one of the best hackers in the world." Greyson explains and I manage to turn my head and look at them.

"When was Edison hired?" I ask. Dr Greyson starts putting the needle in and I wince.

"Sorry, Thea. I should have said it's going to hurt. But you're going to feel better." He explains softly. I instantly start to feel the medication work, whatever he used. "I gave her morphine. It will work quicker. You feeling okay, Thea?" He asks and I manage to mutter a yes.

"Edison was hired over a year and a half ago, before any of you were." Tuck explains, his arms crossed as he stands a little bit away from Sawyer. "He was on his way to being the Criminal Prevention Manager." Tuck explains.

"That's motive." I say while Dr Greyson moves my head forward.

"I need you to stay still, Thea, I'm doing to try and make you feel better."

I decide not to answer and let him work his magic. I'm starting to feel better, but I know it's just the drugs.

"I didn't know this. Why didn't he get the job?" Sawyers asks.

"Because he was becoming too reckless, and he hit a rough few months. He came back a new man."

"Nancy introduced me to him and said he was a newbie." I explain. Although the pain meds are working for my headache, they aren't working whatever Dr Greyson is doing to my head.

"Cause he came back as a newbie. He's been back about three months." Tuck explains. "He was meant to be on my team, but he didn't pass a couple of tests."

"So, he's getting revenge? And it's all aimed at Sawyer?" Greyson asks. "Seems a bit crazy if you ask me."

"Crazy people do crazy things." Tuck says.

"I'm done, Thea." Dr Greyson says nicely tilting my head back to the head rest. "Does that feel better?" He asks and I manage to nod.

"Thank you." I say reaching up and feeling the dressing on the back of my head.

"You'll need to change this every couple of hours. But like I said, she needs to be checked out properly when that's an option. Otherwise, this can turn bad long term." Dr Greyson explains.

"Thanks, Doc." He says extending his hand. Dr Greyson shakes it, giving Sawyer a warm smile before moving out of the way.

"Tuck? Are Mary and Frank alright?" I ask

softly. He leans over giving me a sweet smile.

"They almost got arrested." He smiles. "But they're fine. Nancy managed to convince the team to let them go. All is well." He says.

"Wait, who's heading up the team to try and catch us?" Sawyer asks. And I watch Tuck's face change from playful to worried.

"Connor Brock." He says turning around to see the disbelief on Sawyer's face.

"No…"

"Yes. Sorry man. They called him in out of retirement." Tuck says placing his hand on Sawyer's shoulder.

"Who's that?" I ask raising my eyebrows.

"Let's just say that if Connor Brock is the one hunting us down, he has one outcome in mind. And that is to see us both dead." Sawyer says. His face is pale, meaning this is worse than he thought if this guy is now involved.

"So, what do we do? Wait?" I ask and Sawyer shakes his head.

"No, we're going to outrun the hunter. Cause if he catches us, we will never be able to live to tell our truth."

My blood goes cold, who is Connor Brock? And why does he have this reputation?

THIRTY-SIX

Sawyer

Never did I think that Connor Brock would be the one leading the team to track us down. The man is a legend but has a serious reputation of breaking the rules. There has been multiple investigations into his previous assignments after people turned up dead, with no explanation, or people went missing. He has a short fuse from what I'm told.

I never met him, he was asked to leave I.C.C.O after one of the assignments he had in his final few weeks got quite a bit of public interest and he was questioned by the local police, in regard to three unresolved murders.

He's been here as long as Sinclair has. Sinclair worked his way up to Director in about ten years, after the last Director died of a heart attack. They wanted an Agent who had worked in multiple departments, like Sinclair, and with his passion for right and wrong and doing right by the people of Sin City. Sinclair fit the bill.

He clearly wants us dealt with quickly and accordingly, and the only way he does that is bringing in someone extremely controversial, like Brock. I'm not dying at the hands of a man who could be classed as a serial killer, and I am certainly not letting him hurt someone so innocent in all of this.

It makes me angry how Sinclair has painted her the way she has. I don't care about me, I'll be alright. But she had worked so hard to get where she was and because of me, she's currently being hunted by a man who is notorious for doing something and asking the questions later.

He won't let us explain, and if I'm thinking correctly, he was probably in on the whole situation with Delsavo and Sinclair and was getting his part of the cut.

"You're awfully quiet." Thea says, giving me questionable eyes. "What are you thinking about?" She asks. I think she's still high off the drugs Dr Greyson gave her, and that makes me laugh.

"How the hell we're going to get out of this." I say driving through a dirt road.

We left Greyson, his brother and Tuck back at Rosewell Bank. They explained that they've searched my apartment, well. The one I stay at mainly. They never checked my other one.

My tiny little one bedroomed apartment in downtown Sin City remains untouched as far as I'm aware. Because I rented it out, it doesn't come up that I own it, and my brother is listed as one of the previous owners. I just do the maintenance. And right now, no one is living in it, meaning that Thea and I can head there for a little while.

She needs to rest so I can work out how the hell I'm going to be able to defeat and take down Connor Brock. This is now worse than any of us thought, and not only do we need to prove to I.C.C.O that Sinclair is corrupt without getting the rest of the group put in a jail cell, but we also need a location on Brock.

"I think that no matter what we do we're going to end up dead and not being able to tell our story." She says softly, her eyes struggling to stay awake.

"Don't be negative." I plead with her playfully, shoving her a little to keep her awake and keep me some company. "Give me a Thea theory, a real one."

She begins to laugh, a sound so sweet that I get a sugar rush. "I never knew you had a name for my theories." She laughs hysterically. "That is brilliant."

"What can I say, I come up with some great names." I explain giving her another nudge.

"Like Agent Trouble." She smiles.

"Exactly, just like Agent Trouble." I laugh.

"Why do you hate me?" She asks softly, the smile slowly dropping from her face.

"Believe it or not trouble, I don't hate you." I say looking over at her.

"You're right I don't believe you." She says honestly. "Because if you didn't hate me, you wouldn't do what you do to me."

My heart breaks. "Ever think that I do what I do because I like you?" I smile at her.

That smile begins to grow back on that face of hers. "You're not capable of liking anyone, unless it's to win a bet, or to get your ten seconds of fun." She admits.

Ouch. But true. "I can assure you, Thea. If you were with me, you'd be having a lot longer than ten seconds of fun." I admit.

Her eyes widen, and a playful grin begins to take over. "Well, you must have quite the reputation." She teases.

I laugh. "Yeah, you've got that right."

She turns over to look at me again. "I'll never let you win the bet." She says with a smile.

When she says it, it doesn't hurt my feelings, because this conversation is something that I've only ever dreamed of having. I'm not sure if I like her, or if I'm just feeling this way because I'm severely sexually frustrated, and the place I'm taking her to is my 'sex dungeon,' one girl called it.

"So, where we going?" She asks looking out to the road to see the city.

"We're going to my apartment downtown. We can stay there for a few days while we work something out." I explain.

"So, we're going back into the city where we're currently being hunt down?" She asks sarcastically. "This is why I should hear your plans first."

I snort. "Really think I could ask your opinion while you were snoring like a man on the other side of the car?" I question playfully.

She turns back to look at me, her expression horrified. "You're lying, Sawyer! I do not snore." She objects which causes me to cackle.

"Trouble, you do. Trust me." I tease looking over to her. Even with the darkness in the car I can see she's blushing. "I'm kidding." I say trying to make her feel less embarrassed.

"You better be." She snaps, and I can hear the humour in her voice, staring back at me.

"Or what?" I tease. She turns away from me, slightly embarrassed. Whether or not Scott is right, and the sexual frustration is just coming from me, even she won't be able to deny that there is something here between us.

"How come they haven't found this apartment?" She asks changing the subject which kills the mood a little.

"Because I'm technically not on any documents for this property. I rent it out a lot, and to be honest, I've been the only one to stay in it for a while."

"Why's that?" She asks curiously.

"You'll see." I say as we pull into the drive, and I turn off the engine.

We both proceed to get out of the car, her a little slower than me since she's still high on pain medication and no doubt she's starting to feel the effects of dropping down 40 elevator floors. I'm sore and bruised, but she got the worst of it which does make me feel bad about the whole thing.

I make sure to get my duffel bag out of the trunk of the car and a bag that Nancy sent for Thea. Nothing for me, but for Thea; a bag that weighs more than her. We walk up in silence to the top floor, where I pull the key out on my keychain and put it into the door. "It's late, I have some frozen pizzas we can have to eat and then we can sleep it off." I say as I open the door and stand aside to let her in.

"You've got a lot of different aesthetics,' Sawyer." She teases while looking around the apartment. "This is hardly a bachelor pad."

I laugh. "I like to surprise people." I say placing the bags down near the door.

"How many women have been here?" She asks peeking into the bedroom. To everybody else it's a regular bed and there is nothing to it. Until you find the extra attachments and proceed to walk into the closest and find my box of toys.

"A couple." I say honestly, opening up the duffle bag and begin placing the guns around the room in different hiding spots in case we're ambushed.

"Is that a lie?" She asks leaning against the doorframe.

I pass her on my way to the kitchen and stand above her a little, with an AR-15 in my hand. "The truth." I say softly.

Her chest begins to rise as I lean a little closer, breaking all the space between us and taking all of the air. "Don't believe you."

I smile down at her. "This is a special place. Only a few have been allowed in the walls." I say softly looking down at her lips.

"Why's that?" She almost whispers. Her eyes are wide as I scour every inch of her face.

"Because this is where woman come to have their pleasure put to the max. See how much they can take." I say quietly. She doesn't move from under me, only shifts slightly to get closer to my face.

"If you say so." She says with a grin. Fuck, I want to stop her from talking and pin her to the bed. I need her to stop smiling at me the way she is. Because I'll tie her up and do anything and everything I want to her.

I decide to try and control myself and move away from her. Her scent is addictive as is her face. This is all a game to her, but right now, I couldn't give a shit about the bet if it meant I could hear her moaning my name.

"I don't see anything that would make me suggest this is some sort of sex dungeon, Sawyer. It's pretty basic to me." She shouts from the bedroom.

"How about you look in the closet. Can you see a box?" I shout through to her. Silence falls between us in the apartment, and I head through to see what she could have possibly found other than the box in front of her.

"What's in the box?" She asks curiously. I reach into my pocket and pull out a key, throwing it in her direction.

She catches it no problem. "Open it and find out, Thea." I instruct. She raises her eyebrows at me but does what she's told.

Good girl.

As she reaches down to open the lock on the box, I make my way over in her direction, as I want to see the look on her face.

"If this is some sort of joke and you're actually making me open your box of toy trains, I will die of embarrassment." She says opening the lock and removing it.

She raises the lid of the box and I watch her eyes widen, taken in the slights of indeed, my box of toys.

Any sex toy, or sex accessory you can think of. I'm proud of what I've accumulated over the years, yet I feel like she's never seen any of this before with the look on her face.

She begins to back up, almost panicking as she bumps right into me. "Disappointed?" I ask curiously, my voice is filled with humour and lust, and it really is another sight being able to show her the things' I've been dreaming of using on her for the past month.

"Curious." She says after a moment, looking

inside the box. "Why did you want me to see this?" She asks turning back to look at me.

"Because one day, I hope to have your legs shaking when I use this stuff on you. And what's more is you'll like it." I say in her ear. She becomes nervous under me.

"I'm okay." She says trying to move but I trap her in. I can sense the curiosity on her, and I can sense the sexual frustration.

"Thea, you're telling me you wouldn't let me use any of this stuff on you, if you were willing? Are you that vanilla?" I tease.

That seems to get a rise out of her, and she turns around to face me. "I'm not vanilla, Sawyer." She says annoyed.

My eyebrows raise as I lean in closer to her. "Want to prove it?" I ask, grinning from ear to ear.

She begins to relax and moves just that little bit closer to me. "Absolutely not." She whispers before shoving me away and begins to walk out of the bedroom.

"You're just not used to getting any, Thea. And that's okay!" I shout after her.

She turns on her heels and marches towards me. "Fuck you, Sawyer."

"Say please, trouble." I tease and she groans.

"You're disgusting." she states heading

towards the kitchen and I'm quick to follow her.

"You'll eventually realize you want me, Thea. It's inevitable." I say with a grin, and she rolls her eyes, leaning down into the fridge and getting herself a beer.

Bold of her to think she can touch my beer, that's strike one. Her attitude is strike two.

"I would rather die." She states clearly which makes me laugh.

"And that can also be arranged if you don't listen to my instructions." I say placing my hands on my hips.

She lets out a long deep breath. "Sawyer, I'm determined to keep myself in order, so whatever sexual fantasies you want to fulfil, please, for the love of god, leave them in that box. Because it isn't going to happen. Not now, not ever." She says opening the beer and taking a sip. Her face turns sour as she walks towards me. "You also need to get better beer." She says handing me it heading towards the sitting room and to the duffel bag that Nancy sent for her.

"I don't want your germs." I say looking over at her and she smiles while opening the bag.

"Said every woman ever, to you." She sarcastically smiles and looks down into her bag. "You know what, I love Nancy more than I have loved anyone else in this world." She says doing a little dance.

"Any reason?" I ask heading over into the kitchen and pouring the rest of the beer into two glasses. I don't have any wine, so she's going to have to have beer.

"She packed me everything I will need. This is like a Sawyer Reid survival kit!" She says enthusiastically, pulling out a gun and pointing it at me.

"Alright, put the gun down, trouble." I instruct, and she playfully shakes her head.

"I should have used this when you showed be the box of torture devices." She says getting up, the gun still raised, pointing directly at my head.

"You don't even know how to shoot it." I say heading towards her with the glasses in my hand. She hasn't turned the safety off, so this is an empty playful threat.

"Yes, I do." She whines. "Even after the academy I still kept my gun licence and I bought myself one to keep in my apartment." She says, still having the gun raised.

My eyebrows raise, didn't think she would need it. But then again Sin City is a very unusual place. When she thinks I'm about to walk away, I take the gun out of her hands, swipe under her feet knocking her to the floor and put the gun to her face. "You're too soft St. James." I say turning the gun to give her the handle and she snatches it out of my hand, anger on her face.

"That was unfair." She objects getting up slowly. "What if I hit my head again?" She asks picking up the duffle bag.

"Might give me a bit of peace and quiet. Put the bag down, Thea. You need to eat, and you started that beer, so you're going to finish it." I demand opening the freezer and pulling out a frozen pizza.

She doesn't object and actually listens to me for once, which just so happened to be the first time ever without an argument, and I see that as progress.

She sits on the sofa and picks up the TV remote. The first thing on the screen is our faces, and how they feel as though we've been spotted on the outskirts of Sin City near Rosewell Bank. You're a few hours behind.

The next picture on the screen shows the one and only Connor Brock doing an interview with Sin City News at 10. This is just what we need.

"We are joined now with former I.C.C.O Agent Connor Brock who is leading up the task force to find the fugitives. Agent Brock, thank you for joining us, I know you're busy." Reporter Daniel Marsh says to him and Brock laughs.

"It's no problem, anything I can do to inform the

public." I mock his laugh and Thea turns to me and rolls her eyes.

"*What can you tell us about Agent Reid and Agent St. James? It looks to us that she might actually be a hostage in this situation is that anything that the I.C.C.O can confirm or deny?*" Marsh asks and Brock shakes his head.

"*Agent St. James is in fact just as dangerous as Agent Reid. She has connections with multiple agencies, and with her being British, she has connections over in England that we are currently speaking to. Her family haven't spoken to her in five years. They said she packed up, changed her name, and moved out to America without a second thought for them or anyone else. She left behind a heart broken fiancé, and there was rumoured she had a boyfriend out in America which was the reason for her move.*" Brock announces and I look down at Thea. *She was engaged.*

"*Wow, so she changed her name. What could the public possibly be looking for in terms of her name change?*"

"I mean you would think I changed my name completely!" She shouts in frustration at the TV.

"*Over in England she was known as Theadora St. James-Monroe. But legally now goes as Thea St. James.*" Brock answers confidently. "*She could use Theadora Monroe, so please keep an eye out for that name and call into the number on the screen if you do see it."*

"And what about Agent Reid?"

"Agent Reid's family who he's estranged from, they have no clue on his whereabouts, however we have spoken to quite a few of Sawyer's ex-girlfriends who said he is a man who used to own property all over the city, so we are currently sending people to each of those locations."

Thea stands up after turning the TV off and places her head in her hands and I walk towards her. "Hey," I say softly removing her hands. "we're going to be fine. They won't find us." I reassure her and she nods her head.

"I can't believe they told the whole of Sin City about my past." She says removing herself from my grip to take the glass of beer. "It's all a lie too! Well… some of it. I was engaged, he just failed to mention he was also married with a wife and two kids, and it was two weeks before the wedding that I saw them out in London." She rambles sitting back on the couch. "It was my fault that I had to find out that way, and when he came over to try and fix it, said he would fix us and we would be married, I told him no and kicked him out." She explains, drinking the beer in one gulp. "My family took his side, labelling me as desperate to move on when I applied for the academy the day before my supposed wedding." She continues.

I decide to sit next to her, curious to hear about the Thea from London who I never knew. No wonder she was so closed off, if anything you can still see the embarrassment when she talks about him, or her family. "That's why you never went home for the holidays?" I ask her and she nods.

"I didn't want anything to do with them." She begins to cry slightly. "They chose his side, over their own daughter. A man who lied and deceived his so-called fiancé. He was married, and I found out not long after that he was seeing another woman too." She says wiping the tears away.

"Do you know who?" I ask curiously.

"Yeah, my own sister." She says abruptly which catches me off guard.

"When did you find that out?" I say trying to keep my composure in the twist and turns of events that has just taken place.

"When I moved out here. She sent me a message with videos, photos of them in bed when I was at work, or when I was going out dress shopping for my wedding. The text said something like, he was only marrying you so he could stay close to me. Thanks for this." She explains and wipes her tears away.

"Have you spoken to her since?" I ask.

She shakes her head. "I cut off my entire

family when I moved out here. I occasionally message my Grandmother, but I don't tend to try and have in depth conversations. It's not something I really want. They just want information." She explains moving away from me and begins to pace the room. "Sawyer, what are we going to do? Brock is now labelling us as these awful people to a world who don't deserve to know. I'm a private person and I don't like having my information plastered all over the internet or the news." She says her hands are in her hair.

I raise from my seat and walk towards her, hoping she will allow me to give her some sort of comfort. I never knew Thea's family, I always thought Mary and Frank were her family. "We will be fine. They won't find us here; I can promise you that. We will wait for something from Tuck and the rest of the team. They believe us. Remember that. Even if you don't believe in yourself Thea, there are a group of people currently going against the code to make sure we are proven innocent. So, anything they need us to do, we help them. Got it?" I instruct.

She nods and proceeds to wrap her arms around me in a hug. It takes me by surprise; however, I gladly accept it.

I'm not one for physical touch, holding hands or even a hug. It isn't something I've welcomed from a woman unless it was my mother. But I'm not going to tell trouble, who is clearly worried about this whole thing that she has to get off me when she clearly needs some sort of comfort.

After a few moments, she pulls away from me, awkwardly and goes to sit on the couch yet again. "Sorry, I just needed that." She says quietly, putting her legs to her chest.

"It's fine. Sorry I was awkward. I don't hug." I admit and she nods.

"I gathered; it was slightly like hugging a tree." She teases, which does lighten the mood.

"You're welcome." I say getting up to check on the pizza. It won't be done for another few minutes, however I'm beginning to feel slightly uncomfortable after that hug, and I'm not sure if it's because I actually liked it, or if it's because it was Thea and it shouldn't have happened. I can't place my emotions.

"Sawyer, you only have one bed. Do you want me to sleep here?" She asks from the couch, and I turn to look at her.

"We are adults Thea; I think for one night we are perfectly capable of sleeping in the same bed." I say amused and I look over at her.

Her faces is laced in disgust. "But what if you decide to try something?" She says.

I raise one eyebrow. "I will make us a divider then. I just hope you won't snore; I need my beauty sleep." I tease.

She throws a pillow in my direction, and it hits my face. "Watch it, trouble." I say, launching the pillow her direction and it almost misses her. Hitting her arm slightly. "Break my TV, I break your face. Understood?" I say.

She only laughs, turning away and putting the TV back on. The news should have moved to something less pressing now.

Brock is a bastard for outing all of Thea's past like that. So, she changed her name to her nickname and dropped a last name, so what? If people found out the questionable things he has done, it would shame the I.C.C.O for covering it up and it will show the corruption within the organization. I couldn't care less about them outing all of my dirty laundry. He's right, I don't speak to my family as much as I should, but labelling them woman as my girlfriends, which is putting them too high on the pecking order.

Somehow, we are going to need to prove Sinclair and his dirty little secrets in help Delsavo in his crimes.

There's a way of proving all of the corruption, but with Thea and I not able to get inside the I.C.C.O yet, we're going to have to work out someway in proving our innocence and proving the corruption of the once much respected organization, which in my opinion now is a bunch of shit.

I can only think of one thing to do that might help Thea's case, but ultimately ruin mine.

Release the elevator security video.

After our not so terrible pizza, it's time to get some sleep. It is ridiculously late, almost 3am, and Thea is still recovering from her head trauma.

I agree with Greyson's brother, she needs to be seen as soon as possible. I've already caused her enough pain; I don't want to cause her anymore and have some long-lasting effects.

As I enter the room, she's built a wall to protect herself from me. She stares at me while I look it over in the doorway. She's in one of my t-shirts, clearly, she's helped herself. "I don't want you touching me." She says bluntly.

I shrug my shoulders. "Fair enough. Eventually you'll let me." I wink at her.

She groans. "Fuck you, Sawyer." She snaps at me turning away as I reach the other end of the bed.

"You know, you should speak nicely to people." I say calmly. That seems to anger the demon across the fort as she turns and glares at me, staring into my soul and for a second, I become frightened.

"You deserve nothing, Sawyer. I wouldn't be in this mess if it wasn't for you." She says again before turning away.

I mean she's not wrong, but then we both wouldn't be in this mess if it wasn't for Sinclair. "Don't point the blame at me." I say getting into bed and placing my gun underneath my pillow.

"Who else am I going to blame?" She snaps across from me.

This is ridiculous. I turn over, ripping the pillow from between us and launching it on the floor. "You aren't going to blame me, that's for certain." I snap back. She turns around, I think she's more in shock that I decided to remove the pillow, when she clearly created boundaries.

"What am I meant to do?" She states, her face full of disgust.

"Shut up and go to sleep. I need my beauty sleep." I say closing my eyes, in the hope she doesn't decide to stab me to death.

I hear her scoff and open one eye to see her get out of bed and head towards the sitting area. "Where are you going?" I demand sitting up.

She turns on her heels in the doorway, placing both hands on either side of the doorway. "Away from you." She states bluntly, turning around again.

"Thea!" I shout after her. I hear her stop and

not move any further. "Come back." I plead. Jesus, I sound pathetic. Normally I don't have to give a woman a reason to come back to bed, but with the little blonde demon, it seems to me like I took on the role of caretaker and she's suddenly a toddler who's refusing to get into bed.

After a few moments of silence, I watch her enter the room, heading round to collect the pillow from the floor and placing it in between us. "Move it and I kill you." She says, glaring down at me.

I know she's being serious, so I just decide to nod. She pulls the cover back over her and turns over. "Goodnight." I say with a grin, hoping this isn't pushing it.

She doesn't say anything back, so I decide to lie down and get my own rest, because I dread to think what's going to happen tomorrow.

THIRTY-SEVEN

Thea

I'm really not sure if I agree with Sawyer's plan. He's about to out himself as an attempted murderer to the world in the hopes that I.C.C.O get off my case and look more into him.

As much as I would have liked to see Sawyer's world crash and burn, recently I have a new view on the man, and I can't tell if it's good or not.

I didn't realise he wasn't close with his extended family. I know his Mum died, but surely you would think that would have brought them together.

Sawyer was tired when we went to bed, so

I decided to wait to approach the subject. Also found out, he snores and it's so loud the bed shakes.

Right now, we've managed to get Nancy to agree to a meet up with Tuck. Sawyer has a plan, some of it he is yet to mention to me, apart from the one he knew I might agree with and that was proving my innocence.

I wasn't one hundred percent on it, and I'm still not sure I want to agree to it. Labelling Sawyer Reid as an attempted murderer. Yesterday I would have said yes, however now I've been stuck with the man longer than I would have liked, I can see he does have a soft side. He just chooses not to show it.

Nancy packed me undercover clothes. A wig, some light makeup, and an outfit starter kit of looking like I'm on the streets. I need to look more homeless and less like Agent St. James. Which I hate.

"Let me do the talking." Sawyer instructs as we come close to the meeting point. His black eye is starting to come through beautifully now, and when I see Mary again, I'm going to have to applaud her for doing such a spectacular job.

I notice Nancy, and I instantly feel calmer, the same when I notice Tuck come out of a corner too. He's got shorter hair and it took me a moment to notice it was him, and that it was also a wig.

"You look like shit." Nancy says greeting me with a hug and I gladly accept it. It feels nice to smell her scent and to be welcomed by another woman. "You on the other hand look like you went into the ring with no gloves and let all the women you hurt have a go at you. And it is brilliant." She teases.

"You done?" Sawyer asks her and she laughs. "We need to hurry up in case you're both being followed."

"That is slightly likely considering we had to out-do three Agents who were watching her apartment." Tuck says looking around. "What's the plan?"

Sawyer looks down to me, curious to see if I will tell him not to go through with his plan, but he decides to avoid my eyes in the end and only look at Nancy and Tuck. "We need you to release the elevator footage." He says.

Tuck's eyes widen. "You are aware the only thing that is going to do is prove that you have severe anger issues, that you tried to kill her, and you took her hostage?" He repeats, hoping that Sawyer will change his mind.

"I'm aware of the implications." He says calmly and I look over at Nancy who looks Sawyer up and down. "What?" He asks frustrated.

"Hmm." She says. "Just not sure if orange is the right colour for your complexion, Sawyer." She teases, nudging me as we both begin to giggle.

"Shut it, Nancy. That's not my only idea." He explains looking around. "We need to out all of Brock's cases where an Agent or someone who was there went missing or died under mysterious circumstances, when he was in the agency." Sawyer explains.

Tuck crosses his arms. "So, you're telling me to look into all of the old files prior to my time as Undercover Operations, and out information about the one man who could happily put me in a grave with a smile on his face?" He questions.

Sawyer shrugs. "He wouldn't be the only one." He admits, which takes Tuck by surprise.

"I told you I believe you." He begins to argue in his defence.

"It didn't seem like it yesterday!" Sawyer begins to shout, and Nancy shushes them both.

"Look you two, this isn't going to help anyone if you two are bickering like an old married couple." She says giving them both a look. "We can't guarantee those cases will be there Sawyer, if anything, any evidence of corruption, Sinclair would have had it destroyed." She explains and I feel like she's right.

"There would be evidence of that, surely. On his emails, a private chat, on his computer maybe?" Sawyer asks and Nancy tilts her head.

"That is a high possibility. But he would want to keep them close, in the case someone was to get a hold of them. He might even keep them in his office at his house." She explains and Tuck groans.

"Which one? The man has six."

This seems to be getting nowhere, and although I do agree with Sawyer on one thing, it has to go in a different way. "The person you need to take down first is Sinclair, Brock's time will follow." I explain and they all turn to me. "Sinclair is the reason we're all in this mess. He's been having meetings with Delsavo, he's been helping him with his criminal business, but something changed. Did Delsavo threaten to expose him? Who knows. But if we prove to the people higher than Sinclair that he's been in on this, then we will be able to move down the train."

Looks are exchanged between the three of them, to which Nancy smiles. "Not bad idea." She says looking back over at the men. "You should listen to her she has good ideas."

Sawyer scoffs. "Okay, so what is the plan then?" He says turning to me.

I roll my eyes. "Surely Sinclair has to have

something planned with Delsavo, unless his plan is to help get him out of the country?" I ask turning my attention to Tuck.

"He can't. He's on a no flight list, a no boat list. You name it. The man and his group of criminals can't leave Sin City." Tuck explains looking back at Sawyer. "Thea's right. Sinclair does have a meeting in his diary. We thought it was with Delsavo, but it could be with one of his minions to pass on the message that it's been done."

"What does it say exactly?" Nancy asks and Tuck reaches into his pocket and pulls out his phone. "Meeting with TS. Which could be for Thomas Strauss, Tony Delsavo's right hand man." He explains, but like the rest of us, catches the distress on Nancy's face.

"Or Tilda Shields." She says looking around at us all. "I spoke to Shields not long after the elevator incident. Shields said she was seeing Sinclair anyway about the situation with the both of you, and she was going to demand that he proves your innocence." She explains before looking directly into Sawyer's eyes. "Even yours." She says softly and I watch as Sawyer's face drops in shock. "You may think she was hard on you, Sawyer. But the woman loves each and every one of us as if we were her own children. She takes care of us. And she said she would take care of you." She explains.

"What if Shields knew about Sinclair's criminal activities and this is a way for her to blackmail him to prove our innocence?" Sawyer asks and Tuck groans.

"There is only one problem with this meeting." Tuck says looking down at his phone. After a moment, he turns it around to show Director Sinclair and Connor Brock heading into the direction of the meeting room. "It's about to happen right now, and Sinclair isn't going in alone." Tuck says, his eyes filled with fear, as is the rest of the groups. Even mine.

"If Shields comes to our defence…"

"Brock will kill her. That's one less person in your corner." Nancy explains. I feel physically sick.

"Sawyer do you think Johnson will be able to keep the camera's running in the meeting room? Sinclair might be one step ahead and he might already have Edison on the job to show that there is no one down the corridor or in that room apart from Shields." I explain and Sawyer nods.

"I'll ask." Tuck speaks up for him. "We haven't got long, so what is the plan?" He asks again and I begin to think long and hard.

"You two head to the office as normal. Tuck I need you to distract Sinclair for as long as you can. Keep him away from his office. Nancy, do you think you could flirt with Brock to try and distract him for as long as possible?" I ask her and she raises her eyebrows.

"Thea, I'm gay, not incompetent. I can have any man worship my feet. Ask Sawyer." She teases giving him a wink, only for Sawyer to roll his eyes.

"Sawyer and I are going to follow, take a different entrance. We need a way to get past security." I ask looking over at Tuck.

"I'll have Scott and Ophelia create a distraction." He explains before looking around and his eyes widen. "Hurry up, I spot Agents."

"Sawyer, you and Johnson head to Sinclair's office and try and retrieve as much data off his computer as you can." I explain and he nods.

"What are you going to do?" He asks curiously.

"I'm going to call some important people. They won't know what hit them when I contact some of the biggest leaders in the world." I say with a grin. They all exchange a look of confusion. "You're forgetting I'm the Communications Liaison; I know people in places Sinclair never would have dreamed of checking."

Everyone agrees. Sawyer then grabs me as he notices someone walking towards us and leads us away from Tuck and Nancy.

"There they are!" Someone shouts and the others make a break for it, just as quick as Sawyer and me.

He leads me away from the area and down a few busy streets in the hopes that we get lost in the crowd. There is a parade on today, which happened to be the perfect day to come down this street as it isn't normally busy.

Suddenly, shots are fired, and Sawyer and I find ourselves ducking, moving quickly away from the Agents who have decided to shoot first and ask questions later.

He takes us back into the direction of Alister's car which thankfully hasn't got so much as a scratch on it.

The shots become quieter as we put on our seatbelts and leave the area where the chaos continues behind us.

That was close, and I just hope Nancy and Tuck were able to get out of there before being captured.

Cause right now, I don't have a plan B.

THIRTY-EIGHT

Thea

This is really the only plan that will work, and it has to be done quick in order to prove Sinclair's extracurricular activities with the biggest crime family and organization Sin City has ever seen.

After we left Tuck and Nancy, Sawyer and I headed back to the apartment to make sure we were ready for what is about to be thrown at us when we head back to I.C.C.O.

Not much was said between us, other than the 'do you have this?' 'are you sure you can shoot?' 'if we're going to die, can't I just have one chance with you?' The usual whining from the man who really doesn't want to listen to a woman.

We're currently five minutes from where we will be meeting Smith and Greyson who will be putting us into the boot of their car to take us up to the I.C.C.O.

The men in the hut are two friends of Greyson's. I was nervous when he said he told them, however, one of them happened to be the Agent I met on my first day and he said he didn't believe for one second Sawyer, and I had anything to do with this. So, he immediately got my vote of confidence that this is going to go through smoothly.

"Trouble?" Sawyer says breaking the silence.

"Yes, Sawyer?"

"Do me a favour? Don't die." He says, with a slight grin on his face. "I mean it. I don't have time to ruin another girl's life, come up with a nickname, torture her as an employee and have crazy sex dreams about her. So please, don't die." He pleads.

I begin to laugh. "Wow, so you now admit you've tortured me as you're employee. Care to answer a few questions I have in regards to somethings that have happened that I don't have answers for?"

"Sure, I'm an open book."

"Great!" I say enthusiastically. "The flowers

that turned up to my office from Johnson?"

"That was me." He's quick to admit.

"Interesting. The flowers that turned up from Rogers and Kent?"

"Yup." He agrees again and I find that this is being incredibly therapeutic.

"Nancy worked that one out. You put a target on your back immediately." I giggle.

He begins to chuckle. "Should have thought it through to be honest. I just wanted to see your face and how you responded to the flowers off them." He admits.

It does catch me by surprise, and I turn to look at him again. "Why would that matter?"

There is no darkness to hide how quick his cheeks turn bright red. He's dropped himself in it. "Because I needed to know that you weren't into them." He admits, still avoiding my stare and not answering the whole question.

"Spill it." I demand and he rolls his eyes.

"Because It would kill me to see you with anyone else." He admits.

Now this admission, catches me by surprise, throws me out of the window and a truck runs me over with how out there that is.

I don't even notice that I haven't answered him as we come to a stop, and I notice Smith and

Greyson standing waiting for us.

Sawyer doesn't bother to say anything else, and I haven't been able to find what words I need to say in order to not make this a little awkward, which I would.

"You ready?" Smith asks as I get out of the car.

"I guess. How is everyone else?" I ask and Greyson places his hands in his pockets.

"Everyone's ready as soon as we give the signal. Johnson is in the bathroom, hiding in one of the stalls on Sinclair's floor." He explains and I nod. "He had to disable the cameras. As far as we're aware, they are still in the meeting with Shields, and we can't do much until they come out."

Sawyer begins to open up the boot of the car. "You two know what you need to do just in case this all goes to shit?" He asks.

"Yes, Boss. Release the video of the elevator and any recordings we manage to get that shows any sort of corruption. Other things will eventually fall into place." He repeats to Sawyer, who looks them both over.

"Good. If this doesn't go to plan. You two were great. I'll tell Johnson the same." He praises them and begins to climb into the back of the car.

I look over at them both, who instantly have worried looks on their faces. "Everything will be fine. Don't worry." I reassure them both, placing a hand on each of their shoulders.

"Are you sure, Thea?"

I take a long deep breath. "As sure as I can be. Come on." I encourage them heading into the boot of the car. I'm about to be in the same closed space with Sawyer for a short amount of time, and I still haven't found the right words to say. He moves as far away as he can to give me some room, which isn't much and our breathes lock as one as I stare deep into his eyes.

"You good?" Smith asks.

"Close it." Sawyer says, and Smith does as their told.

The darkness takes over, but a small ray of light comes through, and I find myself looking deep into his eyes. He doesn't move a muscle, doesn't try to avoid my stare, and neither do I.

The car begins to roar to life and whoever is driving heads in the direction of the I.C.C.O.

"Did you manage to get in contact with the people you needed to?" He asks quietly.

I nod. "Yes, they are meeting us there." I explain and he finally averts his eyes for a moment, and I can breathe.

"Who did you call?" He asks turning back to look at me. His chocolate brown eyes make me melt as I can hear his breathing become more and more rapid.

"The Ghostbusters." I tease with a smile.

He begins to chuckle which I needed as I can tell he is nervous. "Alright trouble." He laughs, calming the mood in the boot of the car. "Can you promise me something before we go through with this?" He asks softly looking directly back at me.

"What is it?" I ask curiously.

He shifts nervously. "When life is back to normal, maybe one day in the future, you'll give me a chance?" He asks and my heart aches.

"Sawyer—" I begin but he cuts me off.

"I don't even mean in sex; I mean let me take you on a date. For dinner or for a drink." He explains, and I'm struggling to take my eyes off him as he scrambles to find the right words. "When I look at you, I see the life I dreamed of having as a kid. With a woman that loved me and cared about me. I let my insecurities and the fact I'm terrified to commit get the better of me, and I would hate to go in this and die without you knowing why I am the way I am, and how I feel about you." He explains softly.

He's really good at leaving me speechless, and instead of trying to word something that will end up being stupid,

I kiss him.

And it takes me by surprise, and him. He tries to pull away in shock but grabs me by my hip in the hopes to move me closer to him.

We pull away in sync. Out of breath as we look into each other's eyes. "Okay." I manage to say, breathless.

"Huh?" He says as a confused look grows on his face.

"Okay, I'll let you take me on one date." I agree and give him a smile. "So, make sure to not get yourself killed?" I tease and he laughs nervously.

"That will be the last thing I want to do." He admits.

Just as I think he's going to lean in and kiss me again, which I probably wouldn't object to. We're interrupted. "We're here guys." Greyson speaks from the front of the car, and I look up to Sawyer who gives me a nod.

We can hear words being exchanged, and I can hear the gates open in front of us. Success.

I feel myself become nervous as they drive up to the entrance where Sawyer and I will be getting in with the help of Ophelia and Scott.

We've decided to keep the lift video for now and publish it only if things don't go to plan. My plan is bring in some of the biggest directors and names in law enforcement and show to them the corruption that is being laced within the I.C.C.O.

Some of these people I really had to convince I'm not a part of this, however I know two of their kids, and because they vouched for me, I managed to earn the trust of the FBI and Interpol.

We suddenly come to a stop and Sawyer looks down at me one last time. "See you on the other side. Love you, trouble." He says with a grin.

I roll my eyes. "Hate you too." I tease.

The boot of the car is opened, and we are met with a smiley Smith who proceeds to help me out of the car. "I think that might be the first time you two have gotten along in a small space." He teases, giving Sawyer a hand next to get out of the boot.

"Trust me, it was cramped. And he smells." I tease. To which Sawyer ignores, handing me a gun from the back of the car.

"You sure we haven't informed security we're here? There's a camera, just above us." He asks putting a gun down the back of his pants. He's dressed in jeans, a white shirt, and a pair of boots. Whereas I'm wearing a black leather jacket, black jeans, and a black body suit with my boots. It's very dull and I'm used to more vibrant colours. But right now, the last thing I want to do is draw attention to myself in my normal attire.

"Johnson disabled them all, I wouldn't worry. He's waiting for you on the fourth-floor stairs." Greyson explains handing us both earpieces and mics so we can speak to each other. "Everyone who's on this has one, Tuck, Scott, Ophelia, Nancy, and Johnson. If you need us, call us. We will be too out of range, but we want to be updated." He asks to which Sawyer nods.

"He will have something at one of his homes, just make sure to tell the housekeeper or if it's his wife, that you're here to collect some files that Sinclair left and a laptop. If they say he doesn't have a laptop here, say that you must have misheard him, but he's asked for the files." He explains.

"Got it." Smith says while nodding. "Thea, what are you going to be doing?" He asks curiously. I place my gun in the back of my jeans.

"Some of the biggest agency leaders are currently on their way here. They've been briefed on the situation with Sinclair, they just need to witness it." I explain.

"That's so cool that you know people like that."

Sawyer scoffs. "The woman knows everybody." He teases, earning an eye roll from me. "Everyone ready?"

We all nod, and Smith and Greyson head back in their car and proceed to drive away. "Remember trouble, don't die." He repeats again and I begin to laugh.

"Same to you, Sawyer." I say and he opens the back door and leads me up the stairs. This entrance Johnson found on the blueprints of the building from when it was built. It's only ever used in emergencies, which so far has been never. It leads us through the floors all the way to the very top. As we approach the fourth floor, I can see Johnson and I somewhat relax even for a moment.

"Alright, Johnson. Anything we need to know?" Sawyers asks as we approach.

"Only that this plan in the last thirty seconds has taken a turn." He says looking at us worried.

"Tony Delsavo is here, he's just about to approach security." Tuck says in our ear,

"Fuck!" Sawyer says punching the wall. "What the fuck are we meant to do now?"

"No! This is good. We just need to make sure they go to one of the rooms where Johnson has placed a bug in it." I explain and Johnson looks to Sawyer.

"Sinclair's office, the meeting room and meeting two as well as all the hallways currently are being monitored." He says as we each head up one more flight of stairs to the fifth floor. "Ophelia and Scott are outside these doors, or they should be." He says slowly opening the door and Scott stands grinning like a maniac.

"Hi there!" He greets us both, giving Ophelia a nod.

"I'm so pleased he hasn't killed you." She says pulling me in for a hug. Out of the corner of my eye I notice Sawyer give Scott a look.

"I am an angel, what you trying to say?" He says playing the victim.

She turns around and glares at him. "The elevator footage tells me differently, Reid. So shut it." She demands.

Sawyer decides not to argue and holds his hands up. I'd like to think he agreed because Ophelia is right.

"We haven't got much time to get you through. Shields, Sinclair, and Brock are still in the meeting, but I passed the room before and some words are currently being exchanged."

"They've been in there a while." Sawyer says looking back at Scott.

"No kidding, and what's worse is I was hoping that Shields would be shouting, but it was Brock and Sinclair." He explains looking down at me.

"The leaders aren't here, so I can add five minutes to check out and see if she's okay, let's hope she leaves that room." I explain to which the rest of the group agrees.

"Come on." Scott encourages, leading us down the corridor of floor five. It's one of the quietest floors, apart from mine. It has only a handful of Agents on this floor, all older, who do less challenging tasks, accounting, case reports, some of them just waiting till they hit retirement.

I'm on high alert for anyone who might notice us, which isn't unusual. This building is currently filled with Agents who probably think we're guilty, especially Sawyer.

"Hey Scott!" Someone calls for him and Sawyer is quick to grab me and push me into one of the rooms.

"Hey, man. Everything okay?" He asks and the Agent approaches. Sawyer places his hand over my mouth, and I try to protest. He only shakes his head at me.

Oh my god, it's Edison.

"Actually, I'm not sure. And I can't seem to be able to override someone's lock on the security system. Do you have someone on your team who might be able to look at it for me?" He asks curiously and I exchange a look with Sawyer.

"Why do you need to get into the security system?" Scott asks.

Edison begins to laugh. "I've been helping Brock and Sinclair in tracking down Sawyer and Thea." He admits casually. "You know, I more than anyone want them two captured. Even if it gets them killed. They ruined Tuck's perfectly good operation on catching Delsavo. Such a shame." He admits openly. Sawyer and I exchange a look. Why is he being so honest?

"You know, I'm friends with them both, as is Ophelia. So, you're opinion on both him and Thea is something we won't ever agree on." Scott says as calmly as he can, but you can sense the change of tone in his voice.

"Come on Scott! You know how Sawyer can be! He probably did this for fun in the hopes that he would ruin Tuck's reputation. He might have been going after yours next." He begins to laugh.

I notice Sawyer become more and more angry above me. I shake my head, hoping he doesn't lose it and ruin our cover.

"I'm not going to agree with you." Scott explains and Edison laughs even harder.

"And don't get me started on that British blonde bimbo. Who the hell decided to give her the job?" He laughs. I raise my eyebrows and I feel a rush of anger through my veins.

"I would stop while you're ahead…" Scott tries to warn him, but he only continues to dig himself a bigger hole.

"Her voice. Urghh! It's the most irritating thing to come out of a woman." He admits. I manage to pull Sawyer off me, both of us clearly annoyed by Edison's admissions. "Someone should really do the world a favour and put a bullet between her eyes—"

I can't even stop him. Sawyer swings the door open with so much force you would think it was going to come off its hinges. Edison jumps out of his skin when he spots us both. Sawyer standing in a stance that shows he's ready to fight him. And I have my arms crossed, hinting I'm not impressed or entertained by Edison's admission.

Edison exchanges a look over at Scott, fear plastered on his face and Scott only shrugs his shoulders. "I told you to stop while you're ahead." He explains.

I move past Sawyer, this time standing in front of him and slowly make my way towards Edison, backing him up against the wall. "Do you want to complete that sentence?" I ask curiously.

He shakes his head repeatedly. For a man with such a revenge plan against Sawyer you would think he would act more like a man. But by the look on his face and the fact there is now a wet patch forming between his legs he's afraid now he has seen us in person. He's afraid of Sawyer, and as he should be. I take his laptop, handing it to Scott who closes it down. That is one bit of evidence we needed.

"It's really funny Edison. You did all this for revenge? Because you had to leave and came back to some changes?" Sawyer says leaning against the doorframe, crossing his arms.

"It should have been me who had that job!" He shouts past me, practically pinned against the wall.

"Edison, the only thing you've proven to this circle today is that you're what the British would call a wimp, or a pussy." I explain. He looks down at me, his nostrils flared. "So, how about you help your case and tell me why you decided to help Sinclair? And I might let you keep your dick, otherwise I'm going to chop it off."

He begins to laugh nervously. "You wouldn't." He taunts, and I turn to Ophelia who already has her secret knife out of her pocket.

"Wanna bet?" I say in a perky American accent, and I can hear Scott laugh behind me. Ophelia hands me the knife and I take it, making sure to slowly glide it over his neck and down his chest. His breathing is erratic, and I stop the knife right at his crotch area and look back up. "Why are you helping Sinclair?" I ask.

"Be-because he told me I could have Sawyer's job as long as I helped frame him." He stutters, but finally admits.

I roll my eyes. "Oh Edison! My seventy-five-year-old neighbour would have worked that out. My question is why now?" I ask again, digging the knife into his crotch a little bit more.

He almost screams. "Because Delsavo has some evidence and photos that can tie Sinclair and Brock to four murders back in the eighties and nineties." He says, his lip quivering and he's beginning to sweat.

"Who's got that evidence?" I ask and he begins to cry, the tears staining his cheeks and his breathing becomes insanely erratic.

"Delsavo, that's why he's here! To hand over the evidence and photos to Sinclair since he kept his end of the bargain." He explains.

I turn round to Sawyer, who after a moment gives me an encouraging nod to leave the man alone. I step away, moving the knife and handing it back to Ophelia. "You may want to clean that." I say standing next to her, giving Sawyer full access to the weasel that stands in front of us. "He's all yours, Sawyer." I say enthusiastically.

Sawyer grins from ear to ear. This is something he's been waiting for. He lunges forward and grabs Edison by his collar, launching him into the empty office we just exited from.

He shuts the door, and screaming and crying can he heard before things go quiet and we can no longer hear the whimpering words and pleas from Agent Edison.

Sawyer emerges from the room again. His hair is all over the place as he slicks it back to its usual sitting place. He opens the door further to reveal a very bloody, tied up and sleeping Edison. "He's not dead. Yet." He announces quite casually, and we all decide to take it at face value. I know Sawyer will deal with Edison later.

"We're behind schedule." I hear Tuck in my ear. We all make our way towards the next set of stairs, which the Agents have had to use since one of the lifts are broken thanks to Sawyer's escape.

"Tuck, where's Sinclair?" I ask him.

Silence falls upon us for a moment and then I hear a crack in the mic. "He's coming out of the meeting room. Thea, it's just him and Brock." He says, his voice slightly filled with panic, and I exchange a look over with Sawyer. Scott hands me a key card so I can get into the majority of the rooms.

"We have Ophelia's and Johnson's go. Take mine." He instructs.

"I'm going to that meeting room. Nancy?" I ask hoping she can hear us.

"Already on my way." She says and I feel slightly calmer knowing that Nancy is here and ready to take on whatever shit Brock decides to spew at her.

I give Sawyer a nod and proceed up to the next floor to check if Shields is alive. I'm hoping, praying, that she is alright. If she's gone in there to protect us and say we're innocent, Brock and Sinclair aren't going to like that.

She has friends in some serious high places. Some linking to the President's office down in Washington.

"Thea, I'd hide in the office coming up on your left, Brock and Sinclair are heading in your direction." Tuck says in my ear, and I do as I'm told.

I close the door lightly, hoping they'll just pass and I'm able to go and check on Shields. "She had that coming." I hear a man in a huskier voice speak, that's Brock.

Sinclair is quick to shush him. "We can say it was accidental, but don't be so quick to announce it Connor." He says and I hear the footsteps stop right in front of the door.

Pulling out my burner phone that Greyson and Smith gave me before we got into the car, I lean down and place it as close to the door as I can so I can get something on record of their overall plan or anything linking to what went on in that room.

"I told you not to hire her as the Assistant Director." Brock complains.

I hear someone scoff, not doubt Sinclair, "I didn't have a choice. It would have suspicious if I didn't hand her the job." He comes to his defence.

"Alright, so she has the highest close rate and she's well respected with other agencies and the President, but surely you saw this coming? That she would have defended the two Agent's you decided to throw under the bus?" Brock explains sarcastically.

"I was hoping she wouldn't care. Besides, Sawyer was on the verge of being fired and it was taking St. James too long to come to Shields about what Sawyer was doing to her. She's too nice. So inevitably, that was her biggest down fall." He says casually.

I'd say that hurt my feelings, but I can't even deny it as he's right. I was nice when it came to Sawyer and not because I thought he deserved it, because he doesn't. But more so that I didn't want the reputation of being the girl who cried wolf. Although look at where it got us.

"Well let's hope we can deal with them soon." Brock says before I hear a phone go off. "Huh." He says after a moment. "Seems that it might be our lucky day. Sawyer Reid was spotted in a café close to here. No doubt he still has Thea and she's there also."

"Go. Deal with them quickly." Sinclair instructs. "I have a meeting with Delsavo, he better hand over that evidence otherwise our lives are finished, and this was for nothing." He says as I can hear him move away from the door.

They don't say anything else, and after a few more minutes, I emerge from the room looking down each side of the corridor to notice I'm free and head for the meeting room Sinclair and Brock have just not long left.

"Nancy, you good?" Tuck asks her in my ear, and I hear her chuckle.

"I'm about to give the best performance of my life and I want a bottle of wine from each of you for the disgusting amount of flirting I have to do." She says sarcastically. I know she's not joking, and for all of my new friends I'll be forever in their debt for helping me clear my name, granted this goes to plan.

I turn off my microphone and head towards the meeting room and slowly open the door, checking behind to see if anyone else is here.

That is when I notice the blood on the floor.

"Oh my god!" I almost scream out loud. I rush to her aid. She's on the floor, clutching to life, as she puts pressure on a bullet wound on her chest. I turn on my microphone. "Shields has been shot." I say placing my hand on her chest hoping to stop the bleeding.

She grabs my arm, her lip quivering as she tries to say something. "It's okay." She reassures me. "It's okay."

"You didn't deserve this." I say to her softly, shaking my head. "Ophelia, I need an ambulance." I repeat.

"Already on the phone."

"Thea." She says which grabs my attention. "He's going to try and kill you." She explains. "I knew he was doing something illegal; I just looked the other way." She admits and tears begin to roll down her cheeks. "I knew what I was walking into. I've made my bed. Please, let me go." She pleads again.

"Shields, please—" I say softly before she cuts me off.

She reaches down and pulls something out of her pocket. "They probably thought that I had no idea this was coming." She says softly handing me what seems to be some sort of pen. "Use this." She says putting it in my hand and shutting it tight. "You'll get justice for me. But please tell my children and my husband I love them." She pleads.

I nod. "Of course." I say and I take the pen from her and hold her hand.

A few moments pass and I watch her take her last breath. Her hand goes limp in mine, and I feel my heart break. I've never had to witness anyone die before and I certainly didn't want to have to witness someone like Shields have to die in such a tragic way.

I owe her my future freedom. She fought for us and put herself at risk even when she shouldn't of. She could be standing here. My whole body feels numb with grief that I caused this. We could have stopped this; it could have been prevented.

"Thea!" I hear Tuck scream in my ear. "What's happening?" He questions.

"She's dead." I say trying to control my emotions. "Shields' dead." I repeat.

A moment of silence falls upon the rest of the group. No one knows what to say, and we all hope this wouldn't have been the outcome.

"Keep going with the plan. Let's just make sure they pay for her death." Sawyer instructs.

I get up from my knees, leaving Shields on the floor. "I don't know what to do." I admit, trying to contain myself.

"Breathe, Thea. You'll be fine. We need you focused." Sawyer instructs.

I head towards the nearest bathroom which is only a few doors down from the meeting room.

I wash my hands, trying to get as much blood off me as possible. Scrubbing so much until my hands are sore and they are no longer red with blood, but red with the pain.

Taking a long deep breath, I begin to focus myself. Sawyer is right. I need to be focused and

I need to be on top form in order for this plan to work.

I exit the bathroom; it's time to put my plan in action and showing the leaders of the other agencies exactly what has been going on within these walls.

Heading towards the stairs, I scan Scott's key card to let me onto that next floor. I hope the others are managing to do their tasks.

THIRTY-NINE

Sawyer

J ohnson and I head for Sinclair's office. The plan is for us to be able to check his devices, Johnson is going to override his password and security system. Since he now knows how Edison works, all the technical hacking stuff, he now knows how to bypass everything and get into Sinclair's accounts, emails, and personal data.

I test the door to his office, and it's locked. Johnson looks over at me, curious on how we're going to get in since I don't have a key.

I decide I don't have time to wait around for

someone to let us in or pick the lock. I charge at the door, the only idea I have right now. I can hear Johnson object and I should have listened to him. Because it doesn't work. And the second I run into that door; I almost knock myself out.

"What the hell was that?" Scott asks in my ear as I groan on the floor.

"Sawyer, he just charged at Sinclair's door." Johnson admits as I raise my hand for him to help.

"Did you get anywhere?" Scott jokes which causes Johnson to giggle.

"No." I admit. "I don't know how we're going to get in here." I explain looking for some way to take down the door.

"I have an idea." Johnson speaks, raising his hand.

I turn to him, hoping he will just tell me, and this isn't a guessing game. I begin to rub my shoulder, a note for future Sawyer – those doors are made of steel.

"I can override my key card and give us access to Sinclair's room." He admits.

I begin to see red as I turn to him. "Why didn't you tell me that before I almost broke my shoulder?" I almost shout at him.

He stutters but gives me a smile. "You didn't give me time."

I roll my eyes. "Hurry up." I encourage hoping I'm not waiting here much longer.

He begins typing on the computer and after a minute, scans his key card which begins to beep green. *Thank the lord.*

I open the door and head straight for Sinclair's filing cabinet, hoping that he's keeping some of his deepest darkest secrets in here, whereas Johnson heads towards his laptop and begins connecting them both to get any data he can find.

"We haven't got long, Boss. We best be quick. Nancy is about to meet up with Brock now. Let's hope this doesn't give her too much of a headache."

FORTY

Nancy

The smell of old cigarettes and bad decisions fills my nostrils, and I can tell that Brock is close. I was always told he smelt like tobacco and whiskey, probably because that is all the man did – smoke 100 cigarettes a day and drink whiskey like water, even on the job.

I'm regretting agreeing to this idea. However, I know one thing from doing my research on him. All of his ex-wives had red hair. So, I'm the only person who will be able to catch his attention.

I lean back on the wall as I hear footsteps approach me and I can tell I have a few moments before I'm going to have to flirt my arse with a man old enough to be my Grandpa.

I ruffle my hair and begin to push my boobs up a little bit in the hopes they distract him. He has a type. Skinny redheads with big boobs. I happen to fit the first two points rather than the third. My breasts are a medium, and I doubt they will be able to distract him for long.

Walking in his direction to the corner of the wall, my hope is to catch him off guard.

We bump into each other, and he must have been walking with some speed because I almost fall to the floor.

"Watch it, Agent!" He barks at me as he turns around.

I straighten myself up and look directly at him. "Apologies." I say, as I'm about to turn away, I notice that his mouth is open as he scours my body.

"I'm sorry, I didn't mean to speak to you in such a tone." He says, walking, breaking the space between us. "Connor." He says with a grin.

Gross. Why do I put myself in these situations.

"Nancy." I say sweetly, also grinning ear to ear. "I don't remember hiring you. Are you new?" I ask trying to make conversation.

He chuckles. "No, sweetheart, I was hired long before you started working here. I'm retired." He explains, and I nod, trying to hint I care, when really; I could care less.

"I see."

"Tell me about yourself, Nancy. What exactly do you do here? Since I joined the I.C.C.O, there's been multiple changes even after I left the agency. So, what manage to ruin," He says with a grin. "I mean run."

I'm going to shoot Sawyer.

"I'm Operations Manager." I say calmly but with a cringed smile on my face. I need to shower, at least twice after being in the same room as this man.

"Oh, so you knew Thea St. James very well then?" He asks curiously.

I nod. "I hired her." I explain. He looks down behind him and looks back at me. Making sure to look at my breasts on his way up.

"Tell me, Nancy," He asks curiously, getting closer so I can now smell the whiskey on his breath. "do you reckon Thea St. James would be capable of killing a leader of one of the biggest crime organizations Sin City has ever seen?" He asks, leaning in closer. He almost speaks as a whisper.

I frown my brows. "Absolutely not. What makes you think that?" I ask, astounded by his question. But then it dawns on me, we've missed out a part in their plan.

"Just curious, love." He says picking up my

hand and kissing it gently. "You know, you look exactly like my last ex-wife." He states flirtatiously.

"Ex-wife? So, you're not married now?" I ask curiously.

"Not anymore. The mailman was her type. If you know what I mean." He explains trying to look lustfully in my eyes.

The more I stand here the sicker I become. He's trying to frame Thea or if that doesn't work, Sawyer for the death of Delsavo. Meaning it's currently being planned, or it's currently in motion.

"Well, that's very sad." I say giving him some puppy dog eyes.

"I better go sweetheart. I've got two criminals to catch. See you around." He says, moving away from me and giving me a wink as he walks away and down the corridor. I follow down in the opposite direction, heading around the corner and turning my mic on.

"Guys, we have a problem." I say heading in the direction of the roof.

"What is it?" Sawyer asks eventually.

"Brock is going to try and kill Delsavo in this building and pin it on either Thea, or you. So, we now need a plan to get Delsavo out of range of whoever he has hiding somewhere in this building.

"Shit." Scott offers. "Tuck, any news on Sinclair?"

"He's coming down to where I'm standing now. I'll give you an update soon. Sawyer you got anything?" Tuck asks on the microphone.

"He has nothing in his files, wizard have you got anything?" I can hear him ask Johnson. I really need to put that man through some therapy. He really does get abused by Sawyer a lot.

"I found an encrypted document labelled 'Operation Indigo'." He says.

"Operation Indigo was when a group of Agent's were killed by who we thought were Delsavo's men." Tuck explains, and suddenly it all makes sense. "Can you decrypt it, Johnson?" He asks.

I push through the door to the stairs, passing people on my way up. I undoubtedly look like a mad woman, but if my hunch is correct, the assassination on one of the worst criminals in Sin City is about to happen in this building and I need to try and stop it.

I'm in heels, Jimmy Choo's to be exact. I've never been a woman to run in heels, but I'm trying my best not to break my ankle.

A few floors later I reach the roof access point,

as I go to look at the security seal and it's been unlocked.

Great.

I pull my gun from underneath my shirt, raising it as I slowly open the door. Looking behind, I begin to walk onto the roof in any sign of someone who really shouldn't be there.

I take one step at a time as quietly as I can, not wanting to inform whoever might be up here that I'm in fact looking for them.

I like the element of surprise.

As I turn round one of the water tanks, that is when I see them. A bald man, hunched over with a sniper rifle. I've not see him before, and I didn't hire him, that's for sure.

I raise my gun higher, pointing it right in the direction of his head as I approach him. He won't be listening out for a woman in heels, he's too focused on someone he has to kill.

Slightly leaning over his shoulder, I notice he has full view of the entrance to the building and Delsavo is in a direct shot.

Sinclair's office is some floors up; however, it is at the back of the building and it's once again in perfect view since this part of the building is classed as higher ground.

I approach him carefully, before pressing my gun to his head, giving me an advantage.

"Anything I can help you with?" I ask curiously as he stiffens underneath me. He doesn't speak, only slightly moves his head to look at me and away from the viewfinder. "You have two options." I say, reaching over and grabbing his sniper rifle. "You can explain what you're doing and who hired you, or I kill you? Completely up to you."

"I'm not going to tell you shit." He laughs at me.

I pout. "That's such a shame." I say softly, watching him move under me so he's facing me. Perfect. I drop my gun and swing so hard I knock him out.

This is the first time in my job I've had to take someone out, yet I'm hoping it's not the last. Because that was exhilarating

"Hey Scott? I'm gonna need you on the roof. I have a large casualty I need helping with." I tease.

FORTY-ONE

Tuck

I wait for Sinclair to come down the stairs. Although I'm also playing a hand in his downfall, I would have liked the heads up that Tony Delsavo, someone who has just killed three of my men, was about to walk into the building.

The lack of communication only proves to me that I was the idiot in this whole undercover operation. Delsavo and Sinclair were doing this under my nose and even I didn't notice it.

There were signs. I managed to find matching meetings in their diaries for the same time, same date, going on for the last year or so.

A criminal like Delsavo, you would think he would have thought this through, although, I can't help but feel as though this is his plan, and the only person who is stupid enough to follow through, is Sinclair.

If Brock really is going to try and frame Sawyer and Thea for Delsavo's end that he has planned, why out it to Nancy the way he did? I mean I get it, he's a narcissist, but people can see that straight up.

As I look over my shoulder to my right, that is when I spot him, Tony Delsavo. The biggest crime lord in Sin City. Runs everything from the drugs to the weapons and lastly runs all of the strip clubs. He's the ultimate pimp.

Sinclair comes into my view, and I decide not to hold back on my distaste for my lack of involvement in my own case. "When were you going to tell me?" I ask stopping him in his tracks. He looks up from his phone, almost as if he's surprised to see me. "Delsavo is here? Why, Sinclair?" I demand.

He raises his eyebrows at me. "I would watch your tone with me Agent Tucker-Barlow—"

"How about I don't, and you tell me what the hell a criminal like that is doing in the I.C.C.O." I demand once again.

"I'm warning you Agent, watch your tone. This has nothing to do with you." He says pushing past me, heading in the direction of Delsavo and I grab his arm.

"Sinclair, if you go through with whatever the hell you're up to, I will do my duty as an Agent for this government to hand over my findings to the relevant people. This is sketchy as shit. You're clearly involved." I begin, his eyes flash with fear or anger as he pulls himself away from me.

"Agent, you have twenty seconds to walk away from me and let me handle this. There has been a breach in our system thanks to your friend—"

"Sawyer didn't do it." I defend him. "We both know he wouldn't. Sawyer is an idiot, yes. But he wouldn't jeopardize his job for this."

"But he would for a girl, that's very interesting." He teases.

"That girl you're referring to is one of the strongest people in this building. So how about you use her name, because all you and Connor Brock have done is dragged her through the mud, aired her dirty laundry and she deserved none of this." I say standing so close that he decides to back off.

I'm bigger than Sinclair, he might be older, and calling him wise would be a stroke to his ego, yet I would like to think I intimidate him.

"Agent, Miss St. James…"

"Agent St. James." I snap. "You were quick to offer her some advice when it came to Sawyer, but also very quick to hand her over to Brock as a suspect. Everyone in this building knows there is something up. We all know Sawyer, and we all know Thea. They didn't do this. Thea, was clearly taken hostage and when that video of the elevator goes to the public, there will be public outcry as to why you didn't protect your Agent's… you just informed the others to start shooting."

He's beginning to sweat; however, he does give me his best poker face. "Get out of my sight Agent Tucker-Barlow, or I'll have your badge."

I pull my badge from the belt hoop of my trousers. "Take it, I would rather work for an agency that doesn't try and kill its Agents and frame them for crimes they clearly didn't commit. I spoke to multiple witnesses the morning that you accused Sawyer of leaking the information, He didn't come into the office till late, he was too busy torturing St. James and watching her receive flowers down here. He was nowhere near his laptop."

Sinclair moves towards me, clearly done with my accusations. "That's enough Agent." And he proceeds to walk away. I decide instead of beating the man to within an inch of his life, I might actually help the rest of the group and keep an eye on Sinclair. He knows I know, which now puts a target on my back.

Because little does he know, that on the back

of his suit jacket, I placed a listening device, small enough that he can't feel it and so that no one else can know it's there.

Considering Sinclair approved them for Undercover Operations, he really should have kept a detailed log of them. Because I kept one, as did most of my team, including the three men who were killed.

They had one on them at the time of their death. Their bodies are currently in the morgue in the city, and the clothes and belongings turned up this morning and are on my desk.

That means more evidence of corruption and if we can, we might be able to catch something else.

I head up towards the roof, pulling out my phone to see any security system watching Sinclair very carefully do his duty as Director and show authority to Delsavo who, with three of his men is escorted through the building and towards the stairs.

Turning my microphone on, I decide to give Sawyer a heads up. "Hurry up Sawyer, they're heading your way." I say and I hear him groan.

"Harry Potter, have you got anything?" He asks Johnson. That poor kid and all of his nicknames.

"I've got what we need. It's enough to show

corruption and enough to show that Sinclair was involved." Johnson says, and I take a sigh of relief, still watching the security feed.

FORTY-TWO

Sawyer

Wizard and I scramble to grab everything we need. I put everything back in the place it needed to be, or at least I have tried.

Johnson closes his laptop after getting the final bits off his laptop which he said really do prove corruption. Some emails and private chat room messages.

"You know, Mr Reid, breaking into a Directors office is a sackable offence. Not to mention you're the most wanted man on the planet." Sinclair says from the door.

Well, Fuck.

"That's a slight exaggeration don't you think? The man stood next to you is wanted for over one hundred murders. You might want to check who you're talking too."

Sinclair begins to laugh. Encouraging Delsavo and his pack of minions to enter the room, closing the door behind them. "Mr Reid, I've been doing my duty as Director for a long time now, longer than you've been alive, actually. Meaning I know people that you wouldn't have even thought to contact about my corruption." He says sarcastically. "I'm going to assume Agent Johnson helped you into this building."

He glares over at Johnson, who ultimately stands just that little bit behind me, looking over at me for some sort of guidance.

"Not exactly. But I do have some questions before you decide to shoot my brains out." I ask to which he laughs again.

"You're not in the position to make demands, Agent Reid."

I begin to laugh back at him. "I am when I have all the information I need in order to ruin your entire life. So, sit down and listen to me." I instruct. I'm sick of the small talk, Sinclair is only in all of this for the money. I dread to think how many debts he's in if he's now collaborating with a man like Delsavo. "Sit down, Mr Delsavo." I instruct this time looking over at the criminal himself.

Sitting in Sinclair's chair, I have Johnson standing next to me. "What would you like to know?" Sinclair asks smugly.

"Why me? Why was I chosen to be your scapegoat?"

Sinclair takes a long deep breath. "Because Edison had a history with disliking you. He was passed up for your job, and decided to take revenge, nearly jumped in my pants at the idea of getting you fired." He says with a grin. "But obviously I knew that you wouldn't go down without a fight. So, I hired Brock to take you out." He admits honestly.

"So, is it because you," I say looking over at Delsavo, "decided to blackmail him to get your entire case dropped?"

Delsavo grins from ear to ear. "I have no idea what you're talking about."

I grin back at him. "Sure, you do! You have evidence he wants to destroy that connects him and Connor Brock to murders years ago. Is there something I'm missing?" I ask smugly.

Sinclair rises from his chair, pulling a gun from behind him. "I'm quite sick of hearing your voice, Agent." He says raising his gun to point it right at my head.

"That's a shame I wasn't done talking." I admit

honestly, trying to ignore the gun being pointed at me. Suddenly he moves it to Johnson and fires a shot. It's as if it happens in slow motion, I push Johnson out of the way, making him hit the floor, almost smashing the laptop.

The bullet goes into my arm, and I begin to scream out in pain. Out of nowhere, Sinclair's door almost flies off its hinges, as Thea and Ophelia appear from behind it. Guns raised pointing directly at Sinclair.

"Put your gun down." Thea demands in that sweet British accent. My heart does a loop when I see her. "Shoot another shot and it will be the last thing you do Sinclair, I mean it." She warns.

Sinclair chuckles. "Like I'm going to listen to a British girl." He says looking over at Delsavo, who looks like he's been caught in the crossfire. His eyes are wide and unsure on the situation.

Ophelia moves and points her gun at him, giving him and his minions the warning that they aren't going anywhere.

"I mean I would." She says pressing the gun closer to his head. "Because how you play this will depend on your jail sentence. Not mine." She explains with a small grin.

I look up and notice five unfamiliar faces approach from left and right of Sinclair's corridor.

"Sinclair, I have some people I'd like to introduce." She says hinting for him to turn around, and after a moment he does.

I move, still clutching my arm, applying pressure. This is my first time being shot, and it was saving Johnson. He better be fucking grateful, or I'll shoot him myself.

Sinclair's face is priceless as he notices the people in front of him. The FBI, Interpol, local Sheriff's office, and a spokesperson for Mayor Meyers. All people who have an influence on Sinclair, and people who are on the committee of who gets hired in this organization.

"I'm assuming these people doing need an introduction really, do they?" She says smugly. "However, they are here after I asked them for a meeting about your corruption and criminal activity involving this man, Tony Delsavo." She explains looking over at him. "Mr Delsavo, care to explain the deal you have with Mr Sinclair."

"It's Director..." Sinclair begins before Justine Matthews of Mayor Meyer's office puts her hand up.

"Not anymore." She speaks clearly. Her voice is firm, and frightening. She's old enough to be my Grandmother, and her opinion matters in this City, purely because she has such a hold on the people. She's Sin City's treasure.

"You've killed three of your own Agents not

to mention countless others. We found messages between you both to confirm it." Ingrid Oliver from the FBI speaks next. "You ordered the hit on two Agents you framed for the leak of information to other organizations which has since been proved to be an Agent you hired who has a grudge against Agent Reid and used his login details to leak said information to the press and to other parties. Who you have just shot in anger. Not to mention the countless bank transfers between your criminal enterprise and your bank account. Your Agents who you framed with the help of others found that out in forty-eight hours."

"You're bluffing. You have nothing." Sinclair states smugly with a grin on his face. A sadistic one, thinking he's going to get away with everything he's done.

"Oh, we do." Johnson speaks next to me. He hints at the laptop which makes Sinclair go red with anger.

"We managed to find that out in forty-eight hours. You really should have had a more structured plan, Sinclair. Preferably one with a less ranking Agent. You may have gotten away with it." I say smugly.

"I'll deny everything." He says smugly, as if he thinks he will get anything off this.

"You can." A voice from behind the leaders

speaks. They move as Tuck comes through along with Scott and Nancy who have some bald man in cuffs. Nancy holding a sniper rifle. "But you forgot that everything you've said has been recorded from the second you walked into that meeting with Shields and Brock, which ended up with her dead." He says coldly, moving past Thea who still has her gun raised at Sinclair. "You really thought you would be able to get away with this. But your own greed and need for power is the reason for your downfall. Brock's too."

He stands nose to nose with Sinclair. "You're lying."

"That's something I don't do." He says confidently. "And I don't take kindly to people killing my team." Tuck says, his face turning into rage before launching Sinclair off the wall.

It happens so quick that by the time Sinclair gets back up, he hasn't even reacted to what has happened. "Three of my men. They were fathers, brothers, sons. You killed them for your greed!" Tuck shouts raising his fists to Sinclair.

No one seems to want to stop him, probably because he's not one to beat the life out of my Director, although he does heavily deserve it.

Scott eventually reaches down to get me off him. Sinclair begins coughing and sneezing blood everywhere. He raises his gun pointing directly at Tuck. "Don't think for one second, I'm going to let you get away with attacking me. You all seen it!" He exclaims.

I scoff. "Go ahead. Did anyone see anything?" I asks curiously.

"Not a thing." A lot of them repeat at once. Even the leaders of the agencies. Thea still has her gun aimed right at Sinclair, and for a moment I'm not worried, until he raises his gun higher, aiming for between my eyes.

"This is all of your fault."

I begin to laugh. "Hardly." I say smugly.

Something catches Thea's attention, and she pulls the tigger on the gun and the bullet goes into Sinclair's hand, making him drop the gun and begin to scream in pain, blood covering the white walls. "Stupid bitch!"

Everyone stands back and looks at her. "He was awfully close to pulling that trigger. I just needed to make sure he didn't."

I'm grateful for her bravery. Thankful for her noticing something people didn't. Also, grateful she didn't kill him, I know she wanted to.

Sinclair is screaming in pain, and in the midst of the chaos, Tony Delsavo tries to escape. But both Thea and Ophelia turn and point their guns at them. "I wouldn't move if I was you." Ophelia says smugly.

Applying some more pressure to my arm, I

walk around the desk to greet Sinclair, who sits on the floor holding his hand close to his chest.

"Fuck you, Sawyer." He spews at me.

Grinning like the mad hatter, I take the cuffs from Scott who hands me them with a small smile. "Maybe you should have thought your plan through."

He rolls his eyes, and tries to get to his feet, Scott giving him a firm hand turning him round to face the wall. I lean in closer; his hairs begin to stand on the back of his neck. "Get it over with, Sawyer." He says against it.

"With pleasure." I say with a smile, putting his hands behind his back, not caring if he's in pain or the fact there is a hole from the bullet. "Thomas H. Sinclair, you're under arrest."

FORTY-THREE

Thea

It's been three weeks since the incident at I.C.C.O. Both Sawyer and I were told to remain on leave until a thorough investigation was completed. Thankfully, we were both being paid for it, and we will both be compensated when we take Sinclair and Brock to court over defamation, loss of earnings and attempted murder. The classic items.

Mary and Frank are so pleased I'm back home. Granted I came home to my apartment a mess from the other Agents who decided to turn it upside down and I need to pay for a new door. But that is the least of my worries.

Alister got his car back and he was thrilled because of some sort of miracle, Sawyer and I managed to keep it in perfect condition. I sent him chocolates, filled it up with petrol and will forever be in his debt for helping us the way he did.

I ended up in the hospital for a couple of days because of my head. There was some fluid on my brain but managed to get rid of it with a needle to the bottom of my skull. With pain medication it still hurt.

I'm still bruised and after a full X-ray they were surprised after the only thing I hit was my head during the fall in the lift.

The local police and FBI interviewed me about the lift situation, to which I told them I'm not pressing any charges on Sawyer. They were surprised and tried to convince me otherwise, yet I stood my ground. But Nancy really did want to see him in orange.

Sawyer was dropped of all charges linked to the leakage of documents and case information including Tony Delsavo. Tuck came by the house to tell me that he's out of the hospital and is milking all of the attention he's getting from anyone.

He got shot in the arm for Christ's sake, and thanks to me he manage to keep his almost tolerable face.

I'm yet to see him at all, and I'm hoping when I'm back in the office we can talk about the whole situation in the back of Smith and Greyson's car.

They both managed to find two extra laptops in two of Sinclair's homes that link him to a few other murders that were quite recent.

Poor Tuck is now having to fix up his task force and has been put into anger management for the situation with Sinclair. He's said he will go, but only because he knows the woman who will be holding the classes and he likes her or used to.

My head is almost healed, and I'm feeling a lot better. I have a return-to-work meeting with a Doctor soon to see if I can go back to work, when and if I'm allowed.

I try not to leave the apartment if I can help it. Almost everyone in Sin City knows who I am, although the news station put out a public apology to both Sawyer and I and have invited us both for an interview. I've declined and I really just want to forget this happened when I know deep down I can't.

My Mum has tried to get in touch. Even going as far to contact the local news station regarding it. She's demanding she speak with me, but I still haven't got a phone and haven't been able to get one just yet.

The news station did one thing right, told my Mum that I'll be in touch when I'm ready, so I need to stop contacting them. I'll never contact her, and I don't need to. I cut off my family years ago, and I really don't feel like hearing what she has to say, when all she did was speak badly in interviews and give information to the press for some sort of sympathy.

So, in a better term of words... she's a bitch.

My family's actions didn't surprise me. I wouldn't be surprised if they started bad mouthing me all over social media along with the strangers of the world who have no idea what happened and how it was dealt with.

I finally managed to put my apartment back together. Somethings needed to go out, but once it was finally clean, I felt so much better than I had been.

They confiscated my gun, which was my biggest annoyance. However, I am due to get that back since I have a licence and the gun has never been used. I still have to sign some papers to get it back, but I can do that if I get back into the office.

Nancy brought food last night and we watched some TV to pass the time. She is also under review on how she handled the sniper on the roof. She is also due to be cleared.

Scott and Ophelia ended up being suspended too while the investigation takes place. But Ophelia was allowed back into the office today with some officers to collect some of the items she needed.

We are all due to be let go of any involvement, but we will have to testify at Brock and Sinclair's trials if they decide to go down the route and plead not guilty.

Brock, on his way to the supposed café to deal with Sawyer Reid, was arrested for planning the attempted murder of two Agent's and another. He put up a fight and got arrested of another few charges of assaulting a government officer and resisting arrest. Both he and Sinclair were denied bail and are currently sat in a Federal prison alongside half of the criminals they put away in their lifetime.

I haven't heard much more about them, and all evidence we had has been handed over with the help of Johnson who is currently working with FBI to get justice for the three Agent's that were killed by Delsavo at the request of Sinclair.

The only thing being spoke about worldwide is the corruption of the Director of the I.C.C.O. How the agency is at its knees and how the staff don't trust one another. Which couldn't be further from the truth. Although I haven't worked at the organisation long, I know that it has a sense of unity between the staff it employs. We all want to see justice to be served and we didn't look the other way when it came to the corruption, it was because the Director was so convincing and so manipulative in the way of him being so nice that not one of us needed to question it.

Fastening up my buckle on my heel, I straighten out my dress in the mirror. Today is Assistant Director Shields' funeral. The forensic team matched Brock's gun to the bullet found in Shields' chest and has also been arrested for her murder on top of every other charge.

There is a knock coming from the entrance of my apartment and when I turn, I find Sawyer standing there. He's in a black suit, his hair is slicked back, and it's gotten longer which does suit him. He's started to grow a little bit of stubble. "Did they kick your door down too?" He asks amused. "No privacy in this building." He says with a wink turning behind him.

I head in his direction to see what he is talking about, and no surprise there, Mary and Frank are the door with a glass of champagne. Frank in a wheelchair since he still hasn't recovered from his accident a few weeks ago. "It was nice of them to leave my apartment in such a state." I say sarcastically, heading over to my kitchen and collecting my bag off the breakfast bar.

"I have something for you." He says which intrigues me as I turn to look at him. He pulls something from his pocket to reveal a brand-new iPhone. "Since I broke your other one." He says sheepishly pulling the broken one from his other pocket. My goodness that really is damaged and beyond repair.

I take them both with a smile and place them in the top draw of my kitchen. "Thank you." I say kindly. "You didn't have to; I would have bought my own."

He scoffs. "Enough with the independent shit trouble, just say thank you and let's leave it at that." He says sarcastically.

I begin to laugh, heading in the way of where my door used to be. "Thank you." I say again.

"You ready for this?" He asks stepping out from the apartment and we both make our way towards the stairs.

"Not really. I was there when she died, I really wanted to do something." I say quietly.

"I know," He agrees. "but she asked you to do something when she died, and you did that. Her family are grateful." He reminds me.

Having to speak to Shield's family really broke me and it took me days to recover. That poor family lost someone so dear, and she really didn't need to die. She left behind a husband, a daughter, and her beloved dog Maxie. The whole situation is such a tragedy, and I hope that the justice system finds justice for all the families involved.

"You two look lovely. Send our condolences to the Shields family." Mary says as we approach them. Sawyer gives her a nod and looks down at me.

In a surprise twist, he extends his hand to her, and she takes it with a confused look on her face. "I deserved the black eye and so much more." He admits.

It really does catch me by surprise. He's thanking her. Sawyer Reid is never this polite, to anyone.

"You're welcome. Just note that if you do anything stupid again, I'll kill you this time." She warns him. Her face is stern and filled with only thing in her mind, certainty.

"I'll help get rid of the body." Frank admits next and I roll my eyes.

"Okay, well we better go." I say, giving them both a kiss on the cheek as Sawyer walks away and towards the apartment door.

Mary pulls me in closer. "He's even more attractive when he's apologizing." She admits with a grin. "Hopefully you don't need to use your device anymore!" She whispers, a gleaming smile on her face.

Mine, however, goes scarlett red, "Bye." I say leaving them standing in the entrance of the building.

"What was that?" Sawyer asks as I join him outside.

"Nothing you need to know about."

He begins to laugh. "They seem sweet."

This makes me cackle as he heads towards the car. "Don't let them fool you. They are ruthless as you've found out." I say with a cheeky grin.

"Yeah, yeah. Get in the car." He instructs.

We decide to take his car, ignoring the stares from the people around us who have no doubt seen us on the TV over the past few weeks.

"Seatbelt on." He instructs.

Apparently, I'm not quick enough and he leans over, catching me off guard and is only a few inches away from my face. He puts my seatbelt on, tightening it so I'm not getting out of it easily.

We stare at each other for a moment. He looks down at my lips and I do the same to his. The sparks flew like nothing I had ever felt with my last boyfriend when I kissed Sawyer to shut him up in the back of the car.

He's the first to move away but as I watch him, his cheeks begin to get redder as he pulls away from the apartment and towards the direction of the funeral.

It's probably best we don't' talk about it right now. Although I don't know when it will be a suitable time, but on the way to the funeral of our previous Assistant Director, isn't going to be the best time.

FORTY-FOUR

Sawyer

I pull back up at her apartment after the funeral, and the atmosphere in the car is dire. The funeral was a wonderful way to honour Shields, and to honour her legacy. She was labelled as a hero today, to the people of Sin City as the funeral was live streamed to millions. She was like our very own Queen of England, although when Thea and I turned up, it seemed to cause some drama.

We quickly made it inside, and although we got some interesting stares from some of Shield's supposed friends, we managed to get through the funeral. She was an incredible woman who accomplished so much and cared for so many. The streets were filled with people from all agencies, far and wide. She had quite the connection. Vice President Bear even showed up to show her condolences.

"I hate funerals." Thea says breaking the silence in the car.

"Same." I agree and begin to look over at her. "My mothers was the last one I went to."

She looks up at me, and sadness fills her eyes. "Sawyer, I'm so sorry. Are you okay?" She asks sweetly.

"Oh, yeah. I'm fine." I admit, shifting uncomfortably. "Don't worry about me." I say.

I look back up at her and give her a weak smile. "Do you want to come in and watch a movie?" She asks.

I'm taken back by the offer and although my heart is doing a dance because this is all I've ever wanted. My head tells me to leave her be.

"Sure." I admit.

Idiot. My subconscious tells me.

We exit out the car, and as she walks towards the pavement, I pull her back, so she doesn't walk into two men carrying what looks to be a door. "Coming through!" They say eagerly as the push through into her apartment building.

We both walk slowly behind them and holding the door open is Thea's neighbour. I can't for the life of me remember his name.

"Hi Alister." She says with a smile. "You off to work?"

He looks over at me and gives me a nod. "Yeah, I got a promotion so it's my first night as manager." He says with a beaming smile.

"That's fantastic! I'm so happy for you." She says grabbing his arm gentle. "Congratulations." She expresses.

He smiles as he notices her arm, but then notices me staring at him. "Thanks, Thea. Nice to see you again, Sawyer." He says giving me an encouraging nod and moving out from under us and out of the door.

By this point, the men are well and truly trying to put that door to Thea's apartment. "What was that about?" She asks looking up at me. I shrug my shoulders unsure on what she's referring to.

"What were you doing to him, he is never that nervous." She admits giving me a glare.

"I was my usual pleasant self!" I express and she rolls her eyes.

"Sawyer…"

"Yes, trouble?"

This catches her off guard and moves away when she notices the men are finished putting the door back on and checking the lock on her apartment.

"Here you go, Miss. Brand new." They greet her with a smile, and she thanks them as they leave the building shutting the door behind them.

"Happy new door day!" I exclaim enthusiastically and she proceeds to laugh, heading up towards her apartment.

"Why are you the way that you are?" She asks opening the door and entering.

"Dashing, good looking, funny?" I question curiously while she shuts the door behind me.

"Weird. You're very weird, Sawyer." She laughs heading into the living room area of her apartment. It's a ridiculously small place, but for her it probably does the job.

The open plan living, dining and kitchen area all looks out to big window's overlooking some of the city. It's not a relaxing view, probably because it can be a very uncertain area. But the whole vibe in the apartment screams Thea St. James. Small, minimalist, and comfortable.

"How long have you lived here?" I ask opening her refrigerator to see if she has anything good to drink. Wine, wine, wine and of course the woman is an alcoholic.

"Just over five years. Moved in just before I started the academy." She explains from the sitting room.

"You don't have a lot of options in terms of

drinks, Thea." I shout towards her, peaking down into the refrigerator. "You've got a fresh bottle of wine, wine with no lid and wine with a ridiculously long straw."

She laughs from the sofa. "Bring me my wine with the straw, please. I have whiskey in a cupboard if you would like it. It's the top one to the right." She says pointing and I turn to look in the direction,

Sure enough, I find a bottle of whisky. And not any sort of whisky. "Thea, do you know what this is?" I ask her, holding the bottle in my hand. "This is a 1996 scotch whisky, it's ridiculously hard to get in Sin City." I explain examining the bottle.

I've only had this drink once, and boy did it change my life. It's one of the nicest whisky's around and because it is from Scotland, and import tax is more than my rent, I find it hard to click buy every time I add it into my basket.

"I got it as an engagement present from my Grandfather before he passed. I think it was more for Aaron than me, but when I left the house we had bought together, I couldn't not take it with me."

It has sentimental value, not only was it a present from her previous engagement, but it was from her Grandfather, someone I can tell was especially important. "I'll have wine." I say as I begin to put the bottle back.

"Sawyer, I am not going to drink it, please by all means help yourself and grab a glass." She encourages.

Not wanting to argue, I do just that and grab one of her tiny glasses that weren't smashed in the raid.

"Do you need a glass?" I ask as I approach the coffee table.

She gives me a look. One that asks are you serious?

"Sawyer, there's a straw." She says, pointing at the bottle.

I groan. "British people are weird."

She laughs at me as I head towards the sofa. "Can't argue with that."

She begins to get comfy on the sofa holding the bottle of wine with a god damn straw while I open the bottle of whisky and pour myself some.

"To Shields and the other Agents." I say raising the glass. She joins in with the bottle and a clink can be heard around the room. Both taking a drink, I try my best to avoid looking at her.

I begin looking around the room, and I notice a photo that looks eerily similar. "Is this from graduation?" I say placing my glass down and heading towards the TV stand where a photo of Mary, Frank, and Thea sits. "I remember this photo."

Suddenly the silence fills the air and I decide to look over at her. She's frowning at me, "Why do you remember that photo?"

Because when you smile it lights up a room and you looked incredibly hot in your graduation gown.

"I thought that they were your grandparents, I was talking about it with someone in our class, they said they weren't sure." I lie.

I couldn't tell her that from afar, I watched as that photo was taken by a girl in our class, Tiffany, I think. Thea was glowing that day. Her hair was in her usual curled style, and she had more makeup on than usual, not that she ever needed it. She looked absolutely beautiful every single day without it.

Not only did she win the top of the class award, but when she graduated from the academy, she also happened to be the first British person to be accepted, graduate and accept the award. A lot of firsts, and although twenty-two-year-old me would argue, she really did deserve it.

"Who was there for your graduation?" She asks as I place the photo back down. "Did you Mum go?"

Getting up from my knees, I head back over to the sofa. I think with her I've spoken more about my Mom than I have with anyone. "No, she was in hospital by then." I say softly. "I called her after the ceremony though. She was thrilled but gutted she couldn't be there."

She takes a sip of her wine through her straw. "Did your brother not come?" She asks.

"My brother and I aren't exactly close." I explain. "He and his wife are fine, that's not the problem, they just want me to change my ways and who I am as a person to fit into their beliefs and I'm not about that." I explain, finishing off the glass of whisky and pouring myself another glass.

"Beliefs?" She asks sweetly while I place the bottle down and lift the glass to my lips.

"They believe in marriage and having children and I don't believe in that. And it's not something I'd want anyway." I say taking a drink.

I watch her expression change from curiosity to sadness. "That really doesn't surprise me." She admits, which is clearly a lie. Her face is telling me something different. That maybe I had changed.

"Good."

The silence falls between us, but all I can hear is her gulping that wine down like a horse with water. "Thea, should we talk about what happened in the car? Is that why you're currently drowning yourself in the wine?"

She looks up at me like a deer in headlights,

removing her mouth away from the straw. "I'm not." She objects, placing the bottle down. "But yes, we need to talk about it."

I finish my drink for a second time and begin to get comfortable on the sofa. "I mean, there isn't much to talk about. Apart from the fact, you kissed me."

Her eyes widen. "You were nervous." She says, narrowing her eyes.

I begin to laugh at her admission. "Trouble, I never get nervous if you're into me. Just say so." I say with a wink.

She raises from her seat, almost grossed out my accusation.

"Into you? Please Sawyer. Get a grip of yourself." She says, crossing her arms. "Like I've said since day one, we're enemies, you hate me, and I hate you."

"Actually—" I stop her in the middle of her supposed rant. "You hate me, I like you."

She suddenly stops and her eyes widen. "No, you don't." She objects which makes me laugh.

"Er- yeah I do." I admit, rising from the seat. "You may not like me very much, Thea, but this enemy's thing you've got going on? That's all in your head, baby." I say walking towards her.

To my surprise she doesn't back away, and she's frozen by my admission. "Sawyer, we can't."

She says almost as a whisper. "It's not right."

"Says who?" I ask getting so close that I want to touch her so bad, stop her from talking.

"Everyone." She says looking away while I scoff.

"Screw everyone else." I say catching her attention and gently grabbing her face. "Screw the rules." I say moving my left-hand round to the back of her neck and grabbing at her hair. "Screw the world." I say tilting her head back to look at me. Getting so close I can almost feel her lips on mine, I'm becoming intoxicated in her presence and if she doesn't let me do even half of the unspeakable things I'm thinking of, I'm going to be incredibly disappointed. "Tell me what you want, Thea." I demand against her lips. "Do you want me to stop?" I ask her again. She shakes her head in my grasp and I groan. "Use your words." I demand. I need consent, I crave it.

"No." She breathes against my lips, and I practically go feral against her. "I don't want you to stop." She breathes.

I crash my lips against hers, taking her by surprise. I melt into her; this is something I've been dreaming of for all those years.

She finally relaxes underneath me, and kisses me back, harder. I'm intoxicated by her, praying she doesn't pull away, praying she lets me continue and praying that she lets me make her mine.

I've craved this, and her for so long that deep down this feels like a dream, a one I've had too many times, but this time it's different. It's not in my apartment, but in hers.

I move my left hand back to her face grabbing it tightly, kissing those sweet lips as though they belong to me already. She eventually places her hand on my hips, and I feel every nerve in my body explode.

My heart is pounding, and my knees become weak at the thought of having her, of even kissing her. Even if I do take this further, everything I do. I need consent. I need her to say yes to me. It's all I've ever wanted to hear, her saying yes to me.

I can physically feel the sparks flying off us, she's electrifying, magnetic and I can't get enough of her.

It's never been like this, not with anyone. Not with the woman I once thought I liked and even used my box of toys on. This is another feeling, this feels unreal.

She begins to pull away and I panic, and she can tell. "Sawyer, are you sure?" She asks softly away from me, her head still in my hands and cupping her face tightly.

"Shut up, trouble." I demand and kiss her

again. Although I love the sound of her voice and the sugar rush it brings me, for the next however long, I need her to be quiet.

I want to focus on every inch of her body, on every beauty mark. Kiss every inch as if she said she belonged to me, fucked her as if she belonged to me.

I don't want to move from this position. I finally slide my tongue in, and she accepts it while I begin to explore her mouth. The sweet taste of her wine tingles my tastebuds and I find myself getting drunk off the lust that's mixed with the alcohol.

I move my hands down, feeling every inch of her body while she stands still holding my hips. As long as she's touching me, I couldn't care less what she's doing. I begin to kiss my way down her cheek and to her ear then down her neck, tracing my hands over that tight black dress she had the nerve to wear today. Her ass looked amazing in it, as did her tits and it's all I've thought about since I entered the apartment to collect her for the funeral.

As I reach her chest and I'm almost on my knees, I reach down to hers and throw her over my shoulder. The squeal that exits her mouth along with the giggles as I head towards her bedroom. The *forbidden* area.

It's small, just like her, but the whole aesthetic

screams Thea St. James. Clean, beige, and normal. Boring, some would say.

I place her gently on the bed and climb on top of her, making sure not to put my entire body on her as I continue to kiss her and every inch of her. Her quiet moans help me continue, it's better than the sex hearing her moan and whimper.

She raises herself and tries to move my shirt and I stop her, shaking my head. "Not yet," I say against her lips. "Soon."

She whimpers, almost as an objection, but I ignore the bratty side. I want to savour every single moment, and I don't want her to feel like a one-night stand. Because with how intoxicated I am by her, I want this to last forever.

I continue to kiss her and grab her hands to place them at the top of her head, restricting her which turns me on even more. My cock is so painfully hard that if she keeps moaning in my mouth, I'm going to cum in my suit pants and ruin the fucking moment.

I remove one hand and begin to trace her entire body, slowly, my tongue still fighting for dominance in her mouth. I reach her thighs and begin to move my hand to in between her legs.

She's soaked.

"Someone wants me." I say with a smile against her lips. She pulls away and places her head back on the bed.

"You wish." She teases which makes me smile wider. I lean over and begin to kiss her all over again like I haven't been for the last ten minutes.

"Your pussy is screaming for me baby, just admit it." I say against her lips again and she shakes her head. I decide to not pull away and give her a chance to respond, she wants to fight like we normally do, which would turn me on but because I know Thea, it would make her realize what this would mean for us, and she'd go off into a deep dive of the implications of sleeping with your boss. And right now, if I don't put my dick inside her, I'm going to scream the place down.

I pull away this time, hoping she will just keep quiet. "How the hell do you get this thing off?" I say pointing at her dress.

She laughs but turns over like a good girl, revealing the zipper. Perfection. I undo the zipper, pulling it down slowly to reveal a black lace bra and the top of some black lace panties.

Fuck.

I take a long deep breath and pull her out of the dress, having her stand in front of me, just in her underwear.

She has the most incredible body I've ever seen on a woman. She notices me staring and is about to cover up and I throw the blanket away.

"Never, ever cover yourself, do you understand?" I say grabbing the back of her hair again forcing her to look up at me. "You really don't understand how unbelievable you are do you?" I say to her against her lips. A gentle smile begins to grow which makes my heart do a stupid dance.

I sit her back down on the bed, admiring her and letting go of her hair in my hand. I begin to unbutton my shirt slowly, with me getting shot, I still have to be careful with taking items of clothing off and I thought I would let her enjoy the show.

She gets distracted and goes down to remove her heels. "Hey," I say stopping her in her tracks and reaching over. "the heels stay on."

She looks up, startled by the demand, however, doesn't argue with me and simply nods. I completely remove my shirt letting it drop to the floor. I crawl back on top of her, having her giggle as I take her mouth against mine once again.

I grab her hands again and place them above her head, restricting her. "You going to be good?" I say against her lips.

She shakes her head pulling away slightly. "No, why would I do that?" She teases and my cock gets even harder. *Thea…*

"Don't be a brat." I demand and she looks up at me, giving me the fuck me eyes.

"Or what?"

Shit.

I can't have her acting like this. "Behave, consider this a warning." I warn her to which a smiles this time, kissing me to shut me up and I feel myself melt all over again.

I move my hands down to her breasts and begin to cup them, roughly. I want this bra off and her panties and I want to be deep inside her. I need to feel her on me, crying out for me.

Her hand begins to move further down my body till she reaches my very swollen and sore cock and begins to play through my trousers. The sensation makes me almost cum, and I have to move her hand away, to which she pouts. "Don't do that yet." I instruct her.

A smile grows on her face. "I think if anyone wants anyone here..." She teases, that stupid gleaming grin on her face. She isn't wrong and I roll my eyes.

"Shut up, before I spank you." I warn her, flipping her over to her front and undoing her bra and remove her panties. I don't want her to talk anymore, I want to taste her, and her sweetness.

Moving her back over to look at me, I begin to kiss every single inch of her body. Taking in her scent as if she was an expensive perfume and I just can't get enough of it. "So beautiful." I say moving my way down her body. Complimenting her after every kiss as she raises her hips to meet my lips.

Sliding my hands underneath her legs, I begin to leave kisses in between her legs, and she squirms.

I tighten my grip holding her in place so she can't go anywhere. This is better than anything I've dreamed of. Her tiny little moans filling my ears better than sex ever could.

I leave sweet kisses leading up to her legs and kiss gently on her pussy, she gasps loudly, almost as if she's in shock but I hold her down. I kiss again, the same reaction. And again and again till the exhales turn into whimpers for me to continue.

I pull away and she looks down, startled at me. "As much as I would like to make you scream my name, trouble," I begin, moving one of my hands from underneath her leg and placing it on her face to have her focused on me. Those big blue eyes entrancing me as if I'm falling headfirst into the ocean with no parachute. "you have very nosey neighbors."

She begins to laugh; however, it doesn't ruin the mood, only kisses me, helping me fall deeper. I pull away again, moving her legs to give me access once again.

The more I move and lick and kiss the harder

she grips the bed sheets. She is absolutely soaked and has already soaked some of the bedding already but who gives a shit. She tastes just as I expected, and she tastes so good. Grabbing onto her thighs, I bury my head further, making sure to watch her carefully.

She's holding her hand over her mouth, probably because she may not trust herself, and Frank might come running to her aid, or more like Mary with a pan.

"Thea." I break away from the sweetness and she looks down to me. *Oh fuck.* "Look at me."

She shakes her head, but I encourage her, going deeper and I watch her eyes roll to the back of her head as she places her head back down on the bed. Foreplay, and making a girl feel pleasure, is something of a strong point, I've always been a giver rather than a receiver.

I feel her legs begin to shake, and that brings me more satisfaction than anything else. She always said I wouldn't be able to... well who was lying? Cause it wasn't me.

Rising from in between her legs, as she breathes heavy on the bed, I remove her hand, pinning her down again and kissing her passionately. I want her to know how good she tastes. She kisses me harder, pulling me closer so I'm completely on top of her, crushing her.

Our tongues dance in sync as I take every inch

of her mouth, tasting the wine, and I begin to get drunk all over again.

I reach to my back pocket, pulling out my wallet. She stops kissing me to see what I'm doing, and I show her the condom. "I'm being safe." I say giving her a wink, and she rolls her eyes at me. "Don't even think to snap back, I will spank you." I say playfully to which she grins, but keeps her mouth shut.

Pulling down my suit pants and underwear, I open the condom and roll it on, she avoids my eyes at first, but then I catch her staring and it makes my cock throb with need. She's giving me the fuck me eyes, even if she doesn't know it.

"Are you okay?" I ask her gently, aiming myself in between her legs so she can feel how hard I am for her, for her body, for her voice.

"Yes." She says breathlessly and I grab her face, causing her to look at me.

"Are you sure, Thea?" I ask her again. I want to be sure that this is something she wants and I'm not forcing her in anyway.

"I'm sure." She reassures me. I aim myself inside of her and move slowly. Fuck she is tight. So tight, I feel as though I'm going to cum already. "Fuck." She cries as I enter slowly.

I place my hand above her head, still entering s I don't want to hurt her, and I have no idea when the hell she last slept with someone, so no wonder she's as tight as she is. "Thea..." I breath almost collapsing on top of her. It feels so fucking good. So good, that if I don't contain myself, I am going to ruin it for the both of us and I'll be known as I one hit wonder.

I begin to slowly thrust inside of her, her moans almost becoming louder, and I move up to kiss her, silencing her almost.

She becomes more relaxed around me, and I feel myself fucking her harder, and the more I do, the more she's holding in her scream. I want to tell her to let it out, be a good slut for me, but those nosey neighbor's downstairs would come knocking.

"Fuck..." I moan against her mouth as a tiny moan escapes her mouth as she grabs the bedsheet so tight her knuckles go white.

I push back, hoping she'll stay quiet, and instead, she moves her hand to cover her mouth, muffling her screams. She feels so good around my cock that I feel like I'm going to implode, but I've barely been going two minutes, and this is not how I want to remember it, that I barely gave her any sort of pleasure, that I couldn't get her to come on my cock because I was so needy and needed to finish first, fuck that.

"Thea." I say in between the thrusts. "Thea," I say again, and she catches my eyes. I lean down again, pressing my hand on her lower stomach so it feels better for her. "Look at me when I'm fucking you."

With my other hand, I grab her soft blonde curled hair tight and force her to look at me. She does, and fuck I'm about to cum. I move quicker, wanting to find my own release and hoping to find hers. I can't hold it any longer, I'm starting to go dizzy with how she's making me feel. "Sawyer," She cries and I have to find all of my strength not to cum just hearing her cry my name.

"I know, baby." I say against her, kissing her passionately. "I know."

She tries to move her head back with the pleasure, but I keep her in the same position, fucking her senseless as well as myself because I know I'm struggling to hold on.

That's when I watch her, orgasm so hard her legs shake, and her body lifts off the bed.

That's all I needed.

I hold her and kiss her passionately, coming so hard that I see stars and I almost collapse on her.

I've thought about this for years, so many years that it went so much better than I imagined. We're both breathing heavy and I'm almost afraid to look at her. I don't feel any shame, or any regret whatsoever, because fuck that felt good. She felt good, and it only made me fall for her even more. But I know how she feels in regard to me, our friendship or whatever the hell we have going on.

She grabs my face, and I'm quick to look at her. Her freshly fucked hair, her rosy cheeks and the mascara slightly rubbed on her eyes makes me feel guilty. She's going to say something that's going to kill me inside.

"That was fun." She smiles. Well done, Sawyer. *Overthinking much?*

"It was." I breathe, removing myself from her slowly. She winces, but I press my hand to her cheek and rub it gently. "You okay?" I ask again and she rolls her eyes.

"For someone who doesn't care about people's feelings, you sure care about mine." She teases. I know she's playing, but I feel as though she still thinks this is a game to me. When I feel like this meant more to me than it did for her.

"I do. I'm scared to hurt you." I admit honestly, which catches her off guard as I head towards the bathroom to bring her something so I can clean her up.

She watches me carefully. "Sawyer, all you do is hurt me." She's quick to say. Although I know she's right, I can't help but feel like we could end up in an argument if I don't speak my mind and soon.

I'm too short tempered with her, it's nothing she's ever done apart from be smarter and more charismatic than me. "I don't mean to." I say emerging from her bathroom. "I know I can be a little bit of a dick."

"A little?" She says raising her eyebrows reaching for the cloth with I remove from her reach.

"No, I'm doing it." I snap playfully at her. She squirms a little at the sensation as I begin to clean her up and for a moment, I avoid all eye contact with her in the hopes we can just drop the argument I can feel about to erupt. I just want to enjoy this moment with her, and I certainly don't want to leave and have her feel like I used her for sex.

I head over to what looks to be her washing basket and throw the cloth in there. Reaching down to my shirt on the floor I hand it to her.

She takes it reluctantly. "Why are you giving this to me?" She asks softly.

"Cause I want you to wear it." I say giving her a warm smile.

"Why?"

I roll my eyes at her. "Because it will be a dress on you, and I plan on fucking you one more time tonight and it will be in the shirt this time." I tease, giving her a wink.

She blinks at me for a few moments and raises an eyebrow. "You sure about that, Reid?" She teases as I see a slight grin grow on her face.

I lean down to her, pressing my forehead to hers. "I know what I want." I say looking into her eyes.

She's giving me those eyes again and I want to grab her by the throat and put her to the bed, kissing her till we're both breathless.

I decide to move away first, only because I'll not be able to control myself if I stand around her. "I bet you're upset you couldn't use your box of toys." She teases as I walk away.

Turning around quickly, I can see the smile on her face as she removes her heels. "You have to earn the box of toys, trouble." I state to which she rolls her eyes at me, before looking down and undoing her heels.

"Got a heel fetish, Sawyer?" She shouts towards me, as I head back into her living room. I pour myself a whiskey, and grab her fucking bottle with a straw, a metal straw for the turtles, and head back into her bedroom.

"No comment." I say handing her the wine, and I take a sip of my whisky.

Her eyebrows raise. "That's funny," she starts, taking a sip and heading towards her bathroom from the bed. "I didn't take you to be a shy man,

Sawyer Reid." She teases. "I thought you knew what you wanted, and you stopped at nothing till you got it?"

I stare blankly at her, giving her a look up and down, tilting my head. "Did I not just prove that?"

She blinks at me, stunned how I would be so honest, but then decides to shut the door anyway.

I know she's not mad at me, because I can see the tiny smile she was trying to hide as the door shuts. I decide to have a look around. She has no family photos, other than the ones in the living room of her, Mary, and Frank. She wasn't kidding when she said she has no friends. No photos of people in the city, just a few photos of her neighbors. That upsets me more.

She's been very isolated all of these years since she left England. I know deep down I probably made her experience in Sin City feel like a chore.

I hear the door unlock, and I turn to greet her with a smile, and she joins in, instantly warming my cold heart. "Everything okay?" I ask her as she picks up her heels and opens up the closet to reveal her wardrobe, before quickly closing the door again.

"Perfectly fine." She says sweetly. "Are you hungry?" She asks, heading into the kitchen, avoiding my eyes. She's acting odd, she would rather have me starve.

"Thea," I say catching her attention, to which she turns to me. I approach her slowly, she's still in my shirt, which is catching the light and is slightly see through. I lift my finger to raise her chin for her to look at me. Snaking my hand round her waist so she can't move and pulling her close to me. "what is it?" I ask, my brows frowned.

She tries to release herself from my grip, which only makes me tighten it harder. "I don't do that, one-night stands or whatever that was." She says quietly, almost as if she's ashamed of her actions.

"Don't think about it like that, please." I beg her. "Because I don't want you to think that it was like that. That I would treat you the same way I would treat someone else."

I can see her become upset in my arms. "Why am I any different?" She breathes.

Moving my hand from around her, I place my hands on her face, tilting her head back, holding her so tight she can't go anywhere. "Because you're the one I realized I wanted, even when I deserved nobody." I say against her lips. "I don't deserve you, your body, your kindness or your compassion." I admit softly.

"Sawyer—" She begins to interrupt, and I shake my head to silence her.

"I've been so awful to you, Thea. You didn't deserve it, not one bit of it." I admit again.

She takes a long deep breath, pulling away from me slightly. I got her consent for the sex. I wanted that much, but being in her presence and her home as made me realize she's the way she is because she thought she could trust someone, and they broke it, and dated her sister. Which is so incredibly fucked up.

"Let me make it up to you. Please. But in baby steps." I say pulling her closer. "And I want you to use your words."

She hesitates for a moment, which I expected. I didn't have her for the kind of girl to agree to any of this, although I have to admit it was so much better than I imagined.

"Okay." She agrees after a few moments. But this time, she kisses me, and I feel my knees almost buckle at the sensation. Letting go of her face, I reach down to behind her legs and pick her up. Kissing her passionately, I lead her towards the bedroom. She pulls away slightly, "What are you doing?" She asks as I hold her tighter.

"Fucking you in that shirt," I begin, she pulls away, staring at me blankly. "I told you I would."

She smiles down at me, and I can see her almost wanting to roll her eyes. "You sure you're not all talk, Reid?" She asks softly, leaning down again brushing her lips over mine. It sends me spiralling all over again and I tighten my grip and head towards her bedroom.

"Oh, I'm sure, trouble. And I'm gonna show you." I say against her.

FORTY-FIVE

Thea

S awyer and I lie in the almost darkness while the light from the street shines slightly through the curtains in the room. It's peaceful and it's not awkward, which happened to be my first thought.

At first, I felt stupid. Letting Sawyer Reid of all people be the first man I sleep with in nearly six years. Deep down, my brain thinks I'm gullible, however my heart is telling me that I'm where I'm meant to be, and it was going to happen anyway.

I'm laying on his chest, his heart still beating as quick as it was after the second round, when I collapsed on his chest. He's playing with my hair, and my biggest worry is that he's going to tell me he regrets it.

It really shouldn't have happened. He's my boss, and I am his employee. Or at least I was. Neither of us know the status of what is going on right now, and when or if we are reinstated back into our old positions, what's to say we will be allowed to work with each other?

"What's going on in your head, trouble?" He asks, breaking me away from my troubling thoughts. "I hope you're not over thinking this?" He queries again.

I look up at him, and he meets my eyes. "Can you blame me?" I ask.

"No." He's quick to answer honestly, moving his other arm to cup my face, stroking my cheek with his thumb. "Because I'm feeling the same, and I'm scared you're gonna kick me out." He teases, grinning like a mad man.

I playfully hit him. "You think I would kick you out?" I ask moving and sitting up on my bed.

"Yes." He answers which takes me by surprise. He looks back at me. "It would be so hot if you did." He grins again. "I'd feel like such a slut and love it."

I laugh, pulling up the cover to above my breasts. I mean he's seen them, twice now. Yet the second round he decided that fucking me in his shirt was a hell of a lot hotter than fucking me without it. And it was hot.

"What happens now?" I ask, completely killing the mood.

He sits up next to me, the other side of the cover barely covering his torso and I notice a tattoo on his waist. "Anything you would like." He admits. "I'm fine to just take this baby steps, as mentioned. I don't want to ruin anything right now, and I know I have a tendency to do so." He smiles, pushing a little bit of hair out of my face.

"Okay."

He smiles even harder. "Okay."

He raises his arm to allow me on his chest. This feels weird, but in the best way possible. Although we sit in silence, it's not making me anxious. I'm used to it being loud and disruptive with Sawyer, and this has to be the calmest I've seen him, ever.

"I have a question, and you don't have to tell me if you don't want to. But I'm curious." He says causing me to move from under him and sit up.

"What is it?" I ask, looking at him. He turns so he's facing me directly, and I begin to feel anxious as to why he feels I won't answer his question.

"Your ex," he begins before clearing his throat. "was he the last person you slept with?"

I blink at him. Is it that obvious? "Yes."

He nods. "Why?" He asks next.

The question catches me off guard and I shift uncomfortably in the bed. "Er- well…" I begin, before he stops me, placing his hand on my leg that's underneath the covers.

"You don't have to answer." He reassures me, to which I shake my head.

"It's okay." I reassure him back. "I think I put my career over anything, a relationship didn't seem right after what happened with my last one. So, I didn't even think about it." I admit.

"Did you go out on dates?"

I laugh. "No, I was too busy dealing with you, that I think you kind of put me off dating." His face drops, and the realisation hits. "I can't fully blame you." I say, quick to try and somewhat change the subject. "It was my fault though, I turned down anyone that asked."

He face softens gently and he gives me a reassuring smile. "I wasn't easy on you." He says.

I scoff. "You were the reason I hated men." I admit.

He shrugs his shoulders. "I can't say I'm surprised." He explains. "I mean, I wanted you," He says climbing on top of me, causing me to laugh. "I'm just pleased no one else got you before me." He says kissing my neck gently. "You were mine, even if you didn't know it." He says against my skin.

It sits wrong with me, that I was his. I turn my head slightly and he notices the change in my demeanour but also the air, it's now filled with tension. "I was yours?" I ask, turning to him, my face saying everything it needs to.

He smiles down at me. "I know it's hypocritical. But I really wanted you to be mine someday." He explains softly, but the sentence doesn't sit right with me at all.

"But you could have anyone you wanted? Seems a bit sketchy." I say wanting to push him off me, but he holds my hands down again.

"Hey," He says to stop me. "no matter what you think of me, I felt the same way I do now, five years ago. I wanted you from the moment I met you, just because I slept with girls, doesn't sway my feelings away from you." He explains but keeps his distance above me.

My brows frown. "And what if it was the other way round?" I ask curiously.

His face drops. "Then I would be a serial killer." He says growing a grin on that stupid face.

"Hypocrite." I say shoving him off me.

"I know."

I lean down and get his shirt from the bedroom floor, putting it back over, and heading into the kitchen, avoiding his eyes. "Just a reminder, I had to save your life!" I shout through to the bedroom. I think the man forgets that if it wasn't for me, he probably would have had a bullet would through his head, rather than just his arm.

"Shut it!" He shouts, I can hear the playful tone in his voice. He likes to act like the man, yet he really is a tiny bit of a baby.

FORTY-SIX

Thea

A fter another hellish two weeks, I'm finally welcomed back into the gates of the I.C.C.O. To Mary and Frank, they were surprised that I would even go back. It's been almost three months since I started here, and in that time, I managed to get labelled as a fugitive alongside Sawyer, which ended up being the deceiving plan of the agencies own Director who was doing sketchy shit underneath their noses.

Getting out of my car, I watch carefully as Agents look my way. I've been cleared of all wrongdoing and have been given a public apology as well as a written one. I'm here to have a meeting with the new Director who has come from MI6. I'm finally not going to be the only

British person here, and if anything, that brings me some sort of comfort.

Avoiding the whispers and the stares, I head in the way back towards the lift, to my surprise is now fully functional. A flashback to Sawyer cutting the wires sends chills to my spine and I shiver. I haven't fully processed everything on what happened, even though it was the most traumatising few days of my life.

I shot someone for the first time, I became a fugitive, and I ended up with a brain and head injury. I really don't know why I've forgiven Sawyer, but I have. Because I only hold grudges on the people that really matters, my family.

They have called relentlessly for the past two weeks since they were labelled an unreliable source and some news outlets started labelling them as the worst family in London, when it came out that I was actually a victim, their words, not mine. They want their name cleared and as my Mother would say growing up… tough shit. My sister even got in contact, and my ex, to try and say how they were doing it as they thought it was something I would do, however that just ended up making them look worse and that was when the phone calls got worse.

Blocking their numbers was quite possibly the best thing I've ever done. I had given them so many opportunities to come and support me, and they do that by labelling me as a dangerous woman to the world.

I've finally been able to leave my apartment and go for runs, although they are still running the story, it seems to be after the more important news and that makes me glad. I'm still having to take things slow and I'm still getting terrible migraines, yet it's not as bad as what it could have been.

Mary and Frank have been great with me, and finally, Frank is out of his cast. He's been doing great, but he's got to walk with a cane and he's furious about it. In his words, the women won't want him anymore, and Mary reminded him that she was the only woman that did and that was by pure luck. He quickly shut up and gave her a kiss.

"Agent St. James?" Someone asks, that breaks me from my thoughts, and I quickly turn, startled by them. "I'm sorry, I didn't mean to frighten you. Are you alright?" He asks nicely. I manage a nod; however, I am shook up. "I'm Jack Donaldson. I'm the assistant to the new Director." He speaks clearly. He's more British than I am, and I feel unsettled, where the hell are these people from?

"Nice to meet you." I say extending my hand and he shakes it with a smile.

"Mr Oliver is looking forward to meeting you, please." He says extending his hand out for me to head in that direction. "Are you pleased to be back?" He asks catching up to me.

"Er- I'm nervous." I admit honestly. He presses the button for the lift and we both stand in silence for a second.

"Well, I believe that Mr Oliver will have your best interests at heart." He explains. I give him a small smile, which he joins in.

The lift arrives and we both step in. He clicks the ninth floor, which catches me by surprise, however, I don't know anything about this place anymore which is why I'm here.

Sinclair's office was on the fourth floor, which makes me think Mr Oliver has decided to choose a different floor to have his office.

Suddenly I hear a phone ring, and it's not mine. Jack pulls out his phone and answers it professionally.

"Yes, no problem. I'll be there in a minute." He says before hanging up. "I need to stop off at the Criminal Prevention floor and speak to a man named Johnson. Do you mind? It will only take a few minutes." He says looking down to me. He's so much taller, at least 6ft 2, and I shake my head to him. Sawyer should be back today, and since the wild night of sex, I haven't spoken or seen him.

It was a good thing, I needed space to figure

out if this is something I would want, and right now I feel confident enough that if Sawyer and I wanted to, we could keep this casual. I'm not wanting to be in a relationship, that frightens me.

We exit the floor and, head in towards the pen. I get greeted with some smiling faces and some looks of disgust. I feel severely uncomfortable walking through as Jack heads towards someone in the pen who hands him a folder.

I begin to make my way towards Sawyer's office, I notice both him and Greyson in the meeting room, in some sort of conversation.

As I approach, I feel my heart stop beating when I can hear their conversation. "How you feeling now it's all over?" Greyson asks him. I hear someone exhale, to which I think is Sawyer.

"I mean, I feel guilty, because she had so much hope and thought it would work out. But I think it was just a matter a time before it happened." He explains. There is no doubt in my mind that they are talking about me, and about the night Sawyer and I spent together, which I was going to keep private, but of course, he likes to out it to everyone on his adventures, so why am I so surprised?

"Here," I hear Greyson speak. I peak around the corner and notice him handing Sawyer some money, about $100. That's when I remember, the fucking bet. Of course. I was a bet. "I think I owe you." He says, and Sawyer takes the money graciously. Of course, he did.

That's when I decide I've heard enough, I'm on the verge of tears and I feel like my heart has been ripped out of my chest. I was a bet, and I forgot. How could I forget?

I'm mentally beating myself up, because I was the one that agreed to sleep with him, I was the one that allowed him in. And he used me for a bet.

All he did was spit out bullshit in my apartment, about how he feels about me, and has for the last five years. It was all lies, what a surprise.

Why I suddenly thought I could trust him is what is the biggest shock, he knew what he was doing, it was a manipulative and I fell right into his trap.

"Are you ready?" Jack says as I approach him. My face must tell him something I'm desperately trying to hide as he gently placing his hand on my arm. "Agent St. James, are you alright?" He asks softly.

Looking back onto the meeting room and seeing Sawyer and Greyson laughing through the window, I decide to keep quiet about what I've just heard. I only have myself to blame. "I'm fine, let's not keep Mr Oliver waiting." I say giving him a reassuring smile and try to relax my brows. I can't go into this meeting with the new appointed Director with a face like a might kill someone.

FORTY-SEVEN

Sawyer

"Thanks, Greyson." I praise him as he leaves the meeting room. It's nice to be back at work and with my team again.

I managed to get my old job back, yet I am on report for harassment against Thea, which is understandable. The police are currently investigating me for the elevator situation and are wanting to press charges for assault. I don't blame them either. But from what I've heard, Thea has refused to press charges. So this is coming from the City.

I know right now; she should be having a meeting with the new Director. Nancy gave me her schedule; however, I was surprised to see that she won't be working the rest of this week, just in for a meeting and back home. Nancy said that they are all heading round to Ophelia's later as she's making dinner but didn't know why Thea isn't back in the office fully, all she knows is she is on full pay until the end of the month.

I haven't spoken to her since the morning after we slept together. Granted, it's all I've thought about these past few weeks and how she kissed me and how she tasted. I wanted to give her enough space to really think it through and not pressure her. I'm the first person she slept with in years, and I know for a woman, sex is a very emotional thing and the last thing I would want to do is mess with that pretty head of hers, I've done that already in the elevator.

"Hey, pretty boy!" I hear Scott greet me as I exit the meeting room, heading towards my office. He pulls me in for a bear hug which I accept. It's nice being back at work with them all. "How does it feel to be back in these walls, legally?" He teases punching me in the arm.

Tuck stands behind him, rolling his eyes. "Leave the man alone, he's probably still getting used to being back. It is his first day after all." He says, extending his hand for me to shake, and I do. He always grips tighter, sometimes I think that it's to show his dominance, but this time he's just being a dick, because he has a shit eating grin on his face.

"It's nice to be back, what are you two doing?" I ask as we head into my office, and I place the money from Greyson on the desk without thinking.

"Came to check on you. Cause we are great friends." Scott says smiling.

The smile makes me nervous as I look at both of them getting comfortable on my couch. "What's going on?" I ask sitting on the edge of my desk.

Suddenly I watch Tuck's face drop just that little bit. And I follow his eyes which leads right back to the money. "Subtle much?" He asks, his face changing from playful, to just furious.

I shake my head at them both. "It's not what you think." I say in my own defence. "I gave Greyson money a while ago for his car, he was like $120 dollars short for the payment, I gave him it. Ask him." I say pointing towards the pen.

Tuck stands and places his hands up as if he's surrendering. "You can't blame me from jumping to conclusions, can you Sawyer?" He asks honestly.

I shake my head. "No. But I'm not like that, anymore. I'm turning over a new leaf. No more bets on any woman, it's unfair." I say going round and placing the money in my top drawer.

I watch them exchange a look between each

other. I don't blame them; they probably think I've gone mad. I'm not one to change my ways, I hate change.

"Why?" Scott asks. Before I can even get a word out, he seems to have figured it out as raises from the couch and slaps Tuck's chest enthusiastically. Tuck obviously doesn't flinch, yet his eyebrows raise as he comes to the same conclusion Scott has.

"When?" He asks, a small smile appearing on his face. Narrowing my eyes, I move away to avoid their stares, and to try and stop the smile growing on my face. Now they've asked, I'm having flashbacks and I can't let them know she's all I've been able to think about.

"Don't know what you're talking about." I say, looking up at them slightly. They see right through me, and when I look up, their arms are crossed, waiting for an explanation. "Fine, a few weeks ago." I say quickly.

Both of them blink at me in disbelief. "Wait," Tuck says, taking a long deep breath. "you slept with her a few weeks ago, and we find out today?" He questions, his eyes filled with curiosity. "We've seen you every other day! Why didn't you tell us?" He practically shouts.

Shushing him as I reach for the door, I shut it carefully. "Can you not shout it please? Besides, it wasn't either of *your* businesses, we haven't really spoken about it." I explain honestly going back the end of the end of my desk.

"Why haven't you spoken to her? Did you have an argument?" Scott asks curiously taking a seat back on the couch.

"No, it wasn't like that. I just wanted to give her some space. It was new for her, so I didn't want to overstep, or overstay my welcome." I explain calmly.

Tuck stands in the middle of the room stunned, barely able to breathe. "I have never been able to understand why you were the way you were with her. But now I get it." He says.

Exchanging a look with Scott, who only nods in agreement with Tuck. "What way? What are you talking about?" I ask him, confusion on my face no doubt.

"Dude," He begins to chuckle. "You love her and have for years so don't even try and deny it." He laughs along with Scott.

I blink at them both. "Don't deny it? I'm not even agreeing with it!"

They laugh even harder. "Dude, think about it. You were mean to her because you liked her, you just didn't realize that you love her."

When he says the word love, my heart beats even quicker and I immediately think of her and her smile. Deep down I've always denied my feelings for Thea, or if that any of it was real or just built-up sexual frustration. But with that out of the way, and how I've seen her in the most intimate way possible, I honestly don't want anyone else.

I want her.

"Okay, so I might deep down. But that proves nothing." I object to them both. Tuck rolls his eyes and joins Scott on the couch.

"Whatever helps you sleep at night." He jokes. But before it's too late, I would talk to her."

He's right, and I know he is. I take a long deep breath and get off the desk.

"I will, she's in a meeting with the new Director, so I can't talk to her right now."

"Oh, I know." Tuck says quickly, which causes me to raise an eyebrow. "I know what that meeting is about." He explains, making himself comfortable.

"Yeah, it's a return to work?" I say sarcastically like it wasn't obvious already. Tuck shakes his head and leans forward onto his thighs.

"Not really, they might be relocating her." He says casually and I physically feel my heart drop from my chest.

"Relocating? To a different department?" I ask standing in front of him. He looks over at Scott, who is just as concerned as me. Tuck shakes his head and takes a deep breath.

"To a different country."

FORTY-EIGHT

Thea

T he door opens, and I notice a man standing, looking out the window, Jack welcomes me in, not far behind me as we walk towards the desk that's almost in the middle of the room. This office is so much nicer than Sinclair's ever was. It's very modern yet has that English twist that reminds me of home.

"Mr Oliver, Agent Thea St. James to see you, sir." He announces as I approach the chair opposite the desk. He's quick to turn around, and I almost find myself frowning as to why I recognise the man in front of me.

"Thank you, Jack." He speaks so very clearly, excusing his assistant who gives me a smile before leaving the room. "Please take a seat, Thea." He instructs, pointing down at the seat. I sit down and begin to get comfortable, but I find myself unsettled as I can't place his name nor his face. "Are you trying to work out where you know me from?" He asks, as if he's reading my mind.

"I'm sorry," I apologise. "is it that obvious?" I almost want to laugh. I'm incredibly nervous.

"Sorry, Thea. It's probably a bit of a shock for you. But I knew your father." He admits to me.

Bingo.

Terrance Oliver, although we called him Terry.

"I thought you worked for the police?" I ask curiously.

He laughs. "I did. I worked for Scotland Yard for many years. But I worked for MI6 for the last nine years, before, well taking over as the Director of I.C.C.O." He says, taking a seat at his desk. "How have you been?" He asks nicely.

I nod. "Good, it's weird to see you." I admit honestly and he laughs again.

"I bet. The last time I see you, you were twelve and it was at—"

"My fathers funeral." I finish his sentence.

He remains quiet for a moment, "It was so tragic what happened." He admits. "Your father was a good friend of mine." He says and I nod.

"Oh, I remember. You used to be at our house every weekend." I laugh.

He joins in, as we reminisce on a better and simpler time of our lives. My home life was nowhere near perfect, I was a sheltered child, however, it felt normal when my parent's friends and their kids came round every weekend.

"This doesn't break any rules, does it?" I ask curiously.

He shakes his head. "No, Thea. I've checked with other agencies. I'm not family, and we have no prior relation other than I was friends with your father. They seem to be fine with it." He admits honestly, which brings me some sort of comfort. "I want to ask how you're really doing?" He asks and I sit back slightly startled, and ready to defend myself. "The whole situation in becoming a fugitive, and with your injury not to mention your mental health, I have to ask an old friend and as your Director ask how you're really doing?"

I take a long deep breath. "Well, in all honesty. I was frightened, and it was an uncomfortable situation to be in. I can go to the local shop without someone stopping me asking me if it was all for publicity or why I'm not in jail. I think that is what mentally takes a toll on you, the gossip, the rumours." I say almost zoning out. "Sometimes it makes me question whether

I should have moved back home." I say before coming out of my trance. "But then I realised I have my own family here. My neighbours, Mary, and Frank. I couldn't leave them behind. They practically raised me in this city." I admit softly with a smile.

"Do you speak to your Mother?" He asks, getting comfortable in his chair.

I have to hold back a scoff. "I haven't spoken to her really since I moved out here. I've blocked her now. She had everything bad to say about me when we were being labelled as everything under the sun. I really don't have time for her. Or the rest of my family." I admit honestly.

He nods for a little while before leaning onto his desk and looking right at me. "I spoke to your Mother after your family released that statement. I told her what I thought."

I blink at him. "What did you think of it?"

Taking a long deep breath, he falls back into his chair. "That no Mother should ever treat their child the way she treat you and threw you under the bus. I told her the only thing she has done is brought shame, because it will eventually be proven that you're innocent. I had seen the footage from the elevator, I knew you were innocent! But she wouldn't have it. She didn't have one pleasant thing to say about you." He says, beginning to get frustrated, and lifts from his chair, looking out to the window. "She is as toxic as that sister of yours. Poison really, the whole lot of them!"

I begin to laugh. "You are very right." I say, giving him a smile. "Did she tell you why I'm in Sin City anyway?"

He shakes his head, not in the sense that she never told him, but more so that he didn't approve. "Said you broke a man's heart because you fell in love over here. I quickly came to your defence, and I had seen your file, and spoken to your colleagues and reminded her that you've never had a boyfriend out here it's never been proven, and it was all lies. She obviously argued with me, telling me I was wrong."

"She likes to hear herself talk." I laugh.

"Don't I know it."

There is a relaxing silence between us. I've never been able to rant about my family to anyone really because no one here ever understood me the way Terry does. He's seen my Mother for the person she is and has known her for years, even after my Dad died.

"Thea, with me now taking over as Director, I have to look at all positions and every department. Not to say that I'm getting rid of you, because your time at I.C.C.O has been so short, they never really got to see you for your full potential." He explains before picking up a file and placing it in front of me.

"What's this?" I ask curiously while he walks round the front of the desk, opposite of my seat.

"This is a case I would like you to work, with a new job title." He explains.

I shoot my eyes up, confused by the statement. "New job? Why?" I ask, almost as if I'm panicked.

"A promotion as such, Thea. Think of it that way, please." He requests and I nod, looking back down at the file and reading over what it says. "The man you would be helping look for is a notorious killer named d3ath. He's a hired hitman who has killed some big names in government, but a lot of innocent individuals." He explains softly.

I give him a confused look. "I'm not trained in anything other than communications." I explain and he shakes his head.

"Your job will be to have your own team in tracking him down. You'll be taking Agent Johnson with you, he's one of the best undercover hackers in the world." He elaborates and I feel a little calmer knowing I wouldn't be going on my own. I'll have sweet, innocent, and kind Johnson with me. "You won't be on the face of anything, and your job will be to bring him to justice. We have a team out there at the moment, some of the best and we even have someone undercover." He explains.

"Is this one of the teams working under Agent Tucker-Barlow?" I ask curiously, to which he nods.

"Agent Tucker-Barlow was the Agent who put your name forward for the operation." He explains and I feel a blow to my chest. Wow.

"I see." I say, suddenly struggling to find the words.

"I understand he is a friend of yours?" Terry asks, to which I nod.

"I thought so." I say looking down at the file.

"I think, Thea, he knows you're capable of doing so much for this agency than you realise." Terry explains softly.

I can't say I want to agree.

"Do I have to make a decision now?" I ask him and he shakes his head.

"You have three days, that's as long as I can give you." He says placing his hand on my shoulder. "There is just one more thing." He says moving away from me and towards the window again. "The job is based in Paris, France."

FORTY-NINE

Sawyer

"I don't know what I'll do if they relocate her." I say opening the can of beer in my apartment. Scott sits opposite in a t-shirt and sweatpants; Tuck is dressed in his work clothes as he stayed later than any of us.

"Did you speak to her?" Scott asks and I shake my head.

"She was gone quite quickly after leaving the meeting with the new Director. Who just to happens to be stealing Johnson from me, just for your information!" I shout, taking a drink. "How can he steal my best man." I say in complete disbelief.

Scott scoffs. "You have that man walking on eggshells." He laughs. "He probably jumped at the chance to get away from you, even if it is for just over six months."

I roll my eyes. "He would never leave me. I'll speak to him tomorrow." I say taking another sip.

"You can't." Tuck speaks next to me.

I turn my head. "Why not?"

He clears his throat. "Because he's already on his way there. He left this afternoon after you got out of your meeting." He says opening his can and taking a drink, quite a large one. Dickhead.

"You put the wizard on a plane and didn't think to tell me?" I say, a look of disgust on my face.

"I had to." He says in his own defence. "You wouldn't have let him get on the plane."

"Damn right I wouldn't!" I am quick to respond. "Wow, first Johnson? Maybe, Thea? You would think you're trying to take people away from me, Tuck." I laugh, looking over at Scott. He doesn't join in, only sits uncomfortably in his seat and stares at Tuck. I join in, staring hard at him as he avoids my stares.

"I wouldn't say you're far from the truth." He admits quietly and I feel rage fill within me instantly.

"What the hell are you talking about?" I ask through my teeth. The whole atmosphere has changed in the room, and you can cut the tension with a knife.

He takes a long deep breath and rises sits back in the chair. "I was the one who put her forward for the job." He admits.

I feel like I've been stabbed with how betrayed I feel. "Why the hell would you do that?" I ask him, it almost comes out as a breath rather than a complete sentence.

"Because she's good, Sawyer." He practically shouts. "She's good at her job, in fact – she's great. And this operation will really be good for her, and her reputation in this agency. So don't think for two seconds because you finally wore her down that you own her and her future."

I blink at him, stunned by how quick he is to come to her defence. And she's not even here. "Wow," I say walking away to the kitchen. "some friend you are."

I hear a scoff that causes me to turn around. "Do you blame me, Sawyer? You could have killed her! You're lucky you're not behind bars."

"You know I would never hurt her—"

"But you did!"

The tension in the room is so thick that I can barely breathe, or even comprehend what he's saying. But suddenly, a light bulb goes off in my head and everything comes into focus. "Oh, I get it." I say glaring at him. "You like her." Tuck's expressions softens but his eyes fill with both panic and rage. "Am I wrong?" I ask, deep down praying I am.

"No." He answers after a moment. Out the corner of my eye I can see Scott sitting on the couch, his mouth open and eyes wide with shock. "I like her. Can you blame me?" He asks me curiously, yet he frowns his brows.

I struggle to find my words because I can't blame him. She's amazing.

"Okay," Scott says causing us to break away from our tensioned stare. "you both need to chill out." He stays while he stands between us. "You are not ruining your friendship over her. Whatever tension is going on, it ends now." He snaps.

Looking back up at Tuck, he glares down at me, trying to wear me down. He's as stubborn as a mule, so getting him to agree to anything and move on or come to any sort of agreement is like pulling teeth. It's insufferable. "He's sending her away." I say, speaking first.

His eyes widen. "Actually, it's her decision. The job was offered." He explains.

"So, if she doesn't take it?" My brows frown curiously.

"She gets moved to a different department but remains in the agency." Tuck explains.

I look over at Scott, who exchanges a look with me also. "And if she takes it?" He asks for me.

We both look back over at Tuck who takes a long deep breath. "Then she moves to Paris."

I feel like he's just shot me in the heart. "Paris? How long for?"

"Between six months to a year." He announces, staring at us both. "But remember, it's her decision."

I shake my head, placing my hands on my hips. "She won't take it. She won't leave Mary and Frank."

Tuck shrugs. "She might, it will better her career, and you know how she's passionate about it."

As much as I want to argue with him, I know he's right. She's always wanted to do well and be the best at everything. This operation will put her on the map in the agency, will open her up to new work, and might lead her to having her own team. Even I know she would be a great leader.

"Are you going to try and stop her?" Scott asks me while I stare down at the floor. All I've done is get in her way, since the minute she started this job.

"I can't." I say eventually looking up at them both. "Because even I know that wouldn't be right."

FIFTY

Thea

I wait patiently for someone to open the door to Ophelia's apartment. With me returning back to work, she decided to make dinner for us girls which is thought was incredibly sweet. She also said she makes amazing Sushi, and I can smell it though the door so if someone doesn't come soon, I might kick it down.

The door swings open and a fresh-faced redhead greets me. "Hey!" She greets me warmly.

"Hey back." I say as I enter Ophelia's apartment. Seconds later, a glass of wine is placed in my hand by our welcoming host who looks stylish in her hoodie, hair in a messy bun and some joggers.

"Welcome to my crib." She greets with a grin. "I heard you're a sushi gal?"

I nod enthusiastically. "Absolutely." I smile and she grins even wider.

"Excellent!" She gleams, hinting at the table that has multiple versions of maki, sashimi, nigiri and a bunch of different rolls. "I made different ones, not sure what you like. The safe options are on the side." She explains while I take my coat off and hang it up while she stands at the table in the middle of the room.

"Looks amazing." I compliment, and she blushes almost.

"Thanks. So, Thea. How was your meeting with the new Director? Is he nice?" Ophelia asks while taking a seat alongside Nancy and I head over to join them.

"He's great. I know him personally. He was a friend of my Dad's years ago." I explain taking my seat. To no surprise they exchange a look. "He's checked, there is nothing wrong with me working under him as Director." I say and their faces relax.

"That's good. Because we don't want to say goodbye." Nancy says sweetly and it makes my heart almost shatter.

"Actually." I say putting the napkin on my lap.

"Oh no." Nancy says quickly. "Whatever you're

about to say, I don't want to hear it. No, you're not leaving the agency to go back to being a barista. No, you're not moving back to London, I will hop on a flight and kill you!" She begins to ramble, and I reach out and grab her hand which seems to stop her from talking.

"Terry – er. Mr Oliver, the new Director has offered me a role somewhere else for a little while." I explain softly. She grips my hand tighter, her eyes filled with fear and as I glance over at Ophelia's her expression mirror's Nancy's. "It's for around six months."

Nancy doesn't move from her position, only continues to stare at me. "Where?" She asks eventually and I take a deep breath.

"Paris."

Their eyes widen, and Ophelia gasps. "Paris!" They scream in unison.

"Why Paris? Why not the unit we have in New York? That's closer!" Nancy objects pulling her hand away. "Are you considering it?" She asks, but I can sense the objection in her voice.

"I am." I say, looking down at my napkin and fiddling with the edges, trying to avoid their stares.

"Why?" Ophelia asks and as I look up at them, I feel a tear fall down my cheek and it makes this all feel real.

"Because I was only ever a bet, and he won." I watch their brows soften as they realise what I mean by my statement. I begin to try and contain myself, because I refuse the cry over anyone, especially a man.

"When?" Nancy asks reaching out for me to grab her hand which I do slowly.

"A few weeks ago." I say, once again looking down at the napkin. "I'm embarrassed." I admit, lifting the napkin to dry my eyes.

"Sweetie, why?" Nancy asks.

"Because I believed the lies." I say which almost tips me over the edge. "I let him into my home, and I allowed him into my life. And I got bit on the ass, I knew I would. I can't say I'm surprised." I say, wiping the tears that continue to fall.

"How do you know that the bet was still continuing?" Ophelia asks, reaching out for me to take the other hand.

I tilt my head, waiting for her to realise the mistake in that sentence. "Ophelia, it's Sawyer. The man lives off winning and ruining other people's lives." I say sarcastically, before clearing my throat. She doesn't argue with me, I mean how can she? We all knew from the moment I walked into this job I was a way for Sawyer to make money and finally tick me off that list.

"So, you're considering taking this job because Sawyer Reid won his little game? Thea, that is insane!" Nancy objects to which I shrug my shoulders.

"Maybe, but it would be nice to go to a country where I'm not being judged and to a new city where I can be myself. I'm struggling here, I have been for weeks." I admit while beginning to cry.

"Is the therapy helping? Dr Bailey is an amazing therapist, Thea. Please give her some time." Ophelia encourages, and I shake my head.

"Honestly, it's not helping. All it's doing is giving me more reasons to leave and never return." I admit honestly, before I realise my mistake. "But come back for you two and obviously Mary and Frank."

Nancy gives me a weak smile. "Have you spoken with them?" She asks, to which I nod.

"Yes. They are heartbroken, but they understand why. It's not like I'm not coming back. I'm just taking a little work trip. At least, that's how Frank is seeing it."

"So, you told them about Sawyer?" Ophelia ass and my eyes widen.

"Jesus, no! She'll kill him if she finds out he's the reason I'm taking this job." I explain to which she laughs.

"So, you're taking the job to get away from

him? Do you even want it?" She asks and I shrug my shoulders.

"Not really. But it will be good for my career. I can progress in other departments if I do well." I explain which makes them both nod in unison.

"Or you're so bad you get fired. So, don't screw it up." Nancy jokes along. That does make me laugh, and Ophelia joins in.

"I think we can both agree that she won't get fired."

Nancy shrugs, "Sawyer shouldn't be working at I.C.C.O." She explains taking a piece of cucumber maki from the middle of the table. "But that's my opinion."

I exchange a look with Ophelia, "You think he should have gotten sacked?"

"Oh yeah! He tried to kill you, Thea." She explains with her mouthful.

"I mean, I think a suspension yes, but he is a good Agent, Nancy."

She shrugs again, "I just think he gets away with more than he should. But what do I know?" She says, taking another roll from the middle plate and putting it in her mouth.

Ophelia takes a long breath before picking up her chopsticks, "I agree with you. He gets away with too much." She says grabbing a salmon roll from the plate. "But he shouldn't be the reason you leave your job and your family here, Thea. Are you sure this is something that you want?" Ophelia asks.

I take a long breath, "Yeah." I respond. "I think a change of scenery will be good for me." I explain, giving them a reassuring smile. I'm hoping I don't regret this.

They look over at each other and then back at me, "As long as, you're sure. But remember, you have to come back to us."

FIFTY-ONE

Sawyer

I'm sat almost in darkness at my desk. I need to finish my report, but the only thing I can think of is that Thea might take this job overseas.

Deep down, I'm hoping that she doesn't. But then I'm not in the position to ask her to stay. We haven't spoken to each other since what happened between us. I don't know if she regrets it and she's avoiding me, or if she's just not sure what to say. I have no idea what it will mean for us if she doesn't, I haven't made much of an effort since we had sex and that's because I didn't want to overwhelm her. She might decide that she doesn't feel the same way about me, as I feel about her.

Tuck mentioned that she hadn't made her decision about the job yet, which kind of fills me with some hope she's not going to take it.

It's 3:02am. I've been here longer than I should be. I should be home, sleeping. But I have only a few hours till my report is due for the new Director. There was a rumour that Thea knows him personally. I have no clue how true that is, but considering they are both British I could say it's a high possibility.

Just as I decide to get myself together and finish this report, my door flies open and I look over and notice Nancy, charging at me like a bull. "You're an idiot." She shouts at me, before slamming the door behind her. She's dressed casually, no makeup and her hair is in one of those clips. In all honesty, she looks like she's just got out of bed and came here to give me her wrath. "You finally get the girl, and you treat her the way you do. The way Sawyer Reid always does. Like she's nothing." She snaps.

My brows frown. "What are you talking about? I gave her space. I didn't want to overwhelm her." I explain, my hands up to surrender. "How does that make me shitty?"

She scoffs. "You did it again, Sawyer! You treat her the same as you have the rest of us. To win the bet. You are disgusting." I sit back, stunned by her accusation.

"Nancy, the bet was off! Even before I slept with her."

"Bullshit."

I blink at her. "I'm serious, Nancy! I called off the bet after the whole situation with Sinclair and Delsavo. She saved my life, I risked hers—"

"You almost killed her!"

Suddenly a lightbulb goes off in my head. That's why Nancy's been so cold these past few weeks. She hates me because of what happened in the elevator. "It wasn't intentional." I explain in the hopes to defend myself.

She rolls her eyes. "Everything with you is intentional." She snaps quickly. "You do everything with your gain in mind and you don't care about the feeling or the consequences for others."

"Do you think I don't feel guilty about hurting her? It's eating at me that because of my stupid decision, I could have killed her."

"Well, I wish it would eat you quicker because of your bet, she's taken that job and she doesn't even want it."

Is she listening to me? "Nancy, the bet was off! There was no bet when it happened!"

"Then why did she see you and Greyson exchange a ton of money?" She questions.

Oh shit. "Oh no." I say as the realisation hits me. "No, no. Nancy, it's not what she thinks!"

She stands back and folds her arms. "Then what is it, pretty boy? Please, explain to me how she's wrong."

I groan at her tone of voice. "Greyson was low on cash to get his car fixed. I leant him the money for it, he was paying me it back!" I practically shout at her.

I watch her face change from the smug look that currently resides, to a one of panic. "So, the money really wasn't from the bet?" She asks, almost as a whisper.

"No, Thea got it wrong." I say sitting back in my chair. "Oh my god, no wonder she's avoided me." I say feeling defeated. If I had only realised what she had seen, this could all be avoided. "I need to talk to her." I say in a panic, realizing she has to make a big decision about where she will be for the next six months.

"Well, you better do it quick." Nancy says picking her bag up from the floor.

"Why?"

"Because she's at the airport. She took that job, Sawyer." Nancy says which stops me in my tracks from following her. "She took that job because of you."

435

FIFTY-TWO

Thea

This is my fourth hug from Mary in the last ten minutes. Both her and Frank insisted on taking me to the airport, even though it is 3:30am.

After my dinner with Ophelia and Nancy, I called Terry to let him know I'll take the job, to which he said he wanted me out on the first available flight from SCX.

My flight is at 4:30am, so I'm early but early enough to make sure I have the right documents, grab a few coffees, and look over the case file that I have on a memory stick if I get to my gate early enough.

I got to say goodbye to my office, and even

called Scott and Tuck to let them know I'm taking the job and I will see Scott when I get back, but that I will see Tuck soon, probably because I'll be working under him, and he will be needing updates.

It's sad. I really thought that being the Communications Liaison, that my life was finally planned out. But I'm trying to convince myself that this job will be good for me. To work with a new team and to get used to a routine in Paris.

"Will you call us every day?" Mary asks, breaking from the hug.

"Of course, I will. But remember, my times are going to be different –"

"Don't care." Frank says before pulling me in for a hug. He hugs me tight, and it feels so surreal that I won't be hugging them for a while.

"I'm going to miss you." I say softly in his ear.

"Right back at you, kid." He says softly kissing me on the cheek.

I pull away, hoping to control my emotions and not become too upset. "Do you two promise to behave?" I ask, clearing my throat.

"Does that mean you'll come home?" Mary asks softly. "If we don't behave, you'll come home?"

My heart shatters. "I might have to. I'll need to bail you both out." I tease, which does make her laugh just as she begins to cry.

"Well, I'll make sure to do something stupid to get us both arrested." She grins. Frank quickly turns to her and back at me.

"If you're going down, you're doing it alone!" She announces. She turns slowly to look at him, her eyes narrowed as she gives him a warning, although they are full of tears.

"You married my stupid ass. You're going down with me, you old fart."

Laughing forms around us and I look at them, bullying each other like they did the first time I went over for dinner. They are the best family I could have asked for. They treat me like a daughter. Even though they didn't want a child of their own.

"I love you both." I announce, pulling them both in for a hug at the same time. But making it quick, so I can't decide to change my mind.

"We love you more." They almost say in unison.

Giving them one last wave, I head towards security after saying goodbye. Trying to contain my emotions, I take multiple breaths to try and not cry all my way through security,

This is the worst feeling in the world, and I feel even more guilty for leaving Nancy and Ophelia too. They were my first real friends since moving here.

As I get through to security, I begin to have second thoughts. Is this really what I want? Can I do this? Am I capable of doing this job?

I begin to panic, wondering maybe this was the worst idea possible, moving to a country where I know only one person and we have one person in common, Sawyer.

But suddenly it dawns on me, that he's the reason why. He's the reason I'm doing all of this. He'll never change. He will always be the worst person to be around, and I will never be able to make a name for myself in this agency if my name is always attached to Sawyer's.

His face is the reason I continue to move towards security. I don't want to see it for a long time. I feel embarrassed which is fuelling my feet to keep moving.

Security doesn't take too long, and they let me through quicker than I expected. All of my forms were fine and checked and the woman who I spoke to was nice enough, so that makes this a little easier.

Thinking about it, Terry wouldn't have agreed with Tuck if he didn't think I could do it. Although I haven't seen Terry in years, I'm grateful for how he stood up for me in front of my family and defended me. He was incredibly good friends with both of my parents. It's been a long time since someone stood up for me in the way he did. Especially to them.

They never saw an issue with their actions, or the way they spoke to me or treated me. It's disappointing, that they chose my ex-fiancé over their own daughter. They just had to twist the knife in more when my sister started sleeping with him. The thought makes me shiver as I head to grab a coffee. I dread to think what my life could have been like if I had went through with the wedding.

Ordering my usual from a Starbucks I managed to locate, I head to make my way to my gate. People should be able to board shortly, and from how quiet the airport is, I don't think there will be many people on this flight. I turn my phone off and put it in my bag.

I'm at gate 12, which thankfully is just down a long cold corridor, and take a right. This is my first time since arriving that I've been back to the airport, other than to drop Mary and Frank off. It's not a gigantic airport, but with my sense of direction, I would probably get lost.

As I approach the gate, I realise that there is barely anyone apart from two other people. This might be a quiet flight and brings me with a little bit of peace. It's a long flight, and I need as much peace and quiet as I can get.

I'll be in France later tonight. I've never been

to Paris, and I'm hoping that I might be able to have a few days off to possibly do some sightseeing at some point. I'm also secretly hoping that we're able to locate the person responsible. But since this is a new team of new Agents looking over an infamous case. It makes me think that this might take longer than needed.

FIFTY-THREE

Sawyer

I pull the car into the bay and practically launch myself out, Nancy not far behind me. Her flight leaves in less than ten minutes, and I need to make sure she doesn't leave the tarmac.

"She's not answering, Sawyer!" Nancy shouts from behind me.

Running up to the desk, I approach a zombie looking woman who is in a desperate need of coffee sit at the desk. "Hi," I say as I come to a stop. "I need a ticket for the flight that leaves for Paris in ten minutes."

Her eyes widen. "I'm sorry, Sir. You can't buy tickets for that flight."

"I just need to make sure that someone doesn't get on that plane. Can you call the gate and ask for someone to come back, I'll know she'll be there." I explain softly and she shakes her head. *I wish I had my badge; fuck I wish I had my badge.*

"I'm sorry, Sir. But they will already be on the plane now."

I feel my heart shatter. "So, there is nothing you can do?"

She shakes her head again. "Sorry, no."

I decide to turn away from her and I look over at Nancy "Anything?"

She shakes her head sadly.

Behind her I watch as the doors fly open, and Tuck and Scott stand there staring over at us. "Come on!" Tuck encourages.

Exchanging a small look with Nancy, we head in their direction, running as quick as we can as we head back to the cars. "What are you doing here?"

"Fixing this. I called my friend; he's going to open the gates to the runway. We need to try and catch that plane. It's going to leave in any minute."

Individually, we all pile into Tuck's car, and he begins to drive like a mad man, easily hitting 130 miles and hour to head to the runway that's at the other end of the airport.

We approach the gates, and he stops at the end of the runway. They've just taken the stairs away.

No.

I practically jump out of the car and make a run for it, hoping to catch one of the men and ask on the radio they open the doors.

"Sawyer!" I hear Tuck, Scott, and Nancy call after me. I ignore them all, only sprinting towards the plane that has now started to move down the runway. For some reason, I believe I can catch up to it and try and push myself faster.

But I feel my heart stop as well as my feet as I watch the plane lift off into the sky, and I watch her fly away from me. Falling to my knees, I struggle to catch my breath or fathom what's just happened. Why did I let her get away.

"What have I done?"

Loathe you
entirely.

Book 2 of The Troubled Series

Torrie Jones
Coming Soon...

*Even in death... the body
is never fully happy.*

Why, you ask?

*Because I like the to make sure
my victims don't find peace
in the afterlife. I like the
feeling of knowing they will
suffer, even in death...*

after all... that is my name.

D 3 A T H

Loathe you entirely.

Book 2 of The Troubled Series

Torrie Jones
Valentine's Day 2024

ABOUT THE AUTHOR

Torrie Jones

Torrie Jones is a North-East author who mainly writes young adult mystery, crime, and romance. Her debut novel, The Lies We Tell, became a No.1 Amazon Best Seller in multiple countries. She's a content creator, make up artist and a avid reader of anything and everything. She grew up watching crime shows with her Grandad which encouraged her to go into the mystery and crime genre.

She has a dog called Penny and a cat called Sheldon who keep her entertained, and she's a lover of iced coffee.

BOOKS AND OTHER WORKS

The Hidden Jules Series:

The Lies We Tell – **Out Now**

The Secrets We Keep – **Out Now**

The Betrayal That Follows – **31st August 2023**

The Troubled Series:

Hate you too.
Loathe you entirely. - **Valentine's Day 2024**

Novels:

Dealing with the Outcast – **3rd November 2023**

Social media: **@torriemaryjones** on TikTok
Instagram - **@torriejonesauthor**
Book Club – **Trouble's Book Club** on Facebook

www.torriemaryjones.com

ACKNOWLEDGEMENTS

To my wonderful family who are my biggest
supporters in everything I do.

To all the girls, who no matter what, show me the endless
amount of support and always show me a lot of love.

To my cover artist Hayley (@h0wl.art.) who
absolutely smashed the cover out of the park and
really brought Thea and Sawyer to life.

To the troublemakers who have stuck by this story
since it was Loving the Shield. Did I ever think this
would make it into a novel? Did I F***!!!! Agent Trouble
only exists because of the many of you who loved her
storyline, her dedication, and the love she had to give.
I am forever grateful for you all. So, thank you.

And last, but not least. To my fabulous boyfriend Joseph,
who has supported me since day one of meeting me.

Printed in Great Britain
by Amazon

26698706R00264